PASSIONATE PATIENCE

Last night had been madness. But now the madness was over. "I want it to end," Lady Mary Gregg said. "It is to end."

"It will not end," Lord Edmond Waite said quietly. "You know it as well as I, Mary. Something began last night and it is very far from its end. Very far. But I can wait." He laughed. "I am named suitably. I can wait for you to accept the inevitable. We will be lovers. You will be my mistress. I am not by nature a patient man, but I can patiently await something I really want."

"Then you had better be prepared to wait until your dying day," Mary said.

"I think not," said Lord Edmond, "I think it will be sooner than that."

And who was Mary to argue with the voice of so much experience in love . . . so much irresistible expertise . . . ?

MARY BALOGH, who won the *Romantic Times'* Award for Best Regency Writer in 1985, has since become one of the genre's most popular and bestselling authors. She also won the Waldenbooks' Award for Bestselling Short Historical in 1986 for *The First Snowdrop* and the *Romantic Times* Reviewer's Choice Award for Best Regency Author in 1988, the Waldenbooks Award for Bestselling Short Historical in 1989 for *The Obedient Bride* and a *Romantic Times* Lifetime Achievement Award in 1989.

SIGNET REGENCY ROMANCE
COMING IN OCTOBER 1992

Emily Hendrickson
The Fashionable Spy

Carol Proctor
Theodora's Dreadful Mistake

Charlotte Louise Dolan
The Black Widow

Georgette Heyer
Faro's Daughter

The
Notorious
Rake

Mary Balogh

A SIGNET BOOK

SIGNET
Published by the Penguin Group
Penguin Books USA Inc., 375 Hudson Street,
New York, New York, 10014, U.S.A.
Penguin Books Ltd, 27 Wrights Lane, London W8 5TZ, England
Penguin Books Australia Ltd, Ringwood, Victoria, Australia
Penguin Books Canada Ltd, 10 Alcorn Avenue, Toronto, Ontario, Canada M4V 3B2
Penguin Books (N.Z.) Ltd, 182-190 Wairau Road,
Auckland 10, New Zealand

Penguin Books Ltd, Registered Offices:
Harmondsworth, Middlesex, England

First published by Signet, an imprint of New American Library,
a division of Penguin Books USA Inc.

First Printing, September, 1992

10 9 8 7 6 5 4 3 2 1

1

THE THUNDERSTORM was entirely to blame. Without it, all the problems that developed later just would not have happened. Without it she would never in a million years have taken him for a lover.

But the thunderstorm did happen and it raged with great ferocity for all of two hours, seeming to circle London instead of moving across it and away. And so all the problems developed.

Because she had spent the night with him.

Because of the thunderstorm.

She had never been afraid of storms as a child. While her elder sister had gone racing into the comforting arms of their nurse at the first distant flash of lightning, she had always raced for the nearest window and flattened her nose against it to enjoy the show until the storm got closer and she had been warned away from her perch. And then she had sat in the middle of the room, waiting in eager anticipation for the next bright flash and counting the seconds until the crash of thunder told her just how close the storm was.

It had never occurred to her to fear storms until she was in Spain with her husband during the Peninsular Wars, camped out in wet and muddy misery with the rest of his division. Lightning had struck so close to their tent that it had killed the four soldiers in the very next one to theirs. She had screamed and screamed in Lawrence's arms, returning to sanity only when shouting voices beyond their canvas shelter had indicated that tragedy had struck with the lightning, though miraculously it had missed them.

She had been calm then in the face of death. But ever after that, storms had paralyzed her with terror. And Lawrence was no longer there to comfort her. He had been killed more than seven years before.

Mary Gregg, Lady Mornington, had accepted an invitation from her friend Penelope Hubbard to make up a party of eight to Vauxhall Gardens to listen to a concert and to enjoy the beauty of the pleasure gardens. The party had been organized by the new wife of one of Mr. Hubbard's friends, and the lady had found herself with an uneven party of seven at the last moment. She needed another lady, whom Penelope had promised to provide.

Mary really ought to come, Penelope had said. She had been down lately and was in danger of becoming a hermit. A rather ridiculous fear in Mary's estimation, since she still held her almost weekly literary evenings and never refused an invitation to an entertainment that promised stimulating conversation.

But she *had* been down. Dreadfully down. Marcus had met his wife again after a fourteen-year separation and had fallen in love with her again—not that he had ever stopped loving her. Mary had always known that. He had never made a secret of the fact. Just as she had never made a secret of the fact that she had loved Lawrence and still grieved for him.

But she and Marcus had been close friends for six years. They had not been lovers, though it seemed to be the general belief that they must have been. But now they could no longer be friends, just because they were of different genders and he was hoping for a reconciliation with his wife. Mary was finding the emptiness in her life hard to bear. She had not realized quite how much he had meant to her until he was gone.

Yes, she was very down. And so she accepted Penelope's invitation even though the prospect of an evening at Vauxhall did not appeal to her a great deal. It appealed even less when she discovered who one of the other guests was. Lord Edmond Waite! She could not understand why Mrs. Rutherford would have invited such a man.

Lord Edmond Waite, youngest son of the Duke of Brookfield, was everything that Mary most despised. He was a libertine and a gamester and a drunkard—and a jilt. She did not know the man, of course, and she was willing to concede that rumor and gossip were not always reliable sources of information. But not everything she had ever heard of him could be untrue, she thought. And she had never heard any good of him. None. It was said that he had been all but betrothed to Lady Dorothea Page, that they had been intended for each other since her infancy. And yet he had gone running off with Lady Felicity Wren, if rumor was correct, and had in his turn been jilted when she had married Mr. Thomas Russell. Lord Edmond was not held in high repute by the *ton*. Only his wealth and rank ensured that he was still received at all. And not everyone received him even so.

Mary did not relish the thought of spending an evening with a party that included Lord Edmond in its number. But she had no choice except to make a scene and go home. Good manners prevented her from doing that. She set herself to avoiding him and conversing with the other members of the party.

"I believe it is going to storm," she remarked to Mr. Collins before the concert came to an end. The air was still and heavy. Ominously so.

"I do concede you may be right, ma'am," he said, looking up at the sky, dark and invisible beyond the light of the colored lanterns that lit the boxes and hung from the trees. "We will have to hope that it does not break before we return home."

"Yes," she said. Rachel would have to sleep in her room with her. It would be some comfort to have her maid there, though not nearly as satisfactory as a man's arms. Marcus had always come when there was a storm brewing, and he had always stayed with her until it was safely past. She returned her attention to the music of Mr. Handel.

It was very obvious to her that a storm was approaching, though no one else seemed at all concerned about it. Rather, everyone appeared to be enjoying the unusual warmth and stillness of the evening. And Mary did not know whether to be impatient to be gone and home to the relative safety of her house or to be glad that she was in company with seven other people and surrounded by dozens of others. But then, of course, she had been surrounded by many thousands of other people in Spain. Numbers did not ensure safety against lightning.

Penelope and her husband got to their feet when the concert

was over and suggested a stroll along the lantern-lit paths of the gardens.

"It is such a beautifully warm evening," Penelope said.

"It is going to storm," Mary said.

"Do you think so?" Penelope too looked up to the invisible sky.

"Good," Mr. Hubbard said. "A storm will clear the air. It has been very hot and muggy for two days now."

"But let it wait another hour or two yet," Mr. Collins said, also getting to his feet and offering his arm to Mrs. Rutherford on his other side.

The four of them went off walking. Mary glanced at the other three occupants of the box. They were arguing with great animation over something, and Miss Wetherald was doing a great deal of laughing. Without at all meaning to, Mary caught Lord Edmond's eye and he got to his feet.

"Ma'am?" he said, reaching out a hand for hers. "Would you care for a stroll?"

She certainly did not care for any such thing. Not with him, at any rate. But how could she refuse without seeming thoroughly rag-mannered? She could not.

"Thank you," she said, smiling and taking his hand so that he might help her to her feet.

He was a handsome man in a way, she supposed. He was tall, perhaps a trifle too thin, though he had an athletic body for a man who must be in his mid-thirties. His dark hair was thick, not thinning at all, his face narrow with a prominent aquiline nose, rather thin lips, and eyes of a curious pale blue. Many women would find him attractive and undoubtedly did. She did not. She took his offered arm.

"Tell me how you enjoyed the concert," he said. It seemed more command than question.

"Very well," she said.

"You like Handel's music, then?" he asked. "I prefer Bach myself."

"Do you?" she said. "Each has his merits, I suppose."

They lapsed into silence. It was not a very promising beginning, the brief conversation they had had having been anything but profound and neither seeming willing to defend a preference.

"You still have all those literary gatherings at your house?" he asked. "Brough attends most of them, does he not? He likes that sort of thing. He tells me that your salon always attracts the best talent."

"That is very obliging of him," she said. "Yes, Mr. Brough is a regular visitor to my salon. I have a gathering there most weeks."

"Poets and such?" he said.

"Yes," she said, "and artists and politicians and people who just simply enjoy an intelligent conversation."

"Ah," he said, and they lapsed into silence again.

Goodness, Mary thought, she was strolling in Vauxhall Gardens with Lord Edmond Waite. She could not quite believe that she had sunk so low. She wished that they would catch up to Penelope and the others, but they must have taken a different path. There was no sign of her friends ahead of them.

"It is going to storm," she said. There was a breeze swaying the upper branches of the trees, making a swishing sound. On the ground the air was still very close.

"Probably," he said. "It will not be a bad thing. It will clear the air."

"Yes," she said.

She wanted to be back at the boxes, where there was the deceptive safety of numbers. She wanted to be at home, where she could hide beneath the relative safety of her blankets, Rachel sleeping in a truckle bed close by. She wanted to be mistaken about the storm. Perhaps it would just rain.

"Perhaps there will just be a good rain," she said.

"Perhaps." He looked up to the sky, still invisible beyond the lantern light. "Though I doubt it. I believe we will have a good fireworks display before morning. But not yet, I think."

It seemed to Mary that she was the only person at Vauxhall concerned about the approach of the storm. But perhaps not. As they walked on, they met fewer and fewer people. Was it just because they were moving away from the crowded area around the boxes? Or were other people being wiser and leaving while there was still time?

"Perhaps it would be wise to turn back," she said. "It would not be pleasant to be caught in a storm."

He smiled down at her. "Could it be that you are afraid of storms, Lady Mornington?" he asked. "Or is it my person that makes you uneasy? You may relax, ma'am. I do not make a practice of ravishing unwilling females."

Mary set her teeth together. She would not answer such words. Oh, she would not so demean herself. How dare he! He was more vulgar even than she had expected.

"If you wish to turn back," he said, "we will do so."

The path was deserted suddenly. There was no one else either ahead of them or behind them. And the trees were rustling in the growing wind. Of course they must turn back. Some heavenly fury was about to be unleashed, even though there had been no distant flashes to warn of an approaching storm.

"I am quite happy to walk on," she said. She would be damned before she would admit fear of any sort to the likes of Lord Edmond Waite.

He chuckled. "I fear you are right, though," he said. "The storm is much closer than estimated. It is these lanterns. They make it impossible to see if the sky is clear or cloudy. I believe we had better return. We seem not to have a great deal in common conversationally anyway, do we?"

Mary turned back with an inward sigh of relief. But as she did so, a large spot of rain splattered on her nose and then another against one eye.

"Damnation," her companion said. "The heavens are about to open. We are going to get soaked."

"We will have to run," she said as two cold spots landed on her shoulders and then more continued to come at her, too numerous to count. The wind was suddenly sweeping through the trees.

"Not back to the boxes," he said, releasing her arm and taking her firmly by the hand. "This way."

And he drew her at a run along one of the darker, narrower paths through the trees, the wind moaning through the branches, the rain lashing down on them, until they reached one of the rustic shelters that were dispersed at intervals through the gardens. He pulled her inside.

"Blast!" he said, shaking rain from his hair and brushing ineffectually at his damp coat. "We will probably be stuck here for an hour or more. I hope we can find some topic of mutual interest on which to converse."

Mary dried her arms with her hands. She felt uncomfortably chilly suddenly. "I think perhaps I was right about one thing at least," she said. "It is just going to be a good rain. There will be no storm."

"I would not count on it," he said, turning to push the wooden table against the inner wall so that they would have more protection from the rain. The shelter was walled on only three sides. Fortunately the wind was blowing against the back wall, so that almost no rain was coming in at them.

And sure enough, even as he spoke, the first flash lit up the sky. Mary sat carefully on the wooden bench that was attached to the table. She folded her hands in her lap. The thunder came a long time after. Perhaps it would not come close, she thought. Perhaps they were just on the fringe of the storm.

"Now, then," he said, seating himself beside her, "what shall we talk about? Your late husband was a colonel with the cavalry, was he not? And you were in the Peninsula with him? Tell me about it. What was the life like? Or does it pain you to talk about it?"

"It was a long time ago," she said. "The pain has dulled."

"You were fond of him?" he asked.

"I loved him."

"Ah," he said. "Love."

There was another flash, brighter and longer than the first. The rain was sheeting down beyond the shelter. The wind was howling around them.

"The autumn rains were the worst," she said. "Or perhaps the heat of summer. When it was hot and dry, we longed for the rains, and then when it rained, we wished and wished that we could have the heat and sunshine back."

The crash of thunder was a little louder and more prolonged.

"I have heard," he said, "that conditions were quite intolerable, that men died of the heat and died facedown in the mud. It amazes me that Colonel Lord Mornington would have voluntarily taken a woman there.''

"It was not voluntary," she said. "I insisted on going. And I am glad I did. Our two years there were the only time we had together. I would not be without those two years."

"Love indeed," he said.

"It *was* love," she said quietly, "despite your tone of sarcasm. There is such an emotion, such a commitment, my lord, even though many poor people choose to heap scorn on the very idea."

"Ah," he said, "I detect a setdown. I am one of your 'poor people,' Lady Mornington?"

"Yes," she said. "I would guess that you have never known love."

He chuckled. "And so you comforted your grieving heart after your colonel's demise with Clifton," he said.

With Marcus. The Earl of Clifton. Lord Edmond's tone made her relationship with him sound sordid. It had not been sordid, though for six years she had been the close friend of a married man. It had not been sordid. But she would be damned before she would justify herself to anyone, least of all to her present companion.

"That is my own affair, my lord," she said, and then she was furious with herself for her choice of word as he chuckled again.

Lord Edmund Waite clearly had a sordid mind.

And then suddenly and quite unexpectedly the storm was close. They could actually see the lightning fork above the trees, and the thunder crashed only moments afterward.

"And they said there would be no fireworks at Vauxhall tonight," Lord Edmond said.

Mary clasped her hands very tightly in her lap, tried to impose calm on her mind, and failed miserably. At the very next flash she launched herself against her companion's shoulder, wailing horribly. Her terrified mind could form no words.

"What is it?" He laughed and set one arm about her shoulders. "It was not my person after all, then? You *are* afraid of storms? It is a good thing you had no children, Lady Mornington. Who would comfort whom?"

The thunder rocked their shelter. Mary clawed at his shoulders and burrowed her head against his chest, wailing out her hysteria.

"Hey," he said, the amusement gone from his voice. "Hey." She was almost unaware of the fact that he slid one arm beneath her knees and lifted her onto his lap. He opened his coat and wrapped it about her as best he could. "By Jove, you really are frightened, aren't you?"

"Hold me," she babbled at him as the storm reached a rapid crescendo. "Hold me."

"I have you close." His voice was quiet and quite serious now. His arms were tight about her, his cheek against the top of her head. "I have you safe, Mary. It *is* Mary, is it not?"

But she could not get close enough to him. She wanted to crawl inside his clothes, inside his body. They were so very exposed, in an open shelter and amongst trees. And the storm was directly overhead.

"Hold me!" she commanded him, her face hidden against his neck. "Oh, God. Please. Oh, please."

She resisted as one hand lifted her head away from its hiding place. She clawed at his wrist. And then her face was hidden again—against his. His mouth was warm and wide over hers.

"You will be quite safe," he murmured into her mouth. "I have you safe, Mary."

She clung to him for the next several minutes as he alternately kissed her and murmured to her. There was some comfort. If only she could have him closer. Her back felt so very exposed to danger despite the strength of his arms about her. But there was some comfort. She opened her mouth to his tongue, which came warm and firm right into her mouth and stroked her own tongue.

"I have you safe," he told her as he laid her head against his shoulder eventually and held it there with a warm and steady hand as the storm receded somewhat. The rain too had eased a little, though it was still falling far too heavily to permit them to venture out in it.

Some sanity began to return. She knew that she was on Lord Edmond Waite's lap, her head cradled on his shoulder, held there with one hand that played gently with her short curls. His other arm was protectively about her. She knew that he had been kissing her and putting his tongue into her mouth—something Lawrence had never done. It was perhaps what one might expect of a libertine. She closed her eyes and relaxed. The storm would be over soon.

"Have you always been like this?" he asked her.

"Four men from my husband's regiment were killed by lightning one night in the very next tent to ours," she said. She swallowed. "There was the smell of scorched flesh."

"Ah," he said. "You have every right to be afraid, then. It is almost over."

"Yes," she said. But she did not move. She felt safe where she was. "Thank you."

He chuckled. "No need, ma'am," he said. "There are compensations for offering comfort to a frightened lady."

Such ungentlemanly and ungallant words should have infuriated her. But if she were furious, she would have to lift her head and remove herself from his lap. It was safer and more comfortable to let the words pass.

And then it was obvious that the storm was coming back.

"Oh, no," she moaned, and her head burrowed against his neck again. His hand stroked over her head and shoulder.

"It will pass again," he said.

"Please," she said as the thunder cracked only moments after the lightning. "Oh, please."

After that the sounds she made became less coherent. She was unaware of the fact that he shrugged awkwardly out of his coat and wrapped it about her. She burrowed inside it. There was a little more warmth at her back, but still terror was there. She expected at any moment the unknown pain that lightning would bring as it struck. She tried again to climb inside him.

And then he stood up with her in his arms and turned so that his own back was to the open side of the shelter rather than hers. The tabletop was hard against her back, but enormously comforting. She reached for him blindly while he raised her gown to her waist and loosened his own clothing.

And then the blessed comfort of his weight was on her, the hardness of the table beneath, and she felt shielded from the terror. Her mouth found his and opened to it. And then he was between her thighs and pushing up inside her, hard and warm, and he came reassuringly deep. She felt almost safe.

"Hush," he said against her mouth, and she realized that she was still wailing and obeyed his command.

The simultaneous flash of lightning and crack of thunder shook the earth, or so it seemed. But he was moving in her with slow deep strokes and his weight was so heavy on her and the wooden top of the table so unyielding that she could scarcely draw breath. She felt as if she had finally succeeded in crawling inside him, and she felt almost safe. She heard someone whimpering and forced herself to be quiet again.

"It will be all right, Mary," he said against her mouth. "It will pass again."

"Yes," she said. Yes, it was going to be all right. There was an ache—an ache that made her clench inner muscles and that rose into her throat so that breathing became even more difficult. Yes, it would be all right. He was going to take her into himself, and she would be safe. "Oh, please," she pleaded into his mouth.

"God!" he said suddenly. "Oh, God, woman."

And he drove into her, bringing her an agony of pain as he pounded her against the hard wooden surface, a glory of ecstasy. She cried out, and he thrust once more very deeply into her and relaxed his weight on her.

The storm moved gradually off again.

The removal of his weight woke her. The air was chill. His coat was spread beneath her, her thin evening gown bunched above her waist. She pushed it down as he stood with his back to her, adjusting his clothing while he stared out into the rain.

"Will it come back again?" she asked.

"Your guess is as good as mine," he said. "I have not had much luck in predicting this night's events."

She sat up on the edge of the table and wondered when embarrassment and horror—all the normal feelings—would return. At that moment all she could feel was gratitude. Gratitude that Lord Edmond Waite had taken possession of her body!

"How long has it been?" she asked. "An hour?"

"About that, I suppose," he said. "I wonder how many other people ignored all the signs as we did and are trapped somewhere about the gardens."

"I don't know," she said.

He laughed. "All sorts of interesting things might have been happening hereabouts," he said. "This is far more exciting than the usual fireworks display, is it not?"

There it was again—his vulgarity. She wished he had said nothing, had merely stood silent while staring out into the darkness. She did not want to be reminded just yet of exactly whom she had been stranded with and what she had forced him into doing. And not in her wildest imaginings would she ever be able to persuade herself that she had been the victim and he the aggressor.

"It is coming back," she said after a few minutes, her voice shaking. "It can't be, can it?"

"But it is," he said.

He stood with his back to her until the storm came close again, and then he stepped over the bench, lifted her from the table, and sat with her, his back to the open side of the shelter.

But this time she was less mindlessly terrified. She was tired, with the pleasant ache inside that came from a good loving. She did not think such thoughts, only felt such feelings. He held her head against his shoulder, and she closed her eyes and drifted into a state that approximated sleep—as far as one could sleep in a crashing thunderstorm.

It stayed overhead for a long time, but when it moved off this time, it went to stay. And eventually the rain stopped too.

"Well," he said, looking down at her light slippers, "the paths are going to be rather muddy, but at least we can move out of our prison house. I profoundly hope that my carriage is still waiting for me."

He carried her along the narrower and muddier path despite her protests, and they walked side by side, not touching, along the main path. She needed her hands to hold his coat in place about her shoulders. He had insisted that she wear it, though he must be cold in his shirtsleeves, she thought.

His carriage was still waiting, one of three. It seemed that they had not been the only ones trapped by the storm. He helped her inside, gave some instructions to his coachman, and then climbed in to take his seat beside her.

2

THE CARRIAGE HAD trapped the earlier heat of the evening and not lost it during the storm. Lord Edmond Waite settled gratefully into the seat beside Mary. It was chilly outside in only shirtsleeves—and a somewhat damp shirt at that.

He looked across at her. Huddled inside his evening coat, she looked even smaller than she was. He felt all the unreality of the moment. Lady Mornington of all people. And not only was she seated in his carriage, alone with him, his coat about her shoulders, but she had cuddled on his lap and given passionate kiss for kiss. And she had made love to him on the table as fiercely as he had made love to her.

Lady Mornington! He felt rather like laughing—at the whole bizarre situation, perhaps. At himself.

Lady Mornington was everything he had always most shunned in a woman. She was independent and proud and dignified—not that she had any reason to think herself above people like himself. It was common knowledge that she had been Clifton's mistress for years until he had dropped her quite recently. Or until she had dropped him—in all fairness, he did not know who had put an end to the liaison.

And she was an intelligent woman, one who liked to surround herself with artists and brilliant conversationalists. Her literary salons were highly regarded. The woman was a bluestocking, a breed he despised. He liked his women feminine and a little mindless. He liked his women for his bed.

He had always looked on Lady Mornington with some aversion. Not that he knew the woman, he had to admit. But he had had no desire to know her. She was not even physically desirable. She was smaller and more slender than he liked his women to be. There were no pronounced curves to set his eyes to roving and his hands to itching. And she was not pretty. Her dark hair was short and curled—he liked hair to be set loose about his arms, to twine his hands in, to spread over ample breasts. She had fine gray eyes. That had to be admitted. But they were intelligent eyes, eyes bright with an interest in the world and its affairs. He far preferred bedroom eyes. And then, the woman must be thirty if she was a day.

He had not been pleased to discover that Lady Mornington was one of Mrs. Rutherford's party to Vauxhall. Or the Hubbards, for that matter. He had not expected any fellow guests of high *ton*. He was still smarting from the *ton's* censure over his jilting of Dorothea—the iceberg. Not that they had been officially engaged, of course. But everyone had been expecting it, and the obligation had been there. He could not deny that.

And he was still nursing a broken heart over Felicity's desertion. Beautiful golden-haired Felicity Wren, whom he had wanted for years, even before she was widowed, and who he had assumed was his earlier in the year, though she had teased him with a pretended preference for her faithful hound, Tom Russell.

She would not be his mistress. Finally he had had to realize that she really would not be. But by that time he had been too deeply infatuated with her to give her up. Instead he had jilted Dorothea and gone off to elope with Felicity. For her sake he had been willing to behave in a manner that even for him was dastardly.

But she had sent Tom Russell to the place where she had agreed to meet him. Tom Russell to announce that she was to marry him within the week—from choice. It was to be a love match. And Russell had looked at him with all the contempt of a man who has never given in to any of the excesses of life, and had offered to fight him if he were not satisfied.

He had declined the honor, and had returned to London to lick his wounds, to face the collective scorn of the *ton*, to drink himself into oblivion. And to find himself a new mistress, someone to help him forget all that he had lost in Felicity.

"You are warm enough?" he asked Lady Mornington, looking down at her.

"Yes, thank you," she said. "Would you like your coat back?"

"No," he said. "Keep it about your shoulders."

He had always wondered what Clifton had seen in Lady Mornington, since it was was clar as day that Clifton could have had just about any female he had cared to cast his sights on. But he had chosen the plain bluestocking Lady Mornington and had remained with her for what must have been five or six years.

He had his answer now. Beneath the plain and demure image she presented to the world, Lady Mornington hid a wild and earthy sexuality that had taken him totally by surprise earlier and had all but robbed him of control despite the extreme discomfort of the tabletop, which had not been quite long enough to accommodate their legs.

Of course, he thought, the woman had been quite distraught with fear of the storm. He had never seen anyone so beside herself with terror. Perhaps her behavior had been atypical. Perhaps her usual performances in bed were as passive and as decorous as he would have expected of her. He looked at her again and thought with some unease of the instructions he had given his coachman.

"Is that thunder again?" she asked, her knuckles tightening against the edge of his coat.

"It is very distant," he said. "I don't believe it will come over again. Though of course I have been known to be wrong before."

She looked up at him, and her eyes lingered on him before being lowered again. Was she looking at him with as much amazement as he was looking at her? He still could not quite believe the reality of what was happening. Devil take it, he had taken her walking only because their eyes had accidentally met when she was sitting a little apart in the box and he had felt that it would be unmannerly to leave her sitting there.

He did not like the woman, or she him, without a doubt. They had nothing whatsoever in common. They had not even been able to sustain a polite conversation during their walk. They had nothing to say to each other now.

The carriage drew to a halt and the coachman opened the door and set down the steps.

"Where are we?" she asked as he vaulted out onto the pavement without the aid of the steps and turned to hand her out.

"At my house," he said. The words were true, strictly speaking, though it was not his home. It was the house where he lodged his mistresses, when he had one in keeping, and where he brought his casual amours when he did not. It was in a quite respectable part of London and the staff he kept there were above reproach and were paid well to keep their mouths shut.

He was ready to sneer and climb back into the carriage with her if she protested. But after a moment's hesitation she took his hand and descended to the pavement and looked up in some curiosity at the house. He blessed a very distant flash of lightning.

He led her up the stone steps and through the door, which a manservant was already holding open for them, and into the tiled hallway. He took the coat from about her shoulders and handed it to the servant. She looked quietly about her.

"You would like some refreshments?" he asked her.

She brought her eyes to him and they rested on him for a long moment. "Tea, please," she said.

Lord Edmond nodded to his servant, took her arm, and led her upstairs, deciding to forgo the formality of leading her into a salon first. He had done that once with Felicity and had never got her beyond the salon.

"You will wish to refresh yourself," he said, taking her into the bedchamber and across it to the door leading into the dressing room, which was decked out with all the conveniences a woman could need. "Your tea will be brought to you here. Come back out when you are ready."

"Thank you," she said, stepping inside the dressing room and allowing him to close the door behind her.

He expelled his breath. She could not possibly have mistaken his intent. An imbecile would have understood it, and Lady Mornington was no imbecile. And yet she had made no resistance at all.

Was she still caught up in leftover fright from the storm? Did she need a man to help her live through the night? Or was she missing Clifton as he was missing Felicity? Or did she feel perhaps that she owed him some debt of gratitude for the comfort he had undoubtedly brought her at Vauxhall? Or did she fancy him—did she derive some sort of sexual thrill out of consorting with a rake?

He stripped off his shirt and pulled off his boots. After some consideration he left his pantaloons where they were.

And as for himself, why had he brought her here? Lady Mornington was as out-of-place in this house as an angel would be in hell. He smiled grimly at the simile and glanced about him. All the hangings of the room were red. For the first time he rather regretted the vulgarity. He glanced up at the scarlet draperies beneath the canopy of the bed.

Why had he brought her here? To find out if the passion would still be there now that the storm had gone? To console himself for Felicity? To revenge himself on a scornful society with one of its most respected hostesses—respected despite the fact of her amour with Clifton? To punish himself with the scorn he had expected from her when the carriage drew to a halt outside?

He did not know.

She was still fully clothed when she stepped out of the dressing room and closed the door quietly behind her. Her hair had been freshly brushed. Her cheeks were flushed. She looked very small and slender and respectable in this room. Her eyes looked curiously about the room and then came to rest on him. She looked him up and down, though there was no notable contempt in her eyes.

"Your tea was brought up?" he asked.

"Yes, thank you," she said.

Come here, he was about to say to her. But he swallowed the command and crossed the room to her. She watched him come. An opportune and distant flash of lightning lit the room for a moment.

"It is far away," he said.

"Yes."

He set his arms loosely about her, found the buttons at the back of her gown, and began to undo them. She stood still, her eyes on his chest. When he had finished his task, he lifted the gown off her shoulders with the straps of her chemise, and down her arms. Both rustled to the floor, and he stooped down on one knee to roll down her silk stockings. She lifted her feet one at a time while he removed them with her slippers. And she took a step away from her clothes.

She was pleasingly proportioned even if she was not voluptuous. Her breasts were small, but firm and prettily shaped. Her waist was small, her hips wider, her legs slim and well-shaped, though they were not long. He cupped her breasts in his hands and set his thumbs over her nipples. He kept them there until they hardened, and then stroked them. She raised her chin sharply and closed her eyes.

He lifted her up and carried her to the bed. He stripped off his remaining clothes before joining her there.

He explored her mouth with his tongue, and she surprised him by responding with her own so that he was able to entice it into his own mouth and suck inward on it.

"Mm," he said. "How do you like it, Mary? Do you have any special preferences?"

She opened her eyes and regarded him as if she was thinking carefully of her answer.

"Slow," she said eventually. "I like it slow."

He kissed her openmouthed again. "With lots of slow foreplay?" he asked without lifting his mouth from hers. "Or is it the main event you like to be slow and long?"

Again the pause before her answer. "Both," she said.

He gave her both, imposing an iron control on his body. It was not easy. After the first couple of minutes, once his hands had gone to work on her as well as his mouth, she gave herself with a wild abandon. But she gave herself not only to be loved, but to love. Her hands moved on him, and her mouth and legs and body, with as much eroticism as his on her. Except that she had the luxury of two separate climaxes, one before he mounted her and one after, before the final shared cresting as he spilled his seed in her.

Well, he thought, removing himself from her after a minute or two of total exhaustion and settling her in the crook of his arm as he drew the blankets up over them, he would never again be able to look at Lady Mornington and see her body as sexually unappealing. And he would never look at her again and be a little afraid of her as an intelligent woman somewhat beyond his touch. Intelligent she might be. But she was also an all passionate, uninhibited, feminine woman.

Strange, he thought. He had been in search of a new mistress for several weeks. And finally he had found her where he had least expected. Lady Mornington! It was almost laughable.

He followed her into sleep.

She woke him twice during the night, once when the storm moved briefly overhead again, and he turned her over onto her back once more and mounted her without foreplay and loved her swiftly while she held him close. And again when dawn was beginning to light the room. She was standing beside the bed, touching his arm. She was dressed.

"My lord," she said, "I wish to go home if you please."

"Edmond," he said, laughing.

She turned her back on him and walked unhurriedly to the window as he threw aside the blankets and stepped naked out onto the carpet.

She was unwilling for him to accompany her home. "I would be obliged for the use of your carriage," she told him, "but there is no need for you to come too, my lord."

But he insisted, of course, and they sat silently side by side during the drive to Portman Place, not quite touching, looking out at the early-morning streets, still partly wet from the downpour of the night before.

"At least no one will be complaining of dust for a day or two," he said.

"No," she agreed. "It will be the mud."

That was the extent of their conversation.

He stepped down from the carriage at Portman Place and handed her out as his coachman rang the doorbell.

"Thank you," she said, looking up at him. If she was embarrassed by the appearance of a curious servant in the doorway to her house, she did not show it. "Good day to you, my lord."

He held her hand for a moment longer. "I shall do myself the honor of calling on you this afternoon," he said.

She hesitated for a moment, looking down at their hands. "Yes," she said at last, looking up into his eyes again. "I shall be at home."

He raised her hand to his lips before releasing it.

Mary was usually an early riser. The morning was too exhilarating a part of the day to be wasted in sleep, she always told anyone who was startled to discover that she frequently walked in the park at a time of the morning when only tradesmen and maids exercising the family dogs were abroad. But it was midmorning when she awoke on the day following Vauxhall. And even then, when she opened her eyes and saw her cup of chocolate looking cold and unappetizing on the table beside her bed, she would have gone back to sleep if she could.

But she could not. She lay on her stomach, her face buried in her pillow, and remembered. And felt quite physically sick. She wished it could all be written off as a dream—as a strange, bizarre nightmare. But she knew that it could not. There was that unmistakable, almost pleasant aching in the passage where he had been and worked. There was the tenderness of her breasts, which he had touched and fondled and sucked and bitten. There were the dryness and slight soreness of her lips. And somehow there was the smell of him on her arms and in her hair, and the taste of him in her mouth.

No, it had been no dream. Vauxhall had been real. The storm had been real. And he had been real.

She sat up and reached over to the bell rope to summon her maid. She had to have a bath and wash her hair. If only it were as easy to wash him out of her memory and out of her life, she thought as she swung her legs over the side of the bed.

She cursed the thunderstorm for the first time. Without it she would have arrived safely back at the box, having had a quite horrid time walking with him, and she would have been able to part from him with the fervent hope that she would never have to be in company with him again.

But the storm *had* happened, and it had come at just the worst possible moment. The memory of it had her gripping the edge of the bed in blank terror for a moment. Never since that dreadful night in Spain had she been forced to live through a storm out-of-doors—or as near outdoors as to make no difference.

"A bath, please," she said when her maid appeared in the room. "And some tea, Rachel. No, no more chocolate, thank you." Her stomach revolted at the very thought.

Dear Lord, there had been no one to cling to but him. And she had clung, desperately and mindlessly. And she had been so intent on climbing right inside him that eventually he had climbed right inside her—with her full consent and cooperation. Indeed, she was very much afraid that she had given him little choice.

With Lord Edmond Waite! He had been inside her body. She spread one palm over her mouth and closed her eyes. Dear God, inside her body. Where only Lawrence had been before. And no one for seven years. And now him.

When her bathwater had arrived, she sent Rachel back down to the kitchen to fetch a brush. And she scrubbed at her skin with it until the soapsuds were almost overflowing onto the floor and her skin looked rather like that of a lobster. But he had been inside her. She could not scrub him away.

He had said he would call on her during the afternoon. But she did not want him inside her house. Perhaps he would not come, she thought. But perhaps he would feel obliged to come. Perhaps he would feel obliged to offer for her. Would a libertine and a jilt feel obligated to offer marriage to the woman who had seduced him during a thunderstorm? The thought of marrying Lord Edmond Waite made Mary laugh most hysterically as she stood up and wrapped a towel about her shoulders.

Or perhaps he felt he owed her some apology. Did such a man ever apologize? Perhaps he would not come. She hoped and hoped that he would not come. Ever. She hoped she would never have to face the embarrassment of coming face-to-face with him again.

And it could not be avoided any longer, could it? she thought, wiping the suds angrily from one foot and losing her balance and hopping around on the other. There had not been only that encounter at Vauxhall, for which perhaps she could forgive herself. There had been that horridly sordid house, which was obviously his love nest, and that sickeningly vulgar room with its scarlet velvet hangings and wide soft bed. And her almost inexplicable lack of resistance to being taken there.

With how many other women had he lain in that bed? she wondered, and felt again as if she must vomit. It had been a certain gratitude, perhaps, a certain embarrassment that had taken her there unresisting. He had done her an enormous favor at Vauxhall. There could be no arguing about that, sordid as their encounter there had been. Dear Lord, on a tabletop . . . She shook her head clear of the thought. And there had been some leftover terror, the need to cling, the fear of being alone. And a certain lassitude left over from that first encounter. A certain curiosity, perhaps? She shuddered. For whatever reason, she had found it impossible to refuse him.

And you enjoyed what you got there. The inner voice was almost audible in the room. *You enjoyed every moment of it.* Mary shook her head again, but the voice could not be hushed.

She had always been something of a passive lover, though she had always given herself with willingness and tenderness. Certainly Lawrence had never complained or accused her of coldness. And men, she had always thought, liked to do the loving. Women, she had thought, were the receptacles for their pleasure. Not that she had ever lacked pleasure herself. Lawrence had pleased her.

She had not been passive the night before. Her frenzy was understandable at Vauxhall when the storm was raging. But there had been no storm that first time in the scarlet room. And yet . . . And yet . . . Oh, God.

You enjoyed every moment of it. And you gave every bit as good as you got.

She closed her eyes very tightly. She could not have. She could not. The man repulsed her. He was everything she found most repulsive.

And most attractive, the voice said, unbidden.

Surely he would not come that afternoon, she thought. Surely, like her, he would wake up that morning appalled by what had happened between them the night before. But he had said he would come. She would not be there, she decided. She would go out. But she had told him she would be at home. She could not go out.

She dressed herself with shaking hands and brushed through her damp curls. She could still feel where he had been inside her. Well, she had asked for it to be slow, and slow it had been. The resulting soreness was inevitable. It had been seven years.

She rang for the bathwater to be removed.

The bottom felt rather as if it had dropped out of Mary's stomach when the doorbell rang during the afternoon and she waited in the downstairs salon for her visitor to be announced. But when the door opened, she found with enormous relief that it was Penelope who was following the butler into the room, not Lord Edmond Waite.

"Mary," Penelope said, reaching out her hands to take her friend's, and kissing her on the cheek. "What a relief to find you at home. I was half-afraid that you were still wallowing in some mud at Vauxhall. What on earth happened to you? Adrian had to almost drag me home. There was no point in our waiting around for you, he said, when doubtless you had taken shelter somewhere and were not alone anyway. But, Mary . . ." Her eyes grew saucer wide. "You were not alone! You were with Lord Edmond Waite, of all people. Do tell all."

"We waited out the storm, and then he brought me home in his carriage," Mary said, and hoped she was not blushing.

"I am so very sorry," Penelope said. "That you were subjected to his company at all, I mean. I feel very responsible, since I invited you. It never occurred to me that some of the Rutherfords' guests would not be respectable.

She is new to town, you know. He did not ravish you or anything unthinkable like that, did he?'' She stifled a giggle.

''Nothing like that, I do assure you,'' Mary said firmly. ''We found shelter from the rain and passed the time in conversation.''

''Conversation?'' Penelope said. ''From all I have heard, the man is capable of only one kind of converse with women. But then, I daresay he stands somewhat in awe of you, Mary. Many men do because you dare to be openly intelligent. That is what Adrian tells me, anyway. Did you know that he killed his brother?''

''Adrian?'' Mary frowned.

''Lord Edmond, silly,'' Penelope said with a laugh. ''Ages and ages ago. He was jealous of him, apparently, and killed him. And killed his mother indirectly too. She died of a broken heart. I am surprised you had not heard.''

''People do not die of broken hearts,'' Mary said. ''And surely it did not happen quite as cold-bloodedly as you make it sound, Penny. No, I had not heard.''

''Well,'' Penelope said, ''it is ancient news and I do not know any of the details of it. I am glad you arrived home unravished.'' She laughed. ''But you have a terror of storms, do you not? Did he offer you comfort, Mary? Oh, I should not laugh, should I? It must have been quite dreadful for you, and I am sorry. I came to drag you out for a walk.''

''I cannot,'' Mary said, and this time she knew that she had not avoided blushing. ''I am expecting someone.''

''Oh, bother,'' Penelope said. ''But I will forgive you if he is tall, dark, and handsome. Who is he?''

''I did not say it was a he,'' Mary said.

But the door opened again at that moment and the butler announced Lord Edmond Waite.

Mary noticed only her friend's eyebrows disappearing up into her hair before turning to greet her visitor.

3

HE TOOK HER HAND in a firm clasp. He did not, Mary was relieved to find, raise it to his lips.

"Lady Mornington?" he said. "Mrs. Hubbard? I came to satisfy myself that neither of you took a chill or any other harm from last night's storm."

"None whatsoever, I thank you, sir," Penelope said, looking curiously from him to Mary as he took the seat indicated. "But then, Adrian had the foresight to get us back to our carriage before the rain started. Was it not a dreadful storm? I cannot remember one that lasted so long."

He was again Sir Edmond Waite, Mary thought, looking at him appalled. A stranger, elegantly attired, tall, rather too thin—no, "lean" was the better word, memory told her treacherously—with a harsh, thin-lipped face and strangely pale blue eyes. He was a man with a reputation that had always made him best avoided. A man to despise. A man who was not in any way a part of her world.

A man with whom she had spent a night of wild and abandoned passion. She shuddered.

"Nor, I," she said, and his eyes turned on her and burned their blue ice into her. "I am quite well, thank you, my lord."

"I blame myself," he said, "for having ignored the signs until it was too late. I did not know about Spain, of course, but even so, the experience of a severe thunderstorm with only a frail shelter for comfort is not a pleasant one for a lady."

"But at least Mary had you for company, my lord," Penelope said.

"Yes," he agreed. "At least she had that." He turned back to Mary. "Would you care for a drive in the park later, Lady Mornington?"

How could she refuse? It would be churlish to do so,

especially with Penelope sitting there, listening with interest.

"Thank you," she said. But she really did not want to go. How could she spend an hour or more in company with him, when they had nothing whatsoever in common? How could she let herself be seen driving in the park with Lord Edmond Waite? She would be ashamed to be seen with him.

"I shall ring for refreshments," she said, getting abruptly to her feet. But he put up a staying hand and got to his feet.

"I shall not interrupt your visit with Mrs. Hubbard, ma'am," he said. "I have business that needs to be attended to. I shall return for you at half-past four?"

"I shall be ready," she said. "Thank you."

And he bowed to both ladies and took his leave.

"Well," Penelope said, looking closely at her friend's flaming cheeks after the door had closed. "Mary?"

"How could I have refused him?" Mary asked. "Could I have refused him, Penny?"

"You could have been expecting other visitors," Penelope said. "You could have had another appointment. You could have been indisposed, though of course you had just said that you took no harm last night. You could have simply said no."

"But he showed me a kindness last night," Mary said.

"Did he, indeed?" Penelope said. "What exactly did happen last night, if I may be so bold as to ask?"

"Nothing," Mary said. "Nothing happened."

"Nothing." Her friend looked at her curiously again. "And yet you blush more scarlet than scarlet and feel obliged to take a public drive with London's most notorious rake. Mary!"

"And that will be the end of it," Mary said. "I shall thank him for staying close to me and talking to me all through the storm, and he will be satisfied that indeed I took no harm. And then this whole nasty situation will be at an end."

"He is an attractive man," Penelope said. "I know that many women find him so. And to many his reputation is just an added attraction. You are in a vulnerable position at the moment, with the Earl of Clifton gone. You were very fond of him, I know. I think you were perhaps in love with him, though you would never admit as much. I insisted you come

to Vauxhall last evening mainly because you were in low
spirits. You will not turn to Lord Edmond, will you? Oh,
anyone but him, Mary. There must be any number of
perfectly respectable gentlemen who would be only too
pleased to befriend and even court you. You are only thirty
years old.''

"Turn to Lord Edmond Waite? Penny, please!" Mary
looked expressively at her friend. "The very thought of him
makes me shudder.''

"We are talking about his person, not the thought of him,"
Penelope said. "I am more sorry than ever about not asking
Mrs. Rutherford who her other guests were to be last evening
and about the unfortunate chance that put you in Lord
Edmond's company just when the storm began. But I do
believe that like everyone else, he could have predicted its
start and hurried you back to our carriage. It was just like
the man to trap a lady into a forced *tête-à-tête*. He did not
try anything, Mary?''

"No," Mary said firmly. "He did not try anything, Penny.
Do you think I would have allowed it?''

"No," Penelope said without hesitation. "Of course you
would not. And amongst all the bad I have heard of the man,
ravishment has never been part of the list. Enough of that
unpleasant subject. Who is coming to your salon the evening
after tomorrow? Anyone of special interest?''

Mary was relieved at the change of subject, relieved not
to have to be telling more and more lies. What would Penny
say if she knew the full truth? she wondered. The full truth
did not bear thinking of. The more her mind touched on it,
the more incredible it all seemed. It could not have happened,
surely.

But it had.

Penelope stayed for half an hour before rising to take her
leave.

"I shall look forward to the evening," she said. "I always
enjoy listening to Mr. Beasley's theories on reform and to
all the animated argument that his radical views inevitably
arouse. If Sir Alvin Margrove does put in an appearance,
there are sure to be sparks flying. It was courageous of you
to invite them both on the same evening, Mary.''

"When a person holds such extreme views," Mary said, "it is always desirable to have someone who holds the opposite, just so that the rest of us ordinary mortals can form a balanced opinion ourselves."

"Well," Penelope said, "I must be going. Shopping tomorrow? Can we possibly persuade ourselves that we need new bonnets or silk stockings or cream cakes?"

Mary laughed. "Definitely not cream cakes," she said. "But I am sure we can find some purchase that we cannot possibly live without. My carriage or yours?"

And then she was alone again, with an hour and a half to kill before Lord Edmond Waite was to return for her. An hour and a half in which to develop pneumonia or typhoid or something equally indisputable. If only she could put the clock back twenty-four hours, she thought, closing her eyes briefly, and find an excuse—any excuse—not to go to Vauxhall. If only she could.

But she could not. And that was that.

Lord Edmond Waite had not gone back to bed after taking Mary home. He had gone to his own home, saddled his horse, and gone for a brisk gallop in the park, there being no one else there at that time of the morning to object to his speed. Not that a few objections would have slowed him anyway. And then he had gone to Jackson's Boxing Saloon and sparred for a few rounds.

He would normally have gone to Tattersall's or the races in the afternoon, and then sought out a decent card game at Watier's. Dinner at White's and a visit to the theater or opera house to see what new talent if any had arrived fresh from the country—there had been a dearth of good talent lately. A look-in at some *ton* entertainment if there were no interesting prospects to pursue at the opera house. A perusal of all the young things at the Marriage Mart and a sneer at all their mamas, who would inevitably note his arrival and his raised quizzing glass with some alarm.

As if he were interested in bidding at the Market for a gauche and innocent little virgin.

The life sometimes became a trifle tedious. But then, there was no other that he knew of. He might have been happy with Felicity—he *would* have been happy. He would have taken her all about Europe and the British Isles. He would have wanted to show her off to the world. He would have wanted to give her the world.

Well, he wished her joy of her country swain. She would doubtless settle down with him to a life of dull respectability and half a dozen children and never know what she had missed with the man she had jilted.

But devil take it, he missed her and the chance at happiness he had glimpsed for the merest moment. He might have been happy. But he would not have been. It was not in his nature, not in his fate, to be happy.

One fact about his planned elopement with Felicity he would never regret, anyway. It had enabled him to get rid of Dorothea. Ignobly, it was true. His reputation would probably never recover from the blot he had put there by abandoning her. The note he had sent her had been very stark and to the point. He had not let her down gently.

Well, he thought as he climbed to the driver's seat of his curricle late in the afternoon, at least he was about to embark on a new adventure in his life. It would brighten the dullness for a while at least. Lady Mornington! Who would have thought it? If anyone had told him twenty-four hours before that by this time today she would be his mistress and that he would be more than eager to repeat his bedding of her, he would have laughed with the loudest scorn. Lady Mornington?

But he had seen her with new eyes when he had called upon her briefly earlier in the afternoon. Her small, slender figure had looked pleasing to him because he knew what she looked like without the clothes and what she felt like beneath him on a bed, her legs twined about his. And her eyes had looked lovelier because he had known what they looked like when she was making love. Her hair had looked pretty because he knew how softly the warm curls twined about his fingers. Long hair would not suit such a small lady.

And he had no longer been afraid of her—had he really been afraid? She might be a bluestocking, she might be intelligent. But she was also a woman—his woman.

Lady Mornington—looking as dignified and prim as ever,

and looking totally different than she had ever looked to him before. He had almost laughed aloud, and probably would have if her friend Penelope Hubbard had not bee with her. It was a shame, that. He had been looking forward to being alone with her.

She was coming down the stairs when he was admitted to the hall of her house. She wore a spring-green dress with a matching pelisse and an unadorned straw bonnet. She would, of course, be outshone by a hundred ladies on fashionable Rotten Row. But it did not matter. He had been infatuated with Felicity because she was the loveliest woman he had ever known. Perhaps he was ready now for the opposite. Though not quite the opposite, either.

She smiled at him. "Some fresh air will feel good," she said.

"You have not been out today?" he asked her. "I suppose you slept the morning away."

She did not answer, but concentrated on drawing on her gloves, and waited for her manservant to open the front door.

Outside, he helped her up to the high seat of his curricle. "I hope you would not have preferred a carriage or barouche," he said. "But I always believe that during a drive in the park one must both see and be seen. It is the nature of the game, is it not?"

She smiled again. "This conveyance is fine," she said. "Is it new?"

They conversed so politely on the way to the park that Lord Edmond almost laughed. They were behaving like strangers. Who would have thought that only a matter of hours ago they had been in steamy embrace in his scarlet room? He could hardly believe it. He could hardly believe that she was the same woman.

"You slept well this morning?" he asked her.

She stiffened.

"I am afraid I did not allow you much sleep before you returned home," he said.

"I would prefer not to talk about that," she said.

"Would you?" he said. "Do the memories embarrass you? They need not. You were magnificent."

"Last night was a strange out-of-time experience," she

said. "The storm made me lose my mind. I am grateful for the comfort you offered. I just wish it might have taken a different form."

"But there was no storm," he said, laughing, "when you told me that you liked it slow, that you liked both the foreplay and the main event slow. And you proved to me more than amply that you had not lied. You did indeed like it—as I did."

Her jaw hardened, he saw, and she gazed very rigidly ahead of her. "If you are a gentleman," she said, "you will forget last night, or at least keep your memories strictly to yourself. But of course, you are not a gentleman, are you?"

His eyebrows shot up. "You do not mince words, do you, Mary?" he said. "That was a blistering setdown."

"I am Mary only to my intimates," she said.

"Then I am glad I did not call you Lady Mornington," he said. "I am nothing if not your intimate, Mary."

"Hush," she said. "May we please change the subject?"

He had turned his horses' heads between the gateposts leading into Hyde Park, and almost instantly they were amongst other carriages and horses and pedestrians. It was right on the fashionable hour.

He considered her in silence for a moment. She was rigid with anger or embarrassment or something. He supposed that he might have guessed she would not accept the situation as easily as he had. She was doubtless embarrassed to know that she had revealed her passionate nature so early in their relationship.

"I hope you do not expect me to discuss Virgil or the Elgin Marbles or any such thing," he said. "Shall we discuss bonnets? What do you think of Miss Hodgeson's—she is the lady in blue with the sharp-nosed dragon seated beside her."

"It is elegant," Mary said.

"Do you think so?" He set his head to one side and stared at the bonnet. "If all the fruit is real, I suppose there is practical value to it. She and the dragon can have some tea without having to go home for it. If it is not real, then I would have to say that she is imposing a great deal of unnecessary weight on her neck and it is in danger of disappearing into her shoulders. Wouldn't you agree?"

"I am sure the fruit weighs nothing at all," Mary said.

He chuckled. "You have no sense of the absurd, Mary," he said. "Do you ever laugh?"

"When something is truly funny, of course," she said.

"Ah." He winced. "Another setdown. Do you specialize in them?"

She did not have a chance to reply. Colonel Hyde, one of her acquaintances, signaled to his coachman to stop his barouche alongside the curricle. Clearly he intended to talk. Lord Edmond inclined his head to the man and touched his hat to Mrs. Hyde, who sat hatchet-faced at her husband's side.

"Ah, Mary, my dear," the colonel said. "So you are taking the air too, are you? Waite?"

"Hello, Mary, dear," Mrs. Hyde said. "Are you quite safe up there?"

"I am taking good care of her, ma'am," Lord Edmond said.

But the colonel's good lady chose to ignore his very existence. Just as if Mary had decided to take a ride in the park in the passenger seat of a curricle with only the horses for company.

"Quite, thank you," Mary said. "Have you recovered from your cold?"

"Who is to be at your salon the evening after tomorrow, eh?" the colonel asked. "Dorothy wants to go listen to that Madame Paganini or whatever her name is at Rossford's, but the woman screeches. I would prefer to enjoy some intelligent conversation at your house. Who is it to be?"

"Mr. Beasley for certain," Mary said. "And Sir Alvin Margrove has said he will look in if he can."

"Ha." The colonel barked with laughter. "I would not miss it for worlds, dear. There will be a duel at dawn the following day, for sure. I'll have to bring Freeman with me. He will shoot himself if he finds out later that he has missed such fun. Will you be there, Waite?"

"Beasley and Margrove?" Lord Edmond said. "They can set the House on a roar, I have heard. They may just be too much for Lady Mornington's salon. I shall be there to protect her if it should come to fisticuffs."

"Marvin," Mrs. Hyde said frostily, "we are blocking the thoroughfare. We must drive on."

The colonel touched his hat and gave his coachman the signal to drive on.

There was a short silence in the curricle.

"Your literary—or political—evenings are not invitational?" Lord Edmond asked. "You hold open house?"

"Anyone is welcome," she said, her voice stiff.

"Then I shall be there," he said. "If you have no objection, of course."

"I am not sure the entertainment will be quite to your taste," she said.

"Ah," he said. "Your meaning being that there will be no gaming tables and no deep drinking and no willing barmaids, I suppose."

"The words are yours, my lord," she said, "not mine."

"Sometimes," he said. "Not always, I must admit, but sometimes I can live without those things. Perhaps for one evening out of seven. I am not utterly depraved, you see, Mary, only almost so."

"I wish you would not talk so," she said. "It is not seemly."

"But then, you yourself said that I am no gentleman," he said. Two of his acquaintances, he saw, had been about to bring their horses up alongside his curricle. But both looked askance at Mary, raised their eyebrows at him and rode on.

And yes, he thought, it would seem strange to them that he was taking her of all people for an afternoon drive. But then, they did not know. He felt as if he were hugging a precious secret to himself. He drew his curricle away from the most frequented part of the park.

"It is strange," he said, "how people can be quite different from what we expect them to be. You are very different."

"You do not know me at all, my lord," she said.

"On the contrary," he said, "I think I know you very well indeed in the biblical sense, Mary. I think it unlikely that there is one inch of your body, inside or out, that I did not explore to my great pleasure last night."

She looked away to the trees beside the path.

"I would have expected you to be cold," he said, "or at least only decorously warm. I have known many women, Mary, but none as passionate and as uninhibited as you."

Her teeth were white and even, he noticed as they bit down into her lower lip.

"You are different from what I would have expected," he said. "Wonderfully different."

"You do not know me at all," she said again.

"Was it your husband who taught you?" he asked. "I did not know Lord Mornington, I regret to say."

"This is insufferable," she said.

"Or was it Clifton?" he asked. "I must confess that I used to wonder what he saw in you, Mary. Now I know. And I know why he kept you for so long. I think I might want to keep you longer."

Her eyes blazed at him when she turned her head, and he saw yet another facet of Lady Mornington's character.

"This is intolerable!" she said. "Set me down at once."

He raised his eyebrows. "Alone in the middle of the park?" he said. "I am enough of a gentleman not to do that, Mary."

"Gentleman!" she said. "You do not know the meaning of the word. Let me be very clear, my lord. Despite what happened at Vauxhall, I was and am grateful to you. I believe I might well have gone out of my mind if you had not taken it upon yourself to comfort me. What happened afterward happened because it was a strange night and because the storm lingered in the distance and because . . . oh, because everything was strange. I do not blame you for anything that happened. I was as much to blame as you—more so, perhaps. But what happened was over when you took me home last night. I wish to have no further acquaintance with you. None whatsoever. Do I make myself clear?"

"Mary," he said, "you enjoyed it as much as I."

"It brought me comfort," she said. "Enjoyment was no part of it."

"You are a liar," he said. "Next time, Mary, I shall force you to admit to your enjoyment before I allow you release.

You will tell me in words as well as with your body.''

"If you will not set me down," she said, "then take me home, please. I thought when I awoke this morning that I had awoken from some nightmare. But it is still with me. I want it to end the moment you set me down outside my own door. It is to end.''

He turned his horses in the direction of the gates. Yes, he should have expected it, he thought. A woman of Lady Mornington's pride could not be expected to give in unprotesting to her physical nature. Doubtless she was a Puritan and considered physical passion to be sinful. She had been married for a number of years—he did not know how many. And she had been Clifton's woman for five or six years. She had probably not had any other men except him the night before. Having been bedded by three separate men—and only one her husband—would doubtless seem sinful to someone like her.

Well, he would have to teach her. Slowly. Lady Mornington must learn as she loved—slowly.

"It will not end," he said quietly to her. "You know it as well as I, Mary. Something began last night, and it is very far from its end. Very far. But I can wait." He laughed. "I am named suitably. I can wait for you to accept the inevitable, as I have. We will be lovers. You will be my mistress. Perhaps for longer than you were Clifton's. I cannot imagine growing quickly tired of what we shared last night. But I can wait—for a while. I am not by nature a patient man, but I can patiently await something I really want.''

"Then you had better be prepared to wait until your dying day," she said.

"Perhaps," he said. "But I think not. I think it will be sooner than that.''

He was content to be silent for the rest of the distance to Portman Place. And he was glad when he got there that he had brought his curricle. Had she not been perched so high above the road, he did not believe she would have allowed him to assist her to the ground. As it was, he lifted her by the waist and slid her down his body. He felt her shudder.

"I shall attend your salon two evenings from this," he said.

"I wish you would not." She raised her eyes to his.

"But you said yourself that you hold open house," he said. "You would not turn me away, Mary, or have me thrown out?"

"Please do not come," she said.

"You will be ashamed to have me seen there?" he asked. And he smiled at her, although he found it a little difficult to do so.

"Yes," she said fiercely. "If you will force me to be so ill-mannered, yes. I will be ashamed."

"Ah," he said, his eyes glittering down at her, "but no one will know that we have lain together, Mary, unless you choose to make the announcement yourself. Or that we will lie together again more times than you can count."

She turned sharply away from him and rapped the knocker on her door before he could do so himself.

He watched her straight and rigid back until the door opened and she disappeared inside without another word or a backward glance. He smiled and climbed back into the seat of his curricle.

But he was not amused. Felicity too had fought him, and he had refused to believe that she did not mean to have him eventually. He had even offered her marriage in the end because it had seemed to him that there was no other way of having her. Was he being just as blind and just as foolish with Mary? Was he inviting rejection just as surely?

But he had never had Felicity. He had had Mary, and she had wanted him then. No other woman had wanted him as she had wanted him the night before. No other woman had loved him as she had loved him.

It could not be the end. That could not have been both a beginning and an ending. There was a feeling of near-panic at the very thought.

Devil take it, but he would have her. And she would like it too. He would make her tell him so the very next time he had her beneath him and mounted. He would keep her writhing with unfulfillment until she had told him that she enjoyed it. And that she loved him.

He would make her tell him that she loved him. By God, he would. And she would mean it too.

4

MARY'S ENTERTAINMENTS were known to most people as
literary evenings, though that was not, strictly speaking, a
true description of them. Sometimes she did have poets or
playwrights in attendance, but very often it was politicians
or artists or musicians. Occasionally there was no special
guest at all, but just those who liked to gather for an evening
of good conversation without the distraction of dancing or
card playing.

She was proud of her literary evenings and of the class
of people who attended them.

She had told no one that Lord Edmond Waite planned to
attend this particular one—not even Penelope. Perhaps he
would not come, she thought. Surely he would not, on mature
consideration. He would be vastly out-of-place. And she must
have made quite clear to him that she had no wish or intention
of furthering their acquaintance.

But she looked forward to the evening with a trepidation
she did not normally feel. Normally she would have been
excited at the prospect of having Mr. Beasley and Sir Alvin
Margrove in a room together—in her salon. She knew that
the gathering of guests would be larger than usual as a result,
though it was by no means certain that Sir Alvin would be
able to find the time to come. Even Mr. Beasley alone would
draw people to her house, however.

But her eagerness was tempered by anxiety. She wished
she could be back to the old days, when Marcus would be
coming, as like as not, and staying afterward too when
everyone else had gone home. He had stayed just so that they
might talk and relax cozily together. It had not been discreet
of them, perhaps. Inevitably there had been some gossip.
And that gossip might have had foundation. There had been
one occasion early in their acquaintance when he had

embraced her and she had responded. She had even led him to her bedchamber, but once there she had faced him with outer embarrassment and inner shame, and he had laughed, breaking the tension, and agreed that, no, such a relationship was not possible between them. She had joined in his laughter, relieved and a little shamefaced.

After that, surprisingly perhaps, they had developed a deep and warm friendship. She wished she could have those days back. But she could not.

And Sir Edmond wanted her to be his mistress, had confidently predicted that it would be so. It would be laughable if it were not so annoying—so infuriating in the extreme.

She dressed with greater care than usual, wearing an apricot-colored gown more suitable for a concert or the theater, perhaps, than for a literary evening. And she washed and fluffed her hair so that the curls were softer and glossier than usual. She did it to boost her confidence, to enable her to feel good about herself.

There was an anxious hour when her salon filled with familiar and a few less-familiar faces, while neither of the main guests appeared. But Mr. Beasley arrived finally and apologized for being somewhat late. Mary breathed a sigh of relief. If he was somewhat late, then so was Lord Edmond, and probably that meant that he would not come at all.

Young Mr. Pipkin had arrived unfashionably dressed, long hair unkempt, one pocket bulging with copies of his latest poetry. Mary built a group about him and stayed there herself, listening to his theatrical readings of very mediocre poetry, and was pleased to find that most listeners were able to give positive and tactful criticisms of the poems. Perhaps he should try writing in the more modern vein instead of feeling himself confined to the heroic couplet, Lord Livermere suggested. He would find more rein for his talents.

Mary began to relax and enjoy herself. Although there was no sign of Sir Alvin Margrove, the group about Mr. Beasley was large.

And then she saw him—Lord Edmond Waite, that was. He was standing in the doorway of her salon, a quizzing glass in one hand, dressed with exquisite elegance in black evening clothes. He looked rather satanic, Mary thought, anger warring with dismay as she moved away from Mr. Pipkin's side. He was looking about him with a supercilious expression, as if he had walked in upon a colony of worms.

"Ah, Lady Mornington," he said as she approached him, "I am sorry to be so late. You must have been afraid that I was not coming at all."

He reached out an elegant lace-covered hand, and she was aware as she placed her own unwillingly in it that his arrival was attracting a considerable amount of covert though well-bred attention. She felt she would surely die when he bowed over her hand and raised it to his lips.

"Not afraid," she said, appalled at her own lack of manners. "Hoping, my lord."

"Well," he said, and he still retained her hand in his. He even covered it with his other hand. "Sometimes, Mary, one feels the compulsion to see how the other half lives. Your literary evenings are quite famous."

"Thank you," she said. "May I direct you to a tray of drinks?"

"On the assumption that I cannot live without a glass in my hand?" he said. "Perhaps you should give direction that a tray of drinks be placed at my personal disposal. And you do not need to direct me. I can see with my naked eye three trays with servants attached to them. To which one shall I escort you?"

"I do not like to drink," she said. "And I must return to Mr. Pipkin's group, if you will excuse me. He is reading his poetry and will perhaps be hurt if I desert him so soon."

"And I will not?" he said. "Pipkin? The one who likes to look and live the part of a poet but has a lamentable lack of talent to go along with the image?"

"His work is interesting," she said.

"If I were an aspiring poet," he said, "and you called my work interesting in that best hostess voice of yours, Mary, I should drown both it and myself in the nearest duck pond. Go, then. I shall see to my own entertainment."

Mary returned gratefully to the group she had just left,

and felt all the bad manners of her behavior and hated him for having forced her into it. It was inexcusable of her to abandon a late guest without first of all seeing to it personally that he had a drink in his hand and had been introduced into some group.

She hesitated, as there was a flurry of polite applause to herald the end of one of Mr. Pipkin's longer and more impassioned pieces. Perhaps she should return to Lord Edmond? Even considering who he was, she would have treated him with the proper courtesy if those events surrounding Vauxhall had not happened. Of course, her salon would be the last place on earth he would be if it had not been for Vauxhall.

She was relieved to find when she looked behind her that he was half-hidden amongst the large group about Mr. Beasley. The look on his face had changed to one of amusement. How dare he? she thought, giving in to a wave of anger. How dare he find one of the country's most prominent and progressive politicians amusing? How dare he find her entertainment amusing! Doubtless he would be far more comfortable and serious if she had a few half-naked dancers cavorting on the tables.

"Mary!" Penelope Hubbard tapped her on the arm and drew her to one side. Their mutual friend Hannah Barrat was with her. "Whatever is this?"

"Lord Edmond Waite?" Mary did not pretend to misunderstand. "He said that he has a curiosity to know how the other half lives."

"I could have died when he walked into the room," Hannah said. "Julian will not like it above half when I tell him, though Julian is a thoroughly dry old stick, of course, and I never pay him any mind. The whole idea of women being interested in politics and matters of the mind shocks him. But Lord Edmond Waite, Mary. He is somewhat beyond the pale, is he not? Poor Lady Dorothea Page."

"I told you about Vauxhall," Penelope said.

"So you did," Hannah said. "I think I would have developed smallpox and returned home when I saw that he was one of the party, Penny. And you were caught in the rain with him, Mary? That was most unfortunate. But could you not discourage him from coming here this evening?''

"My guests come not by invitation only," Mary said. "I would not turn away a guest. Besides, he is behaving with perfect propriety." For some reason her anger was suddenly directed against Hannah.

"Mary," Penelope said, "Vauxhall less than a week ago; a drive in the park the day before yesterday; here this evening. The man is not conceiving a *tendre* for you, is he?"

"How ridiculous!" Mary said. "Of course he is not."

"He must be sent about his business without further ado, Mary," Hannah said. "It will do your reputation no good to be seen consorting with him, you know."

"Oh, come, Hannah," Penelope said crossly, "sometimes you can be as stuffy as that husband of yours. And yes, of course I apologize for the insult. But friends can be excused for some plain speaking. Is he bothering you, Mary? Do you want me to be sure to be the last guest to leave?"

Mary hesitated. What if he really did as Marcus had always done and lingered after the other guests had taken their leave? Except that Marcus had always done it with her consent, of course.

"Yes, please, Penny," she said. "I would be grateful."

Penelope gave her friend a penetrating look. "He is being troublesome, then," she said.

"I must go and see if the refreshments are ready in the dining room yet," Mary said, and she smiled and turned away from her friends.

"A wonderful evening, Mary," Colonel Hyde told her at supper. "It is a shame that Margrove was unable to come, and a shame perhaps that most of us are in such awe of Beasley that we put up no argument against his theories. But one must confess that they are interesting theories. And as usual you have attracted the cream of London society here."

"Thank you," she said.

He leaned a little closer to her. "Waite is the one who puzzles me," he said. "What on earth is he doing here, Mary? The man does not have two serious thoughts to rub together, does he?" He chuckled. "Dorothy was put out that

I stopped in the park the other day. People would talk about our showing civility to such a man, she said. But how could I ignore our little Mary, I asked her.''

Mary's smile was a bit forced. "I hold open house," she said. "Anyone is welcome to come, provided he is appropriately dressed and well-behaved, of course.''

"Of course," he said, patting her hand. "I did not mean any criticism, Mary. It is a thoroughly pleasant evening, as usual.''

Provided he is well-behaved. The words echoed in Mary's mind less than an hour later. They were back in her salon, in three groups this time. Mr. Pipkin was surrounded by a new group of the curious or of those who felt that good manners dictated that he not be left in isolation. Mary had maneuvered some people into his group herself. A second group had gathered spontaneously to discuss the play at the Drury Lane they had seen the night before. The third and largest, of course, was about Mr. Beasley.

Mary joined the third group, despite the fact that Lord Edmond Waite was still part of it and still a silent and amused spectator. Or so he was for a while, at least. Mr. Beasley had been delivering a lengthy monologue in which he was expounding some of his most radical theories. He gazed about on his gathered disciples with condescension and satisfaction. There were several murmurs of surprise and disapproval, even of shock, but no one spoke up against him as Sir Alvin Margrove would surely have done. Not until Lord Edmond spoke up, that was, his voice bored and quite, quite distinct.

"Beasley," he said when the great man paused for breath, "you are an ass.''

Everyone, including Mr. Beasley, froze. But the politician had not been a member of the House for several years for nothing. He recovered himself almost immediately.

"I beg your pardon, sir?" he said in a tone that boded ill for his critic.

"You are an ass," Lord Edmond repeated, and Mary closed her eyes, white with fury. "I cannot imagine how so many apparently intelligent people can stand here and listen politely to such utter drivel.''

"My lord." Mary stepped forward. She was using her best hostess voice, she realized, instinct having taken over, though she had no idea how she was going to smooth over the moment.

But Mr. Beasley held up a large staying hand. "Don't distress yourself, pray, ma'am," he said. "Doubtless the gentleman will explain himself."

"Redistributing wealth equally will make everyone equal in value and happiness," Lord Edmond said. "Utopia will have been arrived at. Heaven will be on earth. It is an idea as old and as asinine as the proverbial hills."

"Of course," Mr. Beasley said, looking about him for approval, "the speaker is one of the wealthy and privileged. One who would have much to lose under the new order. The same would apply to most of us in this room. Most of us, however, have a spirit of humanity and justice."

"Spirit of cow dung," Lord Edmond said. "If you seriously believe that by artificially making everyone equal, Beasley, you will make them content to remain equal and to live happily ever after, then obviously you have a pea for a brain."

"I have ever found," Mr. Beasley said, inhaling deeply so that he appeared to swell to twice his size, "that those people of dull mind and brain invariably attribute like intellectual powers to those they cannot understand."

"And I have ever found," Lord Edmond said, "that asses consider themselves to be intellectual giants. If you are to bring justice to the poor, Beasley, you do not abolish all property rights and title and position. Do you seriously think that by setting a gin addict and pickpocket down on a few acres of land and stuffing a wad of money into his hand you are enabling him to live a happy and productive existence for the rest of his life? He will spend the money on gin and sell the land for more and steal from his neighbor to secure yet more for his future."

"A liquor addict." Mr. Beasley pursed his lips. "From one who knows, sir? I would have no experience of such matters myself."

"And have sealed your own doom and confirmed me in my estimation of you by admitting as much," Lord Edmond said. "If you do not understand people, Beasley, then you cannot concoct theories for their happiness. Have you learned nothing from the Revolution in France and from the career of Napoleon Bonaparte? A wonderful exercise in univeral liberty and equality, would you not agree?"

He turned away from the interested group as Mary squirmed with embarrassment and impotent fury. How dare he? Oh, how dare he!

"I must be leaving, Lady Mornington," he said. "I wish I could stay and converse longer, but I believe I have made my point, and I would not wish to monopolize the conversation."

She could have let him go. She could have stayed to smooth over the situation as best she could. There was no compulsion on her to see him to the door. But she turned and preceded him from the room.

"A delightful evening, Mary," he said, closing the salon door behind him.

She rounded on him, her eyes blazing.

"How could you!" she said. "How could you so have embarrassed me and ruined the evening?"

He raised his eyebrows. "As I understand it," he said, "these evenings are meant for conversation, not for the delivery of monologues. I seem to remember that Colonel Hyde was looking forward to the evening because a few sparks would fly if Margrove had come. Well, Mary, I rescued the evening from dullness for you. I believe I stirred up a few sparks, did I not?"

"You called him an . . ." She drew in her breath sharply.

"Ass?" he said. "And so he is too. A horse's ass, to be more precise. How can you listen to him spouting such poppycock without shouting with laughter, Mary? Politeness must be very deeply bred into you."

"And perhaps it is as well," she said, her voice tight with fury. "Or I would tell you precisely what I think of you."

"I wish you would anyway," he said, smiling at her and flicking her cheek with one long finger.

"You are unspeakably vulgar," she said. "Your language belongs in the gutter."

He considered. "In the farmyard, I believe," he said.

"Asses and cow dung are to be found there, Mary. Duck ponds too. Have you never been into the country?"

"I believe you were leaving," she said with icy courtesy.

"I must take you there sometime," he said, looking down to her lips. "It would be an education for you, Mary. You would not believe, for example, the number of uses there can be for a haystack. I will show you at least one of them."

"Please leave," she told him.

"When will I see you again?" he asked. "Will you come to Kew Gardens with me tomorrow? There are no duck ponds there, or haystacks either. Nothing to shock your sensibilities. Will you come?"

"No," she said, "thank you."

"Because I called Beasley an ass to his face and a horse's ass to yours?" he said. "My apologies, Mary. I was angry with the man. Forgive me?"

"Please leave," she said.

"You will not come to Kew?"

"No."

"No without the thank-you this time," he said with a sigh. "You must mean it, then. But I shall see you sometime soon, Mary. I do not like this primness. It is what I have always disliked in you. I like the other Mary—the real Mary. Good night."

He took her hand in his, and she steeled herself to having it kissed again. Instead he leaned forward and kissed her firmly and briefly—and openmouthed—on the lips.

"Get out!" she whispered fiercely. One of her servants was at the door, just out of earshot, waiting to open it for him. The man must have seen. "If I never see you again, it will be too soon."

"A cliché unworthy of you, Mary," he said, his pale blue eyes boring into her for a brief moment before he released her hand and turned to leave the house without a backward glance.

If she were any more furious, Mary thought, she would surely explode into a thousand fragments. She was . . . furious! Feeling had shivered downward from her mouth, just as if it were a physical reality, past her throat, through her breasts, down into her womb, and lower, leaving an uncomfortable throbbing between her legs. They felt rather as if they might collapse beneath her.

And she remembered again all that she had remembered with great and physical clarity each night since Vauxhall. She turned quickly and hurried back into the salon.

He did not know quite why he was pursuing her with such determination. She seemed seriously to want to have nothing to do with him, and her world was not his. He could not understand how she could take people like Pipkin and Beasley seriously. He had always found the deliberate pursuit of intellectuality either amusing or tedious. Could she not see that it was all hogwash?

He had been sent down from Oxford once upon a time for saying as much to a don—though his language had been rather more colorful on that occasion and had strayed somewhat from the farmyard. And he had bloodied the man's nose. Mary would have had ten fits of the vapors—though perhaps not. She had followed the drum for a few years with her husband, had she not? She must have heard it all, and more, then.

The Oxford episode had been atypical of him at that time, of course, happening as it had a scant month after Dick's death and at a time when his mother's life had hung by a thread. Lord Edmond's mouth formed almost a snarl as his mind skirted the memories. The don had been fortunate not to have had his neck wrung. Sanctimonious fool!

Why was he pursuing Mary? For the sheer challenge of overcoming such obvious resistance? Perhaps. He had pursued Felicity for similar reasons. So that he might degrade her and show his contempt for her world? No, not that. He felt no hatred for her, only a certain amusement at the fact that he might be the only man in existence, with the possible exception of Clifton, who knew that a more worldly and more earthy—and damned more interesting—Mary lurked below the demure surface.

Because her performance in bed had left him aching for more? Yes, definitely that. Women, in his experience, did not enjoy sex. Either they lay still and limp as fish, submitting to having their legs thrust wide and their bodies penetrated, and smiling like sweet martyrs afterward—that type he rarely bedded twice. Or else they twisted and gyrated and panted and shouted out with ecstasy and then adjusted their hair and held out a palm for payment. At least such women worked hard for a living, and often they knew how to give exquisite pleasure. He occasionally returned to them for more. Twice he had employed one of them as his mistress, one for a year and a half, the other for longer than two.

Mary fell into neither category. She was the only woman he had had who had quite openly and honestly enjoyed having sexual intercourse. And so she was the only woman with whom his own pleasure had been unmarred. Just the memory of that first bedding in the scarlet room could make his breathing quicken and his temperature soar—the time when she had asked for it slow and had been given it slow.

Yes, that was the reason. There could be no other. He wanted her. But not as an occasional bedfellow, someone with whom to while away the tedious hours of a useless existence. More than that. As a long-term mistress—very long-term if her performances continued to match those of that night. He wanted to have her to start his days and as dessert to his luncheon, as a midafternoon exercise, as an appetizer before whatever entertainment the evening had to offer, and as a nighttime lullaby and a middle-of-the-night drug.

He wanted to teach her more—much more. And he wanted to learn all she had to teach.

He wanted her. And by God, she must want him too. As far as he knew, she had had no one since Clifton. And a woman of such passion and appetite could not possibly find fulfillment from abstention. She was just too prim and too respectable for her own good—despite Clifton. Doubtless his reputation bothered her. Many ladies had avoided him even before he had dumped Dorothea. After that, many had totally shunned him—like Mrs. Hyde in the park the other day. The old fool! As if he cared.

Perhaps Mary had heard about Dick. It was a fifteen-year-old scandal, dead almost as long as Dick himself. But perhaps she had heard about it.

She must be made to realize that reputations and labels do not make a man. The man she saw and thought she knew was no more the real person than she was the woman he saw. The two people who had met and loved during all the frenzy of a bad storm were not the two people that the *ton* knew and the two people they had thought each other until that night. He could see that clearly. She must come to see it too.

And if she did not, well, then, by God, he would make her see it. He wanted her. And he needed her. And he would have her too.

And so he set about discovering where he might meet her within the following week. She would be at the theater with the Barretts and a few more of their friends two evenings after her literary evening, he discovered by devious means, which were second nature to him. And she had accepted an invitation to the Menzies' ball three nights after that. He had not himself received an invitation, but he would not allow that to deter him from going. They were scarcely likely to make a scene by turning him away. And if they did, well, then, it would give the tabbies something else to gossip about for a few days until another scandal came along to amuse them.

Lady Mornington had not seen the last of him by any means.

5

SHE HALF-EXPECTED HIM to call her the next day to try to insist on taking her to Kew. It was an enormous relief when he did not. He did not appear all day, or all the next day. He had finally taken the hint, she thought, though the words she had used to him could hardly be classified as a hint. He had finally accepted the fact that she wished to have no further dealings with him.

Life settled back to normal. No one, she had found, seemed to blame her for Lord Edmond's dreadful breach of good manners to Mr. Beasley. Indeed, several people had commented when she returned to the salon that the brief argument had livened the evening. Colonel and Mrs. Hyde made no mention of the incident when she called on them the following day, and when she dined with Penelope, Mr. Hubbard being from home, her friend remarked only that actually it had been rather funny.

"And though I may quarrel somewhat with his choice of words, Mary," she said, "I could not help agreeing with the sentiment. It seems he was the only person present willing to cross swords with Mr. Beasley."

She would put the whole ghastly episode behind her, Mary thought as she prepared for the evening at the theater. There would be dinner at Hannah's first and then on to the Drury Lane, one of a party of six. Hannah had invited the Viscount Goodrich as her escort. Mary had known him for several years and had always liked his quiet good manners and sensible conversation. He was about ten years her senior, about the same age as Marcus, in fact. Hannah had confided in her that he had shown definite interest in learning that her "friendship" with Marcus was at an end, and had asked his friend, Hannah's husband, to pair them up for some occasion.

"He has been a widower for eight years, Mary," Hannah

said, "and is ready to make another match, if Julian has understood the matter right. It would be splendid for you."

Mary tended to agree. She had not really thought of marriage since Lawrence's death. She had grieved for a long time. And then there had been her new life to set up in London, and her long friendship with Marcus had satisfied her need for masculine companionship—while it had lasted. But she was thirty years old and childless. And she had needs—needs that had lain dormant in her since Lawrence's death, but that had recently flared again.

She quelled a vivid and unwilling memory of just how well those needs had been satisfied during the notorious Vauxhall night. But she needed more than physical contact with a man; she needed a relationship. Perhaps she could have both with the viscount. Perhaps she could have another marriage. It was too early to plan yet, of course. But the possibility was enough to add some pleasurable anticipation to her preparations for the evening. She wore her new rose-pink silk.

Dinner was everything she could have hoped for. The food was superior—the Barretts' cook had had several covert offers from other households but had remained loyal to her employers. The company was good—the Waddingtons were the other couple—and the conversation stimulating. And the Viscount Goodrich was flatteringly attentive without being embarrassingly so.

"You should always wear such vivid colors, Lady Mornington," he had said in the drawing room when she had first arrived. He had looked at her appreciatively. "They become you."

She had felt good about the evening from that moment on.

The play that evening was to be *The Tempest*, by William Shakespeare. It was not one of his more entertaining plays, Lord Goodrich gave as his opinion during dinner, though it was one of his most thought-provoking. And of course it could be a visually pleasing play, provided it was produced well. Did not Lady Mornington consider Caliban one of Shakespeare's most villainous characters?

"I must confess that I have always felt a little sorry for the man—for the creature," Mary said. "But it happens in great literature, does it not? The most satanic characters can be so well-developed that one cannot help but identify with them. Satan himself in *Paradise Lost,* for example. Perhaps there is the realization through such creatures that there but for the grace of God go we.''

"And unfortunately," Mrs. Waddington added, "evil aways has a rather fatal attraction for us."

The discussion became lively when Mr. Barrett stepped in to disagree with the ladies.

Mary looked forward to watching that particular play. But she discovered as always on their arrival at the theater that just the place itself, just the atmosphere, was enough to arouse excitement in her. Had life only been a little different for her, she often thought, perhaps she would have been an actress.

"Mary," Hannah whispered, leaning toward her just before the play began, "that dreadful man has just arrived and is staring at our box—at you, I would imagine—through his quizzing glass."

"Where?" Mary had no doubt who "that dreadful man" was.

"First tier of boxes," Hannah said. "Almost opposite. Ah, he has lowered the glass. He has not pestered you since that dreadfully vulgar display he made in your salon? You showed great fortitude, I must confess, in not swooning quite away. I am sure I would have, had it happened in my home."

Mary did not look immediately. But she leaned a little closer to the viscount, who was waiting to make some comment to her, and she smiled warmly back at him and continued the conversation. She felt self-conscious and angry, though it was unfair to do so. Lord Edmond Waite had as much right to be at the theater as she, she supposed.

She looked finally just as the play was beginning. Her eyes went immediately to the right box. He was alone. He did not have his quizzing glass to his eye, but he was looking directly across the theater at her, just as if there were nothing of interest to see on the stage. Mary turned her head sharply away to watch the action, and leaned another fraction of an inch closer to the viscount. Their shoulders almost touched.

She found herself wishing over the next hour that it were one of Shakespeare's simpler plays. She was finding it difficult to concentrate.

The Waddingtons left the box during the interval to call upon acquaintances in another box, and Hannah and her husband stepped into the hallway to stretch their legs. The viscount asked Mary her opinion of the production of the play and proceeded to give his. She wished that she had paid it more attention.

When the door to the box opened, she turned her head, expecting to see Hannah return. She froze.

"Ah," Lord Edmond Waite said, "my eyes did not deceive me. Good evening, Mary. Goodrich?"

Mary? She bit her lower lip.

"Waite?" The viscount's voice dripped with ice.

"Good evening, my lord," she said. And when he reached out a hand to her, she felt obliged to set her own in it. And inevitably he raised it to his lips.

"Your salon was well-attended two evenings ago," he said. "You must have been gratified. Of course, you provided your guests with stimulating company, Mary, as always I came to thank you for an interesting evening and to apologize for having had to leave early."

"I understand," she said. "You had another appointment."

"You were not there, Goodrich," Lord Edmond said, and only then did he release her hand. "You missed a splendid evening. But then, Mary's literary evenings are quite famous. I daresay next week's will be just as stimulating. Perhaps I will be able to stay later next time."

His pale blue eyes were openly caressing her. Mary was rigid with fury. What was he implying for Lord Goodrich's benefit? That they had some sort of relationship? Some sort of intimacy? How dare he call her Mary in someone else's hearing? Or even when there was no one else to hear, for that matter.

"I have always intended to sample one of Lady Mornington's entertainments," the viscount said, his voice stiff and cold. "Perhaps I shall do so next week."

"And how are you enjoying the play, Mary?" Lord Edmond asked. "A little dry, would you say?"

"By no means," she said. "I find it quite stimulating to the mind." Her words sounded pompous even to her own ears. And they were quite untrue.

"Prospero likes the sound of his own voice too much,"he said. "He should be content to allow the Bard's words to speak for themselves."

"But is not the whole point of performed drama to breathe life into words that are dead on a page?" the viscount asked, not even trying to hide his contempt.

Lord Edmond considered. "I have never found words on a page particularly dead," he said. "Only perhaps the mind that reads them."

It was a masterly setdown. But quite unnecessary. And very unmannerly under the circumstances. And who was he to talk of dead minds? And to the Viscount Goodrich, of all people?

The viscount shrugged and turned away. The insult was beneath his notice, it seemed.

"Don't you admire Caliban, Mary?" Lord Edmond asked. "And don't you wish that he could rise up and sock all the other sanctimonious characters between the eyes? I would have made a hero of him if I had been Shakespeare." He laughed. "Perhaps it is as well I was not."

"Perhaps," she said. But she could not comment on Caliban in the viscount's hearing. How could she condemn him when she had spoken up in his defense at the dinner table?

"You are not to be drawn," Lord Edmond said. "I think you must secretly like him, Mary. I believe women sometimes do admire what seems ugly and brutish. Beauty and the beast and all that."

"That would seem to imply that women crave brutality and abuse," she said. "It does not show a great respect for either women themselves or their minds."

"Ah," he said, "you become too deep for me, Mary. I do not believe I mentioned abuse. It seems that I am interrupting a *tête-à-tête* here. I came merely to pay my compliments. I shall see you again, my dear."

My dear? Mary's eyes widened.

"Good night," he said. "Goodrich?"

But the viscount, who was gazing down into the pit, did not reply. Lord Edmond looked back to Mary, winked at her, and left the box. She could hear herself exhaling.

"Lady Mornington," the viscount said, "I did not know you were acquainted with Lord Edmond Waite. Are you sure it is wise?"

She looked at him in some surprise. "I have only the slightest acquaintance with him," she said.

"And yet he calls you by your given name?" he said.

"I have never given him leave to so do," she said. "He was being impertinent."

"The man has an unsavory reputation," he said, "especially since he humiliated Lady Dorothea Page so unpardonably. You have heard about that?"

"Yes," she said. "I do not like the man, I do assure you."

"I am relieved to hear it," he said. "If you had only given me the slightest signal, ma'am, I would have requested in no uncertain terms that he leave the box immediately. I do not like the fact that his visit here was made under the eye of half the *ton*."

For your sake or mine? she wanted to ask him, looking at him curiously. But he did not supply the answer to her question.

When the last stragglers had returned to their boxes, she noticed later, Lord Edmond Waite's box remained empty. He did not reappear for the rest of the evening.

The Viscount Goodrich's carriage conveyed the Waddingtons home before Mary, though her house was closer to the theater. She sat alone beside him during the short ride home.

"You are to attend the Menzies' ball?" he asked her.

"Yes." She smiled. "I am looking forward to it. I like to dance occasionally."

"We are all entitled to some frivolous enjoyment in life," he said. "Will you do me the honor of dancing the opening set with me, ma'am, and perhaps a waltz later in the evening?"

"Thank you," she said. "I shall look forward to it."

"But that is all of three days in the future," he said. "May I take you for a drive—tomorrow? Perhaps as far as Kew?"

Kew. She remembered another invitation to drive there.

"That would be pleasant," she said. "I always enjoy a stroll in Kew Gardens."

"Then I shall come for you after luncheon," he said.

He helped her down to the pavement when his carriage stopped outside her house, and squeezed her hand before releasing it.

Inside the house, Mary handed her evening cloak to her manservant and ran lightly up the stairs, well pleased with the evening if she blocked from her mind the one discordant episode. The viscount was a pleasant, intelligent companion. And he seemed eager to see her again—Kew the next day and two sets with him at the Menzies' ball.

It would be good, she thought, to have a beau again, to have someone interested exclusively in her. It would be good to have a man to dream of. To have a possible marriage to hope for. She was ready for marriage again, she thought, for the assurance that her man would always come home to her at night. She was ready for children. It was not too late, surely. She was only thirty years old.

She pictured the viscount in her mind with his pleasant features and slightly receding fair hair. And she saw Lord Edmond Waite's pale blue eyes intent on hers.

Well, at least, she thought, a new man in her life would help her banish the memories. And in future, if Lord Edmond tried to intrude himself into her company while Lord Goodrich was near, he would be told in no uncertain terms to take himself off.

Mary thought of his saying that words were not dead on a page, only the mind that read them. And she smiled despite herself.

So Mary and Goodrich were about to become an item, were they? Lord Edmond Waite thought, viewing the two of them waltzing together. His hand was spread across her back in a proprietary manner and she was smiling up at him. He himself was late. He had had no wish to run the gauntlet of a receiving line when he had received no invitation. But as he had suspected, no one had impeded his progress into the ballroom. And only a few matrons appeared to have noticed him and frowned possessively at their young charges lest they rush at him and elope to Gretna with him without further ado.

Ah. She had seen him. And had jerked her head away and was smiling even more determinedly up at Goodrich. It was a promising sign. At least she was not indifferent to him. She was damned hostile, but that was better than indifference.

Goodrich. He did nothing to keep the sneer from his face as he raised his quizzing glass to his eye and surveyed them through it. She could hardly have chosen anyone duller or more respectable if she had tried. A pillar of respectability. The man had had the same mistress in keeping since several years before the death of his first wife, and was rumored to have been faithful to her—apart from some beddings of his wife while she had still lived, presumably. The mistress was now plump and matronly herself, and the mother of five offspring.

But Goodrich was a respectable soul. If he felt himself in need of another wife, he would certainly not dream of marrying the woman who had given him all for years without benefit of clergy and presented him with a whole bood of bastard children. No, he would marry Lady Mornington, who curiously had preserved her reputation for respectability despite her lengthy liaison with a married man.

Lord Edmond's lips thinned into an arctic smile. He wondered how eager Goodrich would be to lay even the tip of one finger on Mary if he knew just how eagerly and lasciviously she had given herself little more than a week before to a certain gentleman currently out of favor with the *ton*.

The waltz was ending. Lord Edmond inclined his head to Lady Menzies, who had just caught sight of him from a short distance away and was staring at him, somewhat startled. He strolled in the direction in which Goodrich was leading Mary. They had joined the Hubbards and the Barretts before he came up to them. He made his bow to the group.

"A grand squeeze," he said, "for so late in the Season."

"Yes, indeed," Penelope Hubbard said. "We were just saying so ourselves."

Lord Edmond turned his gaze upon Mary. "May I?" he asked, touching the card at her wrist.

"That dance is mine, Waite," the viscount said stiffly.

Lord Edmond raised his eyebrows. "Which?" he asked.

"Whichever one you were planning to claim." The viscount fixed him with a hard stare.

The devil, Lord Edmond thought, there could be a duel at dawn if he was not careful. That would do wonders for his reputation. Especially if he put a bullet between Goodrich's eyes, as he would be sorely tempted to do. Five bastards might have to face the morrow as orphans.

"Indeed," he said, lifting the card from Mary's unresisting wrist and opening it. His eyes glanced through it. "Ah, but you forgot to write your name, Goodrich. And I believe it is just as well. Mary's card tells me that you have already danced two sets with her. Would you sully her reputation by claiming a third?"

They were one step closer to that duel, he saw when he glanced up.

"Her card is full," the viscount said slowly and distinctly, as if he were talking to an imbecile. "There is no dance free for you, Waite."

The other two ladies were shifting uncomfortably, Lord Edmond was aware. Mr. Hubbard was clearing his throat.

"Perhaps that is for the lady to say," he said. "Mary?"

"Lady Mornington to you," the viscount said. "And you will let go of that card if you know what is good for you, Waite."

A few other people close by were beginning to look at their group.

"Oh, please," Mary said. "I will be happy to dance one set with you, my lord."

"Ma'am, there is really no need to give in to coercion, I do assure you," the viscount said.

But Lord Edmond ignored him. He looked through the card. "A waltz?" he said. "The second set after supper?"

"Yes," she said, her voice breathless.

He scribbled his name in the space next to that particular set, made his bow to her, and withdrew to the card room, where luck was with him and he won three hands in succession.

He wandered alone in the ballroom and anterooms and out onto the balcony during supper and returned to the card room when the dancing resumed, a spectator rather than a player. He was listening to the music, waiting for the first set to end.

She was not with her friends this time. She was alone, walking purposefully along one side of the ballroom as if she were on her way somewhere definite. But he knew that she had merely chosen not to be embarrassed again in front of her friends. His lips curled.

"Mary?" he said, touching her on the arm. "My dance, I believe?"

"Yes." Her face was pale, her jaw set. "I have never given you leave to address me by my given name."

"Mary," he said softly, drawing her into his arms as the musicians prepared to play. "I have made love to you. Three times. And you to me. Am I to address you formally?"

She looked up into his eyes. "You will never let me forget that, will you?" she said.

He wondered yet again why he was pursuing her so relentlessly. She was so much older and plainer than most of the other dancers. At least he thought she must be. He could no longer remember if she was pretty or plain, old or young. She was Mary.

"Do you mean that you would forget it if I were not here to remind you?" he said. "I think not. I think that you remember every moment of every day. I think you relive those encounters every single night. You cannot deny it, can you?"

The music began, and he moved with her, noting again how small she was—she reached barely to his shoulder— and how slender. She was light on her feet and responded well to his lead. She was a good dancer.

"I like this gown," he said, looking down to the pale green silk at her shoulder, "as I liked the apricot-colored one you wore at your salon. Pale colors suit you. You have a strong enough character that you do not need to hide behind vivid shades—like the pink you wore at the theater.''

She stared at his shoulder. She was not going to answer him, it seemed.

"Had you given Goodrich permission to send me away?" he asked. "I found his attitude most obnoxious."

"Yes," she said, her face animated with anger again. "I had. But you have no conception of what good manners demand, do you? There would have been a nasty scene if I had not agreed to dance with you. I chose not to make a scene."

"I am glad," he said. "I would hate to have had to punch him in the nose, Mary, or direct a pistol at him tomorrow morning."

She drew in her breath. "You would have done either or both, would you not," she said, "without a thought to the distress you would have caused to a number of people? Without a thought to my reputation?"

"I do not like to have watchdogs set on me, Mary," he said. "Perhaps you should know that now. I would hate to have to harm Goodrich or anyone else. Argue with me face-to-face. Or do you not have the courage to do so?"

"I do not wish to argue with you," she hissed at him, "or to converse with you or to have any dealings whatsoever with you. I want you out of my life. Completely and immediately and forever. But you will not believe that, will you?"

"No," he said. "Or I will not accept it, at least. I want you in my life, you see, Mary. Completely and immediately —and yes, perhaps forever too. I believe this conversation is becoming rather too intense for the scrutiny of all these eyes. It needs a little more privacy."

He danced her out through the French windows onto the stone balcony. It was rather a chilly night. There was only one other couple out there, and they were on their way back inside.

Lord Edmond Waite and Mary danced alone. And in silence. She did not immediately resume their quarrel, and he would not. She closed her eyes, he noticed. And he drew her fractionally closer and breathed in the scent of her.

It was eight days ago. The storm must have been in progress already at this particular time of night. He must have been holding her. Kissing her. Perhaps he had been in the process of laying her down on the table. Perhaps he had already been inside her.

If it were eight days ago, he would have the rest of that night to look forward to. God, if it were just possible to put back the clock. If it were just eight days ago.

Mary!

He looked down at her and knew in some shock that he was falling in love with her.

Had fallen.

6

THE AIR WAS cool on the balcony. Blessedly cool—she had become overheated in the ballroom. The music was lovely, the sort of music one could hardly resist moving to. The waltz must be the most wonderful dance in the world. Mary kept her eyes determinedly closed. She willed her partner to keep quiet. She wanted to believe that she was waltzing with any good partner anywhere.

"Mary." His voice was low and caressing.

She held her breath, but he said no more. She kept her eyes closed and they danced on. Until he twirled her about and stopped. There was something hard and cold at her back—the stone balustrade. Something brushed her cheek— the leaves of one of the large potted plants that stood at intervals along the balcony. She opened her eyes. They must be more than half-hidden behind the plant. He was standing very close to her, his arm still about her waist, his other hand holding hers. He was looking at her intently.

"Mary," he said.

"I have danced with you," she said, anger rising again. "I have even made an effort to be polite to you and to stop quarreling with you. But this is more than enough. I am going to return to the ballroom now—alone. And I would ask you, my lord, to leave me alone in the future. Strictly alone. I do not wish ever to speak with you again."

For answer he lowered his head and kissed her.

Her one hand was not free—he was gripping it tightly. With the other she pushed at his shoulder and slapped at his face, twisting her own away from it. They struggled in silence until he had her two wrists imprisoned. He set her hands against his chest and held them there until the fight went out of her.

"Do you wish me to scream?" she asked him. "Is that what you want? Yet another scandal? You will get nothing else from me, my lord, without a very loud scene, I promise you. Let me go, if you please.''

"Mary," he said, making no move to release her, "we were good together. More than good. The best. We could be so again—and again and again.''

"You make me sick," she said. "Physically sick. Nauseated. Are you so perverted that you like to pursue women who can vomit just at the thought of you?''

"You did not vomit last week," he said. "You gave every bit as good as you got. You enjoyed every moment.'' He looked at her in silence for a long while. "Is it my reputation? Is it that you know I have had many women and have recently jilted one lady in order to run off with another? Is it all the rumors of excesses and reckless living? Is that it?''

"Yes," she said, tight-lipped. "That is precisely it. Strange, is it not, that a woman would shun such a man? And one who killed his brother and his mother too, if all the stories one hears are to be believed.''

She wished that anger had not caused her to add those last accusations. She knew nothing with any certainty. And usually she scorned unsubstantiated gossip. His lips thinned and twisted into a sneer. His nostrils flared, and his eyes bored into hers.

"Ah, so you *have* heard that one, have you?'' he said. "Well, it is true, Mary. I killed them. Are you afraid I will kill you too? Put my hands about your neck, perhaps, and squeeze?'' He suited action to words, except that he did not squeeze. "It would be a new method for me. That is not how I killed them. Are you frightened?''

"No," she said, holding her voice steady. "I am not afraid of you, my lord.'' But she lied. She was, she realized, mortally afraid of him. Not afraid that he would kill her. Not there and then, anyway. But afraid that, say what she would, he would not leave her alone. Afraid that she would never be free of him. And a little afraid of herself, perhaps.

"Liar," he said. "Mary, has it ever occurred to you that all the stories you have heard, all the labels that have been put on me, do not make up the complete man? Do you not think that perhaps there is a great deal more to be known?''

"You would try to deny it all, then?" she said. "You would have me believe that you are a worthy and upright citizen?"

"Hardly that," he said. "No, it is all true, Mary, what you have heard, and a great deal more that you have not heard, I do not doubt. But even so, there is a large part of myself—a very large part—that is not accounted for by such a public image. Do you feel no curiosity to get to know what you do not yet know?"

"No," she said. "None whatsoever."

"Mary Gregg, Lady Mornington," he said, "widow of Colonel Lord Mornington of the Guards, former mistress of the Earl of Clifton, bluestocking, hostess of one of the most respected literary salons in London. Is that all of it? Is that who Mary Gregg is?"

"Of course not," she said. "Those details do not tell you who I am, only what I am or have been. And not all of those are true even. You do not know me at all, my lord."

"Touché," he said.

Her hands were still spread on his chest, she saw, though he no longer held them prisoner there. His own hands were now at her waist.

"I do not want to be having this discussion with you," she said. "I believe this waltz is almost at an end. I have promised the next dance to someone else."

"If it were not dark out here," he said, "I should open your card to find out if you tell the truth, Mary. But no matter. The waltz has not quite ended. Kiss me."

She stared at one of her hands. "Please," she said. "Let me go. I do not want to have to scream."

"Kiss me," he said, and he lowered his head to kiss her neck below one ear.

She closed her eyes and swallowed.

"Kiss me." He whispered the words an inch from her mouth.

"Please," she said.

"Mary," he whispered against her mouth. "Mary."

"Please," she said. And one hand was on his shoulder and moving up behind his neck, and her head tipped to one side, and her lips trembled against the light pressure of his.

"Mary," he said. "Kiss me."

She kissed him, her hand bringing his head forward, her mouth opening as his tongue came to meet it. And the ache was there again, intensified a hundredfold, and she knew that he could satisfy it. That he would satisfy it. One of his hands had slid down her back and brought her against his swelling groin. She pressed herself closer.

And then both her hands were against his shoulders, pushing firmly, and she turned her head to one side.

"Now be satisfied," she said. "Now have done and go away. Please!"

"You were humoring me?" he asked.

"How else can I be rid of you?" she said.

"Mary," he said, "you lie through your teeth. Your body is far more honest than you. Your body admits that it wants me, that it is fated to be mine. Why will you not admit it too?"

She turned her head back to look at him. "The physical is the only aspect of life that matters to you, is it not?" she said. "If I were to admit that, yes, I am attracted to you at the basest physical level, you would exult, would you not, and feel that that was all-sufficient? It would not matter to you that I do not like you, that I do not respect you, and that I would despise myself for the rest of my life for giving rein to my basest instincts."

"You would deny the body, then?" he asked. "It is an unhappy thing to do, Mary. We have to live inside our bodies for the rest of our lives."

"Some of us," she said, "also have minds to live with. And consciences too."

His smile was somewhat twisted. "Ah," he said, "it was obliging of you to explain that. I have often wondered what can give meaning to the lives of those who do not indulge their bodies as I do."

She swallowed.

"I want you, Mary," he said, "and I mean to have you. Not just from selfish whim, but because I know that you want me too and because I hold the strange belief that we can find a measure of happiness together. Stop fighting me. It is a useless struggle, I do assure you.'' He dropped his hands to his sides and took one step back from her. ''But enough for tonight. It is time for me to find a few bottles from which to drink deep, and a few wealthy and foolish young bucks to separate from their fortunes at the tables, and a willing whore with whom to enjoy what remains of the night.''

''I can live without having the details spelled out to me,'' she said coldly.

''Well,'' he said, ''that is what you expect of me, is it not, Mary? Is it not better to know for sure than merely to imagine? If I did not tell you, you might fear that you were doing me an injustice in your imagination.''

She frowned. ''You hate yourself, don't you?'' she said.

He sneered and drew breath to speak. But the words were never uttered.

''Lady Mornington,'' the voice of Viscount Goodrich said from just beyond the potted plant, ''may I escort you back into the ballroom, ma'am? Or would you like me to throw out your, ah, dancing partner first?''

One side of Lord Edmond's mouth lifted in a smile. He stood quite still and looked into Mary's eyes.

''We have been conversing,'' she said. ''But the waltz is at an end, I hear. I would be thankful for your escort, my lord.''

Although she looked at Lord Edmond, she was speaking to the viscount. She stepped to one side and around the former. He did not move, either to help or to impede her progress.

''Good night, Mary,'' he said softly. ''Thank you for the dance and for the conversation.''

''Good night, my lord,'' she said, and she set her hand on the viscount's sleeve.

He did not believe in love. Love brought only pain and bitterness. Love ruined lives, deprived them of all meaning and direction. He believed only in lust, only in the satisfaction of the body's cravings. And yes, she had been right. Only the physical mattered. Nothing else. Not mind. Not conscience. What did he care for conscience? Conscience had tormented him once upon a time, until it had seemed to be a toss-up whether he would end up in Bedlam or in hell, dead by his own hand. Somehow he had steered clear of Bedlam, and his hand had shaken like an autumn leaf when he had set the dueling pistol first against his temple and then inside his mouth. He had been too much the coward to pull the trigger.

Yes, he believed only in lust. She was damned good in bed, better than anyone else he had ever had, and so that was why he craved more. It was her body he craved. He cared nothing for her mind or her feelings or for all those other elements that were a part of her in addition to her body. He wanted her body. Lust was all.

He did not believe in love.

And yet in the two days following the Menzies' ball, liquor seemed to have lost its power to make him drunk and gaming to amuse him and whoring to give his body ease. And so he gave them up, hurling a full decanter of brandy into his fireplace late on the second night—the night of her literary salon, which he had stayed away from—having already thrown in a winning hand at Watier's before the game was quite won so that players and spectators alike had gaped at him in disbelief.

And before going home and smashing the decanter, he had taken a delicious little whore into his scarlet room, sat down to watch her undress, and then ordered her to dress again while he stalked from the room to summon his carriage. He had paid her twice her usual fee—merely for undressing in his sight and dressing again out of it.

Her body had been twice as luscious as Mary's.

On the third day he called at Mary's house and sent up his card. He repeated the call for the following six days. Each time she was from home and he left without disputing the message. Once he saw her driving in the park in Goodrich's barouche. He deliberately redirected his horse so that he would pass her, and he raised his hat and gazed steadily at her until she flushed and acknowledged him with a nod. Then he rode on without even attempting to engage her in conversation.

The word was out that Goodrich was courting her in earnest.

He made no move to discover where she was likely to be during the week. He wanted her body, not her. There were a thousand women in London alone with bodies more attractive than Mary's, and many of them willing bodies too. He would choose another woman and teach her to perform as Mary had performed for him, and better. She did not want him. Well, then, he would forget her. She did not matter to him. He believed only in lust, not in love.

But he sat in his dressing room late one night, staring at his boots and remembering that she had kissed him at the Menzies' ball and that for a few moments she had been hot and willing in his arms, his for the taking. And he woke more than one night aroused for her and remembering her at the ball pressing herself against his groin, wanting him inside her.

He cursed her and damned her. He conjured up a mental image of her and ruthlessly criticized every aspect of her appearance. Her legs were too short, her hips too narrow, her breasts too small, her whole body too dumpy, her hair too unfeminine, her face too plain, her eyes too . . . He shook his head. Well, she had one good feature. One! And she was too old and too prim and too everything else he did not like.

It was almost laughable that he, who had always been considered something of a connoisseur of women, could not shake from his memory a woman whom no one in his hearing had ever called pretty or lovely or attractive or bedworthy. He would be the laughingstock if it were known—as it well might be if he did not forget her soon—that he had determinedly pursued the very plain and ordinary Lady Mornington and been rejected. People already knew such a thing of Felicity Wren, but at least Felicity was breathtakingly beautiful.

But Mary! His lips curled with contempt—contempt for his own reactions to her.

On the night of her next literary evening—she had a lady novelist and a more reputable poet than Pipkin on her guest list, he had heard—he arrived at her house again. But he did not take advantage of the fact that she held open house. He sent in his card with a note scribbled on the back. And he waited for her reply, wondering what he would do if she ignored it or sent a message that she was not at home.

He stood in the hall of her house and bowed to Sir Henry and Lady Blaize as they entered and handed their outdoor garments to the butler before making their way to the salon. He smiled arctically when Lady Blaize openly ignored him and Sir Henry merely frowned and bobbed his head in what might have been a greeting.

Old fools! Did they think he cared?

The outside door opened again to admit the Viscount Goodrich at almost the same moment that Mary stepped out of the salon, Lord Edmond's card in one hand.

"Ma'am?" The viscount made his best bow to her before noticing either her frown or the fact that Lord Edmond Waite stood silently in the shadows.

"Ah," Lord Edmond said. "The eternal triangle."

The viscount turned sharply in his direction, and his eyes narrowed. "Lady Mornington," he said, "is Lord Edmond Waite an invited guest?"

"I send out no invitations for these evenings," she said.

"Do you want him here?" he asked.

She did not reply.

"Waite," the viscount said, "you may leave under your own power or you may choose to be thrown out. It is all the same to me, though I think perhaps I would prefer the latter. Which is it to be?"

"The second, if you wish to have your nose flattened in line with the rest of your face," Lord Edmond said coolly. "I was unaware that this is your house, Goodrich. I wish for a word with Lady Mornington. I am awaiting her answer."

"Her answer is no," the viscount said. "You have five seconds to take yourself off."

"Mary?" Lord Edmond spoke quietly and unhurriedly.

"I shall talk with him for a minute, my lord," she said. "I thank you for your concern, but I am in my own house and quite safe." She looked at Lord Edmond all the while she spoke.

"Perhaps I should stay with you to make sure of that,"

the viscount said, and Lord Edmond smiled into Mary's eyes.

"Thank you," she said, "but that will not be necessary."

"Scurry out of range of my fists while you still may," Lord Edmond said.

"And that will not be necessary either," she said firmly. "There will be no violence or talk of violence in my home, gentlemen. Lord Goodrich, you will find several people gathered in the salon already. Lord Edmond, will you step this way, please?"

She led him across the hallway and into what must be a morning room. There was an escritoire against one window, its surface strewn with papers, several books carelessly scattered on tables, and an embroidery frame with a mound of many-colored silks on the arm of the chair before which it stood. It was clearly a room that was lived in. A feminine and cozy room.

She turned to face him as he closed the door quietly behind his back. "What is the meaning of this?" She held up his card in one hand.

"That if you were from home this time I would be obliged to kidnap you?" he said. "I hoped that it would provoke exactly what it has provoked. I hoped that you would admit me."

"To my salon?" she said. "You know you need no invitation there, my lord. You would not have been turned away. Though of course you would have been unwelcome."

"Mary," he said, "you do not know how you wound me. I am human. I have feelings."

She laughed shortly. "Well, bless my soul," she said, "and so do I."

"I have given up gaming and drinking and whoring," he said. "They have had no attraction for me in the past week. I took a girl to the room where I took you, Mary, and could do nothing with her except send her home with a handsome fee clutched in her hand. I could not lay her on the bed where you had lain and do with her the things I did with you."

She flushed. He watched her swallow. "The great reformation," she said. "Thirty years or more of debauchery wiped out in one week of abstemious living, and now you are worthy to take me as a mistress. Am I to fall into your arms?"

"If you wish," he said. "I would be surprised, but I would close them about you fast enough."

She laughed again. "Get out," she said, "and stop wasting my time. I have guests to entertain."

"Not quite thirty years," he said. "But a goodly number, I will admit. A week has been more than an eternity. More than a week. Will you give me a chance, Mary?"

"A chance?" She laughed incredulously. "A chance for what?"

He shrugged. "A chance to show you that you will not have a drunken womanizer for a lover," he said. "A chance to show you that there is more to me than you know?"

She closed her eyes. "I cannot believe this is happening," she said. "You try to convince me that a miraculous transformation has happened in your life, and yet you can scribble on the back of your card that you will kidnap me if I will not speak with you, and you threaten Lord Goodrich, who would protect me, with violence?"

"He was the first to offer to throw me out," he said.

"Because he knew you were uninvited and unwelcome," she said. "Because he cares for me."

"You are sleeping with him?" he asked.

Her eyes widened and her flush returned. "Get out of here," she hissed at him.

"I will kill him if you are," he said.

She clamped her teeth together, grasped one side of her gown, and moved sharply around him toward the door. But he set one hand on her arm and whirled her around to face him. And he set his mouth to hers, releasing his hold on her for a moment—a moment during which she might have broken away but did not—in order to encircle her with his arms and draw her against him.

She kissed him back with fierce passion for a few seconds and then gradually went limp in his arms. She was crying when he lifted his head, and shaking with sobs.

"I hate you," she said when she could. "And I am so afraid of you. I no longer know what to do, I am so afraid."

He drew her against him and held her there with arms like steel bands.

"Why?" he asked. "Because I want you? Because I have killed? Because you want me?"

"Because you will not take no for an answer," she said. "Because nothing I say or do will persuade you that I want nothing to do with you. Because I am afraid I will never be free of you."

"And because part of you does not want to be?" he said. "Give in to it, Mary. Come to bed with me. Be my mistress. Let me prove to you that I am no monster and that what happened between us less than three weeks ago was merely the prelude to a glorious liaison."

"You see what I mean?" she said, and she was crying noisily again against his cravat.

He held her to him, rocking her until she was quiet.

"Give me one small chance," he said. "Come out with me tomorrow. There is a garden party at Richmond. Lady Eleanor Varley's—my aunt. There is no one more respectable in England. The only less-than-respectable thing she ever did was continue to associate with me when . . . well, after I had killed my brother and mother. She was the only one— the only one." He set his cheek against the top of her head and inhaled deeply. "Come with me there, Mary."

She did not answer for a long while. But finally she lifted her head and looked up at him with reddened eyes. "Yes, I will," she said so that his arms tightened about her again. "On one condition."

"What?" he said.

"That after tomorrow," she said, "if I still feel as I do now—and I warn you that nothing on this earth can change my mind—you will accept my rejection and leave me alone."

He considered. "I don't think I can do that, Mary," he said.

"Then I will not come," she said.

He stared into her eyes for a long moment. "Very well," he said at last. "I promise."

He watched her eyes light up in triumph and swallowed against what felt like a lump in his throat.

"I shall come for you soon after luncheon," he said.

"Yes." She smiled at him. "I shall be ready."

"And eager for the end of the day and the end of an affair that was never quite an affair," he said.

"Yes." She continued to smile.

He dropped his arms to his sides. He felt rather as if every part of his body was made of lead. Including his heart. What had he promised? What had he done? He set one hand on the knob of the door and paused to look back at her.

"I would bathe my eyes with cold water before returning to the salon if I were you," he said.

She was still smiling. "Yes," she said.

"Good night, Mary," he said.

"Good night, my lord."

He left the room, leaving the door open behind him.

7

IT WAS A beautiful day. Of course, Mary thought, it would have to be. It was just too much to hope that anything would happen to put a stop to Lady Eleanor Varley's garden party. The sun was shining from a cloudless sky. And it was hot without being oppressively so, she discovered during a late-morning visit to the library.

She would really rather be doing anything today but what she was preparing to do, but she cheered herself with the thought that it was for the last time. Once the day was over, then so would be all the unpleasant train of events that had begun with the thunderstorm at Vauxhall—if he was anything at all of a gentleman, of course. If he kept his promise. Strangely, the night before she had not considered that perhaps he had promised only because promises meant nothing to him. She had believed him.

Penelope had been disturbed. Lord Goodrich must have told her that Lord Edmond had come to the house and that she was talking privately with him.

"Mary," she had said, "he has a *tendre* for you. Are you quite sure you do not return his regard? Oh, please say that you do not. You can only end up being hurt."

"I have no *tendre* for him," Mary had said firmly. "And he has promised, Penny, that after tomorrow he will leave me alone."

But her friend had looked unconvinced. "It would be better to call on Lord Goodrich's protection," she had said. "Or better still, to betroth yourself to him. Lord Edmond Waite would not be able to argue with that. Though, of course, betrothals mean very little to him either."

But she could not betroth herself to a man who had not asked her, Mary thought.

The viscount had been vexed. "You should give me leave

to give the man a good horsewhipping, Lady Mornington,''
he had said when she had finally returned to the salon after
a lengthy visit to her room to bathe her eyes. "He does not
deserve the dignity of a challenge to a duel. And you need
not have allowed him to bully you into a private *tête-à-tête*.''

"Thank you," she had said, "but I was not bullied."

"You have *what*?" he had said when she told him about
the garden party. "You have agreed to allow him to escort
you? I can only express my deepest disapproval, ma'am."

But her chin had gone up at that. "I would remind you,
my lord," she had said, "that I am free to do as I wish."

He had taken her hand in his then, regardless of the groups
of guests gathered in the salon. "My apologies," he had said.
"I speak only out of concern for you, ma'am. I can see that
Waite has been pressing his attentions on you and that as
a lady you have found it difficult to discourage him in a
manner that would convince him. Allow me to protect you.
Send word that you have a prior engagement with me for
tomorrow that you had forgotten about. And let me stay with
you tonight in case he comes back."

Oh, no. Not that. Was that all Viscount Goodrich wanted
of her, too? She must seem fair game both to him and to
Lord Edmond Waite—and perhaps to others, she supposed.
She was a widow and a woman who had apparently taken
a lover for several years after her husband's death. For the
first time she was feeling sorry that she and Marcus had done
nothing to dispel the rumors about them, but had chosen to
laugh at them instead. But she was not a woman of easy
virtue. They would have to realize that—all of them. And
yet, she had thought uneasily, she was a woman who had
spent a night in the vulgar love nest of a notorious libertine—with no coercion at all.

"Thank you," she had said, "but I have accepted Lord
Edmond's invitation, and I have no fears for my safety."

He had released her hand and they had both turned to
mingle with the guests.

Mary had chosen a bright yellow dress for the garden
party. She had even had her maid take it out of her wardrobe
and iron it. But she changed her mind at the last moment

and dressed in her blue sprigged muslin. He had said that she looked better in pale colors, she thought unwillingly. That had nothing to do with her change of heart, of course. It was just that she had always wondered if yellow was her color. She had a suspicion that perhaps it made her complexion look sallow.

He came earlier than she had expected, though she was ready. The afternoon had scarcely begun. She slid her feet into her blue slippers, tied the blue ribbons of her straw bonnet with the cornflower-trimmed brim, and drew on her gloves. She was pleased with the effect when she glanced at herself in the mirror.

He seemed pleased too. His eyes moved over her in open appraisal as she descended the stairs. It was not a gentlemanly thing to do, but she no longer expected him to behave like a gentleman.

"You look lovely, Mary," he said, reaching out a hand for hers as she stepped down onto the bottom stair. "Like a delicate flower."

"Thank you," she said, placing her hand in his. They looked rather as if they had coordinated their appearances, she thought. He wore a coat of blue superfine over buff-colored pantaloons and shining white-topped Hessians. She felt almost like returning the compliment. Despite his rather narrow face, with its prominent nose and thin lips, he was a handsome man. And his blue eyes, though too pale, were a distinguishing feature. They were compelling.

"You are ready?" he said. "I feared perhaps I was early. But I thought we might arrive before the masses so that you may talk with my aunt at some leisure. Do you know her? I believe you will deal famously together."

"I know her by sight," she said. "We have never met."

Lady Eleanor Varley was a high stickler, known for her strong opinions and forthright manner. Mary had not known that she was Lord Edmond's aunt—and one who had not cut him from her acquaintance despite anything. Perhaps she was not such a high stickler after all.

He had brought an open barouche. It was perfect for the weather. It was also very public. She was to be displayed to view, it seemed, as she had been in the park more than two weeks before.

"It is a beautiful day," she said as the barouche moved away from Portman Place.

"Yes, it is," he said. "My aunt doubtless put in a special order for just this weather. But if I have only one day with you, Mary—half a day—I do not intend to spend it talking about the weather."

She looked at him suspiciously. Where was he taking her?

He seemed to read her thoughts. "And no, I do not mean that I am intending to tumble you in some conveniently secluded spot," he said. "I do not believe my aunt sports such places on her grounds. And I have not given clandestine orders to my coachman to take us to my, ah, second residence."

"It is as well," she said. "I would create a very loud scene."

"And it would not serve my purpose anyway," he said. "I have half a day in which to persuade you that perhaps I am worth getting to know after all."

She turned her head away and watched the buildings on the opposite side of the street.

"Tell me about yourself," he said. "Was your marriage to Mornington really a love match? Why did you decide to follow the drum? Why were there no children? Am I being impertinent?"

Of course he was. But at least he had made it possible for the long drive to Richmond to be made with comparative ease. It would have been a difficult task to fill up the time with small talk.

"It was a love match," she said, "although he was twelve years older than I. I went with him to Spain because I was a realist, I suppose. I was not an adventurer and I hate discomfort, both of which facts make it strange that I went. But I knew and accepted that he was likely to be killed before the wars ended, perhaps well before. And I was unwilling to marry him, enjoy a brief honeymoon with him, and then see him go, knowing that perhaps I would never see him again. So I went. And I am glad I did. We had only two years together. But they were good years despite the discomforts.''

"But there were no children," he said.

"If I had been with child," she said, "Lawrence would have sent me home. As it was, he felt guilty about the life I was subjected to. He wanted children. We both did. But I would not have any until the wars ended. Afterward I was sorry.'' She looked down at her gloved hands. "There was a spell after his death—six weeks—when I thought that after all perhaps I was to have his child. But it was not so. I really knew him to be dead then. I knew it was the end.''

"I am sorry," he said.

"Why should you be?" She raised her head. "You were not responsible for either his death or my false hopes.''

"I am sorry that you suffered," he said. "Suffering can kill. Not always physically. But it can kill dreams and it can deaden hope and the will to live.''

She looked up at him in some surprise. He described it so well, just as if he knew.

"You have never wanted to marry and have children since?" he asked.

The conversation was becoming very personal. She could hardly believe that she was talking thus with Lord Edmond Waite of all people. But then, why not with him? No other gentleman of her acquaintance would be so unmannerly as to ask her such questions.

"Not for a long time," she said. "It somehow seemed disloyal to Lawrence to think of marrying someone else—as if I had not cared. And I began another life and made new friends. I have had little chance to be lonely.''

She could feel him looking at her. He sat relaxed across one corner of the seat, one foot propped on the seat opposite.

"I suppose I should tell you something about my life in return," he said. "The trouble is that there is very little to tell, Mary. Very little that would impress you, anyway. I had a happy childhood.''

"Did you?" She turned her head to look fully at him. It was hard to picture him as an innocent child. He was smiling at her rather mockingly.

"We were three boys," he said. "How could we not have been happy? Of course, I was the youngest and might have been at the mercy of the other two. But Dick—he was the middle one, the one I killed—was so sweet-natured that I was never harassed. He would shame Wallace out of bothering me just by looking reproachfully at him. Dick was everyone's favorite, and no one ever resented him for it."

Mary swallowed and looked down at her gloves again.

"Ask it," he said softly.

"You killed him?" She looked up at him. "Surely you cannot mean it."

"Oh, but I do," he said. "I did. And you see? I cannot even talk about my childhood and have you see me as a person worthy of knowing. You want to know what happened."

"Yes." She bit her lip.

"It was the day after my birthday," he said. "My twenty-first. I had been drinking all day and all night and decided to clear my head with a brisk gallop. Dick tried to dissuade me—said I was still foxed and would do myself some harm." He laughed. "When I insisted, he came with me. He had not taken one drop beyond the glass with which he had toasted me at dinner, of course. I cleared a gate that should have been unclearable—at full gallop. I was watching and laughing when Dick came over after me. He broke his neck."

Mary tasted blood.

"They would not have allowed me to attend the funeral," he said. He laughed. "Not that I was around to attend it anyway. I took myself off from there as fast as I could, and never went back."

It was horrible. She did not know what to say. And yet it was not as bad as she had imagined. It had not been a cold-blooded murder. But it was also worse than she had imagined. How he must have suffered.

"And then there was my mother," he said. "You will want to know about that too."

"Not if it is painful," she said.

He laughed. "She died of consumption a little more than a month after Dick," he said. "My father had taken her to

Italy for a winter, and they were both convinced when they returned that she had recovered. She seemed better too, I must admit. But she outlasted Dick by less than five weeks. He was her favorite, you see, as he was everyone else's. So I killed her too."

"You say it almost with pride," she said. "As if you really wish people to see you as a murderer. Strictly speaking, you are not."

"Ah, but I am," he said, "in the popular estimation. And why fight public opinion, Mary? The truth of the matter is that Dick would be alive now if it had not been for me. And perhaps my mother too. Fifteen years they have missed because of me."

"And yet you behave as if you do not care," she said. "For fifteen years you have behaved as if you do not care. *Do* you?"

He was grinning at her, she saw. And yet the mockery was still in his eyes. "I have a quarrel with learned and intelligent people," he said. "You like to read and to exercise your mind, do you not? You like to converse with other people like yourself. And you pride yourself on your wisdom. Or perhaps I do you an injustice there. Perhaps you do not even pretend to be wise. Wisdom does not come from books, Mary."

"Has the subject been changed?" she asked.

"By no means," he said. "I am merely saying that you would not have asked your question if you had any of the wisdom that perhaps you imagine you have."

"But you have not given up drinking," she said, "or any of the other excesses that must have led to that accident. I would have thought you would have given it all up out of remorse. You might have shown your family your sorrow. Perhaps by now you would have been reconciled with them."

He laughed at her.

"It does not matter to you, does it?" she said. "Nothing matters."

"I remained true to one thing, at least, for many years," he said. "I remained true to my obligation to Dorothea."

"Perhaps it would have been better if you had not," she said.

"Undoubtedly," he said. "I would not have had to escort an iceberg about London several times."

"You are not even sorry about that," she said indignantly. "And yet you say that you wish me to see you as a worthy companion? I can see nothing worthy at all, my lord."

"No." He spread one arm along the side of the barouche and the other along the back of the seat, almost touching her shoulder with his fingers. "There appears to be nothing there to see, does there? Perhaps we should have confined our conversation to the weather after all."

"Yes," she said. "Or perhaps you should see that any interest you may have in me is ridiculous. Perhaps there are some women who would admire your lack of conscience and see something manly in it."

"There are plenty of women who admire the fatness of my purse," he said, "and are willing to perform for a portion of its contents."

She flushed and turned her head away.

"But none of them has ever been as good in bed as you, Mary," he said. "I cannot forget that. I want you there again. I want to make love to you."

She turned her head sharply to look at him in anger. "Perhaps you should offer me payment too, then," she said. "Only, more than you have ever offered before, to match my superior performance."

"Would you come to bed with me for money?" he asked her, his eyes glinting beneath narrowed lids. "You could name your price, Mary. Would you be my whore?"

"No," she said. "Not your whore or anything else. I think you should take me back home, my lord. We are going to do nothing but wrangle all afternoon."

"But you have promised me the whole of it," he said. "And you see what you have done to me, Mary? I set out to impress you, to convince you that really I am not so bad once you get to know me. And yet somehow once again you have maneuvered me into acting deliberately to shock you. How do you do it?"

"Perhaps by holding up a mirror to you," she said, "so that you can see yourself as you really are."

He stared at her through narrowed lids for a long moment.

"You are vastly accomplished at giving setdowns," he said. "Do you ever consider the pain you give with them, Mary?"

"I never seem to feel obliged to set down anyone but you," she said. "And I think you are incapable of feeling pain."

"Another one," he said, "hot on the heels of the last. Are you going to marry Goodrich?"

"That is none of your concern," she said.

"Ah, yes, it is," he said. "I would not be willing to share you with a husband, Mary. No, don't say it." He held up a staying hand. "Are you going to marry him?"

"He has not asked me," she said.

"He will," he said. "You are respectable enough to be married, despite the lapse with Clifton. And I believe the man is on the lookout for a leg shackle. Don't marry him."

"Why not?" She could not resist the question.

"No passion," he said. "The man would not be good in bed."

"Is that all that matters?" she asked scornfully. "Do you think that is the all-important thing in marriage?"

He considered. "No," he said. "I suppose if I were considering marriage—as you probably know I was, not so long ago—I would consider looks and breeding capability. And I would be careful not to choose a shrew or a giggler or someone who has to drag about a large canvas bag full of hartshorn and lavender water and whatnot. And I would not want a timid little thing without a tongue in her head. Or someone who gazed at me reproachfully whenever I arrived home after midnight. But bedworthiness is important too, Mary, despite your scorn for the physical. I could not stomach making love to a cold fish for the rest of my life— or even to a warm fish. She would have to be like you."

"But I would never marry you," she said.

"Certainly you would not," he said, "because I would never ask you. You see how well I learn from you, Mary? That was a setdown almost worthy of you, was it not?"

She smiled despite herself.

"You are pretty when you smile," he said.

"And am not when I do not?" she asked.

"No," he said.

She raised her eyebrows.

He laughed. "You will never get the expected answers out of me, Mary," he said. "I am not a gentleman, remember? You are not pretty. At least, I have never thought you so. I had never thought you attractive or worthy of a second glance until almost three weeks ago. It is strange how one's perceptions can change. Actually, you have looked remarkably pretty to me in the last three weeks, though I know with my mind that you are not. Now, which would you prefer? Mind, which you so value? Or intuition, which you scorn?"

"Your opinion does not matter at all to me," she said. "I do not care how you see me."

"Very well, then," he said. "You are too short and too flat-bosomed and remarkably plain of features. Let us have some plain speaking."

"And you are no gentleman," she said, stung, glaring at him, "at the risk of repeating myself."

"But, Mary," he said calmly, "you do not care what I think of you."

"That's true enough," she said crossly, turning to stare rigidly forward to the horses' heads. She stiffened when she felt the backs of two of his fingers caress her cheek briefly.

"You look lovely to me even when you do not smile," he said softly. "And if your body has imperfections, then I certainly did not notice them three weeks ago. Nor did they mar my great pleasure in you."

She closed her eyes. It did not matter, she told herself determinedly. His opinion did not matter. Whether he found her beautiful or whether he found her ugly—it was all the same to her. She had been hurt only because the words had been brutal and unmannerly. And it did not matter how well he had been pleased by what had once happened between them. *My great pleasure in you.* It did not matter. She did not care. She wanted only to forget.

He sat up suddenly so that his shoulder almost touched hers, and he took her hand in a firm clasp and held it on the seat between them.

"We are almost there," he said. "Time is slipping fast already. Too fast for me. Too slow for you. Right?"

"Right," she said.

For some reason she was remembering sitting beside him during the storm, trying to control herself, trying not to show him her fear. She was remembering trying to climb into him when her control snapped. And the way he had scooped her up onto his lap and proceeded to comfort her in any and all possible ways. A woman he had never considered either pretty or attractive. Just someone who needed comforting.

Was he the sort of man to do something merely to comfort another person?

She was about to ask him, but she was a little afraid of his answer.

Lady Eleanor Varley's house was set in extensive grounds in Richmond. Long lawns interspersed with flowerbeds and shrubberies sloped gently to the banks of the River Thames. Long tables set with crisp white cloths had been set out on the upper lawn just below the terrace. Servants were carrying out trays of food and large bowls of drink. Four early arrivals were strolling down beside the river. Four others were playing croquet on the lawn beside the house.

Lord Edmond handed Mary from the barouche but did not lead her immediately to the garden. He took her indoors to where his aunt was standing in the middle of a morning room, its French windows onto the terrace thrown wide, giving orders to a harassed pair of servants.

"I might as well do it all myself and save myself the cost of servants," she said, shaking her head. And then she spotted her nephew. "Ah, Edmond, dear, there you are. I was not looking for you for at least another three hours. You are always notoriously late."

"Your usual exuberant welcome, Aunt," he said, setting his hands on her shoulders and kissing her cheek. "I am on my best behavior today. I have Lady Mornington with me."

"Ah." Lady Eleanor held out her hand. "Lady Mornington. Welcome. I have been wanting to meet you this age. I keep meaning to attend one of your literary evenings, since the Clements are always full of enthusiasm about them. But I never seem to get around to it. I have seen you somewhere before."

"We have occasionally been in attendance at the same ball or assembly," Mary said, shaking hands with her hostess.

"And since when are you back with the literary set, Edmond?" his aunt asked. "It is about time, I must say."

"I am not with any set," Lord Edmond said. "I am with Lady Mornington, Aunt. I coerced her into accompanying me here today."

"Coerced?" Lady Eleanor chuckled. "That is probably true too, dear. Any lady takes her reputation in her own hands when she is seen with you. I take it you know about the Lady Dorothea Page and the Lady Wren episodes, Lady Mornington? Shocking businesses, both. Though as for Dorothea, I must say Edmond is well rid of her. The girl will rule the man who finally takes her to the altar. And these marriages that are arranged from the cradle are ridiculous affairs, in my estimation. No chance of success at all. What do you think, my dear?"

"I am very glad that no marriage was ever arranged for me," Mary said. "I do not believe I could marry where my feelings were not engaged and where I did not feel liking and respect."

"Very sensible," Lady Eleanor said. "Now, take my arm, my dear, and we shall step outside, where I should have been this past hour. Tell me who has been at your salon for the past few weeks. Whom have I been missing? And who is to be there next? Tempt me. Perhaps I shall look in on you."

"And what am I to do, Aunt?" Lord Edmond asked. "Trot along behind like a faithful lapdog?"

"You may run along and bully the servants, Edmond," she said. "They should have had all the tables set long before now. Growl at them, dear. You are so very good at growling. It will be far more effective than my nagging. When I nag at my servants, they invariably proceed to do exactly what they were doing before, which is not a great deal. Do you have any trouble managing your servants, Lady Mornington?"

The two ladies walked arm in arm out to the terrace, and Lord Edmond was left in the middle of the morning room, scratching his head.

8

IT WAS NOT working well at all. She was the only woman he had ever really wanted to impress, and it was impossible to impress her. Oh, he had wooed other women, but he had always done so with confidence, playing by the rules of the seduction game that he had learned over the years. Only once had he failed—with Felicity. But then, he could not recall wanting to impress Felicity. He had only wanted to lure her to his bed, and had been willing to do so even at the price of a leg shackle. He wanted to impress Mary, to make her like him, respect him, think him worth knowing and perhaps loving.

But it was not working. There was nothing to impress her with, he was realizing. There was nothing likable or worthy of respect about him. Was there really nothing? Had his life been so utterly worthless? Had he so hated himself that he had wasted fifteen years of his life—all his young manhood? He remembered with a jolt that she had commented on the fact that he hated himself.

He had nothing to offer her beyond a certain expertise in bed. It had always been enough with women—enough to please them and enough to satisfy himself. It had pleased Mary too, but she was not the type of woman to wish to build a whole relationship on that alone. And she was right. No relationship could thrive on just sex.

But did he want a relationship? he asked himself, and laughed inwardly. He was incapable of having a relationship.

After half an hour he managed to detach her from his aunt's side. He had thought the two of them would get along famously, but he had not expected that they would leap into such instant friendship. He took her walking down by the river, and when there was a boat free, he rowed her out onto the water. By his request she told him about Spain, and he listened, fascinated, to her accounts of various campaigns and the endless marches to and fro across the Peninsula. He had heard some of the stories before, but never from a woman's point of view.

But it was a one-sided conversation. He had nothing to tell her. Nothing beyond his twenty-first year, and before that time his life had been so wrapped up with family that it was difficult to tell any story that did not involve Dick. And as soon as he mentioned Dick, she would be reminded of how he had killed him as a result of a drunken debauch.

He looked at himself through her eyes and saw a worthless fellow, someone who had done nothing that he might lay with pride at the feet of his chosen woman. Chosen? For what? For his mistress? That was what he had wanted. She attracted him and had proved to him already that she could satisfy him more fully than any other woman he had had.

Had wanted? Was that no longer enough? No, it was not, he realized with numbing shock. It would not be enough to have Mary only in bed, to take her to his house once or twice a week, to stay at hers once or twice more. Not nearly enough. He wanted her in his life, an integral part of it. A part of him. He wanted her as his wife.

"Shall we stroll up to the house?" he suggested when he handed her out of the boat. "You are probably ready for some tea. Perhaps there will be another couple who will wish to join us in a game of croquet."

He no longer wanted to be alone with her. Knowing what he now knew, he realized even more the impossibility of the whole situation. His wife! He would see the scorn in her eyes if he so much as hinted at such a thing. And it would be like the lash of a whip. He would be quite defenseless against it.

"Yes," she said, taking his arm. "That would be pleasant."

The poke of her bonnet reached barely to his chin. She was light and dainty, like one of the delicate flowers on her bonnet. The thought amazed him. If someone had told him a little more than two weeks before that he would ever look at Lady Mornington and compare her to a delicate flower, he would have chuckled with vast amusement. It was hard to remember how he had used to view her.

"Are you enjoying yourself?" he asked, and then wished

he had not done so. Why invite one of the setdowns she was so good at?

"It is very pleasant," she said. "The surroundings are lovely and the weather perfect. Your aunt is very amiable. I am pleased to have made her acquaintance at last."

She was also good at diplomacy.

"Ah," he said. "So I have done something that meets with your approval, Mary. I have effected a meeting between the two of you."

"Yes," she said. "Thank you."

She had said not one cross or scornful word to him since their arrival. It was as if she had decided that since this was the last day she would have to spend with him, she would be pleasant. She had been scrupulously polite. She seemed to have surrounded herself with an impregnable armor. And there was so little of the day left.

But it was just as well, he thought. It would be as well when the day was over and he could return to normal living again. There was a new actress at the Drury Lane, a tall brunette who played some of the more minor roles. He had heard that Crompton had taken her under his protection already. But he would oust the opposition with no trouble at all—Crompton was nothing but a gauche boy with a fortune too large for his own good—and enjoy the girl for a few days, or a few weeks if she pleased him.

It would be a relief to return to normal life. He would feel safe again.

They were not alone again for the rest of the afternoon. They played croquet in company with several other couples and then had tea on the upper lawn with the same people. They were all very merry. No one in the group noticeably shunned him. He supposed they would not feel it appropriate to do so, considering his relationship to their hostess.

A few people were already taking their leave. He would have to order around the barouche soon, he thought with mingled regret and relief. The day was all but over. And nothing whatsoever had happened in it to make her want to repeat the experience. Quite the contrary, in fact.

They strolled up to the terrace with two couples with whom

they had been having tea, and waved their carriage on its way.

"So, Mary," he said, "the day nears its end."

"Yes," she said.

But before either of them could say more, his aunt stepped between them and took an arm of each.

"I do believe the party has been a success," she said, "for which I have the weather and your growls to be thankful for, Edmond. The servants actually behaved like real servants."

Actually, Lord Edmond thought, pursing his lips, his aunt's servants probably found it far easier to perform their duties when she was not constantly hovering in their vicinity giving confusing and contradictory orders. All he had done earlier in the afternoon was stroll up to her butler and say quietly, "Growl. Now I have followed her ladyship's instructions, Soames, and you may go about your business without further interruption."

The butler had grinned at him for a moment before remembering that he was a butler and pokering up quite as if he had never in his life been taught to smile. "Yes, my lord," he said. "Thank you, my lord."

"But I shan't be sorry to see everyone on the way and to be quiet again," Lady Eleanor said. "I have scarcely had a chance to exchange a dozen words with either Lady Mornington or you, dear."

"I shall summon the barouche without a moment's delay," Lord Edmond said. "Never let it be said that I cannot take a hint, Aunt."

"Oh." She laughed merrily. "I would not be so ragmannered, dear. I merely meant that I shall be glad to have the two of you to myself for a few hours. You will, of course, be staying for dinner."

Sweet seductive idea. "I invited Lady Mornington for the afternoon," he said. "Perhaps she has other plans for dinner and the evening."

"There is one easy way of finding out," she said, turning to smile at Mary. "Do you have another engagement, my dear? I do hope not, as I have looked forward all afternoon to having a pleasant conversation with you over dinner. Do please stay. *Do* you have other plans?"

Her eyes met his across his aunt for a moment. She thought he had arranged this, he thought. She thought he was not playing fair.

"I have the barouche with me, Aunt," he said. "It is not very suitable for night travel."

"Then you shall take one of my carriages," she said, "and return it to make the exchange some other day. Do not make difficulties where there are none, Edmond. Lady Mornington?"

"I would be pleased to accept your invitation, ma'am," she said.

His heart leapt with gladness—at a mere delay of the inevitable. He smiled at her, and then thought that the smile would convince her even more that he had arranged it all.

And so after everyone had left, the three of them strolled again down by the river before Lady Eleanor retired to her room to change for dinner and had Mary directed to a guest room to freshen up. And they sat down to dinner together, a long leisurely meal followed by coffee in the drawing room. Conversation did not flag for a single moment.

"You are remarkably quiet, Edmond," his aunt said at one point during dinner. "I can remember the time when your papa used to have to frown at you and warn you *sotto voce* not to monopolize the conversation when it was on topics to your liking."

He smiled. "I am enjoying listening to you and Mary exchange views, Aunt," he said. "I like it when people do not always feel obliged to agree with each other."

"Oh, I believe Lady Mornington and I respect each other's minds too much to do anything so silly," she said. "Is that not right, my dear?"

"And how dull conversation would be," Mary said, "if people always agreed with each other."

"Beasley and the crowd gathered about him at your salon," he could not resist saying.

"What was that, dear?" Lady Eleanor asked, and he was obliged to explain to her what had happened at Mary's house.

"I called the man an ass when I could stand it no longer," he said. "Mary was forced to take me aside and scold me roundly."

"Mr. Beasley?" his aunt said. "He *is* one, dear, but you should never have said so in quite that way. And in the hearing of ladies? I wonder Lady Mornington did not have you thrown out. Edmond hates humbug, my dear, and sometimes is not too careful about how he shows it. It is hard to believe, is it not, that he was in a fair way to becoming one himself once upon a time?"

"A humbug?" he said. "Surely someone would have done me the kindness to shoot me. Instead I did myself the favor of having myself tossed out of Oxford on my ear. Did you know that unsavory fact about me, Mary?"

"There were extenuating circumstances," his aunt said, but he was smiling at Mary. One more nail in the coffin of his faded hopes.

"No, I did not," she said.

But his aunt did not pursue the topic, he was thankful to find. The conversation resumed where it had left off, in a discussion of Wordworth's poetry, which Mary loved and his aunt considered sentimental drivel.

It was late dusk already when they finally took their leave. Too late and too chill for the barouche. Lady Eleanor's traveling carriage was brought around, and she insisted on lending Mary a warm woolen shawl and on having some heavy rugs put inside the carriage to cover her lap.

"Nights can be quite chilly after such warm days," she said, "when there is no cloud cover to keep in the heat. I have enjoyed the latter part of the day more than I can say, dears. You must have Edmond bring you again, Lady Mornington. This has been too pleasant an evening not to be repeated."

"I have enjoyed it too," Mary said, submitting to having her cheek kissed by Lady Eleanor.

"I did not know you had enough sense left to escort someone of Lady Mornington's caliber, dear," his aunt said, turning to Lord Edmond to give him a matching kiss. "I am so glad. It is time my favorite nephew came back from the unpromised land where he has exiled himself altogether too long."

"It was a mere garden party, Aunt," he said.

But she patted one of his cheeks and smiled at him.

The carriage was plushly upholstered inside with green and gold velvet.

"You are warm enough?" he asked Mary as he took a seat beside her. "Do you want one of the rugs over you?"

"No," she said. "The shawl is enough, thank you."

The carriage jolted into motion and they both turned to wave to his aunt, who had come out onto the terrace with them.

And suddenly the interior of the carriage seemed very confined. And very quiet.

She had not bargained on the intimacy of a return home in darkness and inside a closed carriage. She was embarrassed and not at all sure that there was anything else left to talk about.

"Was this all your idea?" she asked.

"No, it was not," he said. "It might have been, I must confess. I have been known to maneuver as deviously. But it was not."

"Oh," she said.

They lapsed into silence.

Just the long drive back into town, she thought. It was almost at an end. And surely he would keep his word. Surely he would. He must have realized during the course of the afternoon that they had nothing in common. And he had been quite unable to participate in the conversation at dinner and in the drawing room afterward. Indeed, much as she had liked Lady Eleanor, she had thought that perhaps their hostess had been rather ill-mannered to choose topics of conversation about which he seemed to know nothing.

She wished it were at an end already. She wished they had not stayed for dinner. By now she would have been at home, all her associations with Lord Edmond Waite just a bad dream.

And then his hand reached across and took hers in a warm clasp.

"A penny for them, Mary," he said.

"Nothing," she said. "I was thinking back over the day, that was all. I like your aunt."

"And she you," he said. "She will wish to continue the acquaintance."

"She will be welcome to attend one of my literary evenings," she said quickly. "I believe I will send her an invitation."

"She wants me to take you there again," he said, and she could see in the near-darkness that he looked at her and smiled.

Oh, no, she thought. She had not seriously considered what she would do if he turned out to be a totally dishonorable man. What if, after all, he continued to pursue her? She turned her head away and dared not ask him. How would she know if he spoke the truth anyway?

They rode for some minutes in silence, until he released her hand and put his arm about her shoulders.

"Please don't," she said, keeping her head turned away from him.

"The day is almost at an end," he said. "Perhaps there is half an hour or a little more left. It is almost over."

"Yes," she said.

"You will be glad?"

"Yes."

His free hand came beneath her chin and turned her face toward him. She could hardly see him in the darkness. Except that his face was very close to hers.

"Don't." She could hear that her voice was trembling.

"So little time, Mary," he said. "Half an hour. How many years do I have left, do you suppose? Twenty? Thirty? Forty? Even if it is only ten or five—or one—half an hour is such a little time to have left before all the emptiness."

"Don't talk like that," she said crossly. "Am I to believe that you have conceived a grand passion for me? Am I to feel sorry for you? You want to bed me. That is all. And I will not be bedded."

"Mary." His hand pulled loose the ribbons of her bonnet and tossed it aside before she realized what he was about. "Give me that half-hour of your time. That is all I ask. I will not bed you here, though the conditions are tempting. I promise. Just give me that half-hour."

Sometimes she tired of fighting. It would be such a relief not to have to fight any longer—after the next half-hour was over. But first there was the half-hour. She let her head relax sideways against his arm and closed her eyes as his hand lightly caressed her cheek and her ear. His thumb feathered across her closed eye, across her eyebrow. Across her mouth.

"Mary."

There was a lump in her throat. She tried to swallow it. She wanted to fight when his mouth took the place of his thumb, first against her eyelid, and then lightly, and closed, against her own mouth.

"Mary."

And she wanted just to stay still and let it happen. It was hard to believe that she had allowed so much at Vauxhall and afterward. She could no longer remember quite why she had done so or quite how pleasurable it had been. When it was dark, as it was now, and when she closed her eyes and her mind to the identity of her companion, when she allowed herself only to feel and not to think at all, she could feel the urge to give in to his caresses.

His tongue was tracing the outline of her lips, sending sensation sizzling through her. It was too raw a feeling. She parted her lips to imprison his tongue between, and opened her mouth to suck it inside. He moaned.

It was so good sometimes just to feel, not to think or to reason. So very good to feel a man's strong arm about her, to feel his other hand stroking over the side of her head and down over her shoulder to her breast, lifting to slide inside her dress, warm and slightly rough over her soft skin. To feel his thumb rubbing over her nipple until that raw ache began again. It was good to feel a man's mouth wide on hers, his tongue exploring and caressing inside.

It felt good to want and know oneself wanted. Good to feel totally and merely woman.

"Mary," he was saying into her ear. "Oh, my God, Mary."

And she knew again who he was. It was impossible to block thought for more than a few brief minutes. But she did not much care, she thought, lifting her hand from his shoulder and running her fingers lightly through his hair.

"I will not bed you against your will," he said. He was running one hand hard up and down her arm. Her shawl seemed to have disappeared. "Tell me you do not want it."

"I do not want it," she lied.

He pressed her head into his shoulder and held it there with one firm hand. His arm about her held her like a vise. They rode thus the rest of the way home. And he held her so for a few moments after the carriage had come to a halt, while the coachman opened the door, set down the steps, and discreetly withdrew.

She did not know whether he had had her conveyed to her own home or to his love nest. She did not much care.

"Mary." He released his hold on her head so that she tipped it back to look up at him. She could see his face dimly in the light from the street—her street. "I must ask you now, though I know the answer. Will you see me again?"

She swallowed and heard an embarrassing gurgle in her throat. She shook her head and watched his jaw harden.

"There is nothing else but this," she said. "I cannot explain this, my lord, but it is all there is. There is nothing else. This is not enough."

"No, it is not," he said unexpectedly. "If you can find nothing else in me to want but my lovemaking, Mary, then I do not want to see you again either. I have a life to get on with."

She looked at him rather uncertainly and made to move away from him, but the arm about her shoulders tightened.

"I wanted you to want me," he said fiercely. "*Me*, Mary, despite everything. But it was a foolish wish, was it not? And now I reap the final harvest of that night of drunkenness. The final punishment. The final hell. If I could go back and change things, I would do it, you know. Do you think I would not change things if I could? For Dick, Mary? And for you. I would change the last fifteen years for you if I could, relive them, put something of some worth into them. But I cannot. And so I have nothing whatsoever to offer you except the ability to give you pleasure, learned appropriately enough in the beds of countless whores. I want to offer you all the precious things the world has to offer, and all I can give you is that.'' He laughed harshly.

She stared at him, dumbfounded.

"You did not suspect that a man like me was capable of love, did you?" he said. "It will work to your advantage, though, Mary. I will stay away from you. I will keep my promise to you because I love you. You have nothing more to fear from me, you see."

He lifted his arm clumsily away from her and jumped out of the carriage. He turned to lift her down, not waiting for her to set her feet on the steps. The front door of the house was already open.

"Go, then," he said, sliding his hands hard down her arms and gripping both hands hard enough to hurt. "And be happy, Mary. That is all I want for you. Please, be happy."

He squeezed her hands even more tightly and raised one of them rather jerkily to his lips before releasing both and jumping back inside the carriage without even waiting for her to disappear into the house.

The carriage took him to Watier's, as instructed. He sat inside, still and silent, for five whole minutes after the coachman had opened the door and stood politely to one side, waiting for him to descend.

"Take me home," he said at last.

He did not want to be alone. But he certainly did not want to be in company. And it seemed there were no other choices.

"Bring the brandy decanter to my dressing room," he told his butler as he passed him in the hallway of his home and began to ascend the stairs. "No." He stopped. "Bring two."

He filled a glass to the brim when the decanters arrived, and took a large gulp of brandy, which burned its way down his throat and into his stomach. And then he stared down into the liquid for a long while. His worst enemy. He had proved it before. It had helped him kill Dick. It had made a terrifying hell out of the months that had followed. He had used it since then only in public, as part of the image he had chosen to give the world of a man who really did not give a damn.

Was he to use it again now in private—his worst enemy in the guise of a friend? Always in the guise of a friend, but in reality nothing but the archenemy. Nothing but the devil himself.

His glass shattered against the washstand a little distance away from him. The two decanters would have followed, but at the last moment he had mercy on the poor maids who would have to clean up the mess. Already it was bad enough.

He got to his feet and wandered through into his bedchamber. So what really had happened? He had been rejected by an unlovely and unattractive bluestocking, and one of not quite impeccable virtue either. She was no great loss. If he could just force his mind back to three weeks ago, before Vauxhall, he would realize that she was no great loss.

He had never believed in love—at least he had not for many weary years. It was no time now to start believing in it. Not at the age of thirty-six, when no decent woman could be expected to afford him a second glance.

What could he do? He must do something to drag himself out of the gloom that assailed him at frequent intervals, this time caused by a foolish infatuation for a woman.

The Season was at an end, to all intents and purposes. He could go to one of the spas as he often did during the summer. Or to Brighton. He thought with distaste of Brighton. He could go to the Continent, travel about for perhaps a year or so. Or he could go down into Hampshire. His estate there was not really far away, and yet it was almost two years since he had been there last.

Perhaps he would go there. It would be soothing perhaps to be in the country with nothing and no one to remind him of a wasted life.

Yes, he thought with sudden decision, he would go into the country—the very next day.

He rang the bell for his valet.

9

MARY WAS ANGRY. A week had passed since the garden party at Lady Eleanor's, and he had kept his promise. Oh, he had kept his promise, all right, but in such a way that she began to despair of ever being free of him. He had done it deliberately. Somewhere he was laughing at her, knowing very well what he had done to her.

She hated him with a passion.

In many ways it had been a gratifying week. She had seen Viscount Goodrich every day or evening—sometimes both—and he had been flattering in his attentions to her. If he had indeed hoped to make her his mistress the week before, he had not pressed the matter since. He had even apologized to her the day after the garden party. He had called on her during the morning.

"You are not well?" he asked her after they had greeted each other. He was looking closely at her.

She had cried for an hour the night before, and lain awake for at least another two. She smiled. "Just a little headache," she said. "Nothing some fresh air will not blow away."

And so he took her for a late-morning walk in the park. And asked her politely about the day before. She told him how she had liked Lady Eleanor and how the lady had said she would try to attend Mary's literary evening the following week.

That was when he apologized. He covered the hand that was resting on his arm with his own and looked down at her. "Forgive me for my manner and words two evenings ago," he said. "I was behaving in a possessive manner that I have no right to—yet. And I am afraid the suggestion I made was very improper. Please believe that it arose purely from my deep concern for your safety and peace of mind."

"You are forgiven," she said, smiling at him. "And I was

indeed upset that evening. But no longer. I will be seeing no more of Lord Edmond Waite." Strangely the words were like a heavy weight on her shoulders.

He squeezed her hand. "I am glad to hear it, ma'am," he said. "Such a man can only mean you harm. I am convinced that there is not a decent bone in his body."

She did not immediately reply. *I will stay away from you, I will keep my promise to you because I love you.* She did not want to remember those words. After she had cried bitterly over them for a whole hour, she had no longer believed them. She agreed with Lord Goodrich. *And be happy, Mary. That is all I want for you.* No, the man was a fiend. The very devil. How could she be happy?

"I believe you are right," she said.

They went walking and driving together over the coming days, and visited the Tower and Westminster Abbey, where they spent a happy hour reading the tombstones and epitaphs in Poet's Corner. They attended the theater and the opera and a concert in the home of the Earl of Raymore.

He talked to her of his home in Lincolnshire and of his two sons, who were away at school and of whose existence she had not known before. He was very close to declaring himself, she was sure. And she would accept, she had decided. She liked him. Life with him offered stability and security and the chance for a permanent contentment.

She wished that he would kiss her, but he never kissed more than her hand. She wanted him to kiss her. She had some ghosts to banish, and she needed him to banish them. But apart from that one suggestion during her literary evening, his behavior toward her was perfectly correct.

It was a happy week. She was deep into what appeared to be a serious courtship, and her friends approved. Both Penelope and Hannah were relieved at the abrupt ending of her association with Lord Edmond, and delighted with the development of her attachment to the viscount.

She was happy. Lord Goodrich could offer her all the companionship she had known with Marcus—though there had been a very special affection between her and Marcus that had not yet developed with the viscount. But it would develop in time. And Lord Goodrich could offer more. He could offer her the permanency and respectability of marriage, with none of the uncertainties and dangers that had marked her marriage with Lawrence.

She was happy. And yet anger grew in her as the week progressed. Lord Edmond Waite—she had grown to hate the very sound of his name—had proved even less honorable and less of a gentleman than in her worst fears. For if he had continued to pursue her, she could have been righteously angry with him. She could have fought him. And if he had broken off his connection with her as he had promised, she could have been exuberant with the relief of being rid of him. But he had managed to do both and neither.

He had made very sure during that drive home that she had felt again all the unwilling attraction for him that she had denied since Vauxhall. He had played on that attraction until she would gladly have lain with him right there in his aunt's carriage if he had chosen to take her. Or she would have gone with him again to that most vulgar love nest. She did not know quite how he had aroused such feelings of surrender, but he had. And she could not even openly blame him for them. He had used no apparent coercion. Indeed, he had given her a way out and then scrupulously allowed her to take it.

So that she would look back in longing? So that she would continue to ache for him long after he had gone? So that she would forever regret that night, which they might have spent together?

To her horror, she had been quite like a puppet on a string. She had done all of those things. All week, while her mind— her real self—was happy with Lord Goodrich and looked forward to a more permanent relationship with him, her body longed for Lord Edmond.

She had cried and cried for him after he had left her that one evening. For one mad hour she had convinced herself that he really did love her. Worse, she had been convinced that she loved him too.

The fiend! He had planned it all. And now he very carefully kept himself out of her sight. She looked for him—unwillingly—wherever she went, but never once set eyes on him. He was doing it deliberately. He knew that if she only saw him again, she would see him for what he was and be free of him.

She began to fear that she would never be free of him.

Mary had sent an invitation to Lady Eleanor to attend her next—and last—literary evening. The Season was over and London was emptying fast of people of *ton*. Many people were removing to one of the spas or to the seaside or to their country estates. Lady Eleanor sent an acceptance and the added assurance that she was vastly looking forward to the evening.

Perhaps her nephew would accompany her, Mary thought, and hoped not and tried not to expect such a thing. He would not come, surely, after keeping his promise for almost a whole week. Unless he wanted to see what effect the week of his absence had had on her, of course.

Lady Eleanor came alone. She sat and listened to one of the two poets who had accepted Mary's invitation, and joined in the lengthy and vigorous discussion that followed. And then she sought out Mary.

"A splendid evening, my dear Lady Mornington," she said. "It is a while since I enjoyed myself so much. What a pity that Edmond is not here."

"I have not seen him for almost a week," Mary said.

"He went into the country the day after my garden party," Lady Eleanor said. "Did you not know? I would normally have been glad, since he does not spend a great deal of time on his estate and needs to be there more often. But I must confess I was sad to find that my guess must have been wrong. I thought that the two of you had a *tendre* for each other, my dear."

"Oh," Mary said, flushing. "No."

"It is a great pity," Lady Eleanor said. "You are just exactly the woman for him, my dear, if you will excuse me for saying so. You are someone who might have brought him back to himself."

Mary looked at her warily.

"And the sort of atmosphere that is here tonight might have

brought him back too," Lady Eleanor said. "If he is to be brought back at all. It has been a long time. Most people, I would imagine, think that he is unreclaimable. What do you think, Lady Mornington?"

"Ma'am?" Mary frowned.

"I was under the impression that you were quite closely acquainted with him," Lady Eleanor said. "Perhaps I was mistaken? Perhaps you know very little of him? I do beg your pardon, but I assumed, you see, that you probably would not have been with him at all if you had not known him well. He does have a deservedly shocking reputation, I am afraid."

"My acquaintance with Lord Edmond is slight, ma'am," Mary said.

"Ah," Lady Eleanor said. "I shall say no more, then." But she sighed and continued anyway. "As a young man, Edmond would have been very much at home here, Lady Mornington. He would quite possibly have been one of your poets, though doubtless his poems would have been written in Latin or Greek and almost no one would have understood them."

Mary stared at her.

"He was too bookish," Lady Eleanor said. "His head was never out of a book. My brother and sister-in-law were worried about him. He would never be able to live in the real world, they used to say. His only ambition was to study for the church, and he was doing so, even though he had not been destined for the church. That was to be his elder brother's position in life—my brother always believed that Richard's sweetness and gentleness would make him an ideal clergyman, though I had my doubts. But it was the life Edmond chose for himself." She chuckled. "He would not have made a good clergyman either, though. He knew nothing of life. Poor Edmond. He was always my favorite, Lady Mornington, though Richard was almost everyone else's."

Mary listened in disbelief. Was the Edmond Lady Eleanor was talking about the same Lord Edmond she knew? He could not be. There must be some mistake. But how could there be? Lady Eleanor was his aunt.

"At the time, I used to wish that he were a little more worldly," Lady Eleanor said. "And yet now I look back and long to see that quiet, serious, studious boy again. If only the accident had not happened. Do you know about the accident, Lady Mornington, or is everything I am saying mystifying you?"

"The death of his brother?" Mary asked.

"Ah, you do know," Lady Eleanor said. "But I must be boring you, dear, if you have no more than a passing acquaintance with my nephew. And I am keeping you from your guests."

But Mary set a hand on her arm as she turned away. "Please," she said, "you called it an accident. Are you merely being diplomatic? Or is that how you would really describe it?"

Lady Eleanor looked at her for a moment and clucked her tongue. "I suppose Edmond has been telling you the usual story," she said, "and the one that seemed to take root here in town. About his killing Richard and all that nonsense? He is quite as bad as my brother and my eldest nephew. The truth is, Lady Mornington, that Richard was not the best of riders, but rode anyway and took a foolish and unnecessary risk and died as a result. It was everyone's fault and no one's. It was an accident. But it changed Edmond's life—totally and unbelievably. And I suppose I am unrealistic to hope that he will ever come back to himself again."

"But . . ." Mary said. She was interrupted by the viscount, who came up behind her and took her by the elbow. He was smiling.

"Ma'am?" he said to Lady Eleanor. "I hope you are enjoying the evening. You have outdone yourself this time, Lady Mornington. Everyone seems eager to be a part of both groups at once."

Mary smiled at him.

"Goodrich?" Lady Eleanor said. "I always discover good things when it is almost too late. But no matter. I shall be a frequenter of your salon next year, Lady Mornington, my dear."

"Supper must be ready," Mary said. "I should go and see."

"Allow me," the viscount said, squeezing her elbow before striding from the room.

"So that is the connection," Lady Eleanor said, smiling at Mary. "And a very eligible one too, my dear. I wish now that I had not thought of you in association with Edmond. I find myself disappointed that it is not so. But no more of that. You are staying in town for the summer?"

"I have no plans to remove anywhere else," Mary said.

"Then I shall see you again," Lady Eleanor said. "I shall send you an invitation. Perhaps I will include Goodrich in it. That would not be out of line?"

Mary blushed. "I think not," she said.

Lady Eleanor nodded and turned toward the group whose conversation she had not yet sampled.

It was later that evening that Viscount Goodrich kissed Mary for the first time and asked her to marry him. He stayed until everyone else had left, even Penelope, who looked from Mary to the viscount in some amusement, shrugged her shoulders, and bade them a good night.

They were in the hallway. Mary turned to look at him inquiringly. He was not, surely, about to renew his offer of the week before. He took her by the elbow, guided her back into the salon, out of the sight of her servants, and closed the door behind them.

"Lady Mornington," he said, possessing himself of one of her hands, "you cannot, I think, be insensible of my feelings toward you."

She looked up at him and said nothing.

"I hold you in the highest regard," he said. "In the deepest affection, I might make so bold as to add."

"Thank you," she said, curling her fingers about his. "Thank you, my lord."

"And if you are in any doubt about my intentions toward you," he said, "let me clarify them without further delay. They are the most honorable. I wish you to be my wife, ma'am."

She stared at him. He was going to be her husband. She was to grow as familiar with him—with his appearance, his speech, his habits—as she was with herself. She was to live with him in the daily intimacy she had known with Lawrence. Her mind felt satisfaction, even elation. It would be a good match. It was what she had wanted for several years. It was what she had never been able to have with Marcus.

"Will you?" He had her hand in both of his. "Will you do me the honor, Lady Mornington?"

He was too bookish . . . He wanted only to study for the church . . . He knew nothing of life. Poor Edmond . . . that quiet, serious, studious boy. The words, in Lady Eleanor's voice, had been revolving in Mary's head since before supper. She had not been able to rid herself of them. She could have wished Lord Goodrich's timing had been a little better.

"I . . . I don't know," she said.

But she did know. She did. She wanted to marry him. She wanted to be married. She wanted to be a mother if she could.

"Ah." He squeezed her hand. "I have spoken too precipitately. You need more time."

"Yes." She smiled at him in relief. She needed time to rid her head of the strange and bizarre images of Lord Edmond Waite that his aunt had put there. "A little more time, if you will, my lord."

"I can wait," he said, "as long as you can assure me that there is hope, Lady Mornington. May I have the privilege of calling you by your given name?"

"Yes," she said, and when she swayed slightly toward him, she realized that she had done so almost deliberately. She wanted the images gone from her head. She wanted to be convinced that Lord Edmond meant nothing to her. "Do call me Mary."

"Mary," he said. And he released her hand, set his hands on her shoulders, lowered his head, and kissed her.

It was not close enough. He made no move either to open his mouth or to draw her closer. It was not close enough. She wanted to feel him against her, holding her close. She wanted to feel his mouth over hers. She wanted desperately to feel the same sensations she had felt the week before. She needed to be convinced that it was a man she needed physically. Not just one particular man. She wanted to be able to choose her man with her mind and know that the physical was very much less important because it was the same with every man.

A foolish wish. It was not the same with every man. Lord Goodrich's embrace was . . . pleasant.

"I had better take my leave," he said, lifting his head away from hers and looking at her with smoldering eyes. "Or I will not be able to leave at all, Mary."

She looked at him in blank surprise. Was he speaking the truth? Had he found their embrace arousing? She had not—not to even the smallest degree. She had not thought she was meant to.

"Mary?" He was looking at her intently. "Do you want me to leave?"

"Yes, please, my lord," she said.

"Simon," he said.

"Simon."

He dipped his head and kissed her again briefly. "Good night, then, Mary," he said. "You will come walking in St. James's Park tomorrow afternoon?"

"I shall look forward to it," she said.

"And I too."

She walked out into the hall with him and saw him on his way. And she wondered as she climbed the stairs to her room why she was not now officially betrothed to him. No, she did not wonder. She knew the reason. How had Lady Eleanor phrased it? He had changed totally and . . . How? Unbelievably. He had been quiet and bookish, too unworldly for his own good. He had wanted to be a clergyman. He had been studying to become one. Lord Edmond Waite? It was impossible, surely. Oh, surely it was impossible!

He had written Latin and Greek poetry. Lord Edmond Waite!

He had gone into the country. That was why she had not set eyes on him since the day of the garden party.

He was the reason why she was not now officially betrothed to Viscount Goodrich—Simon. She could not shake him from her mind. And now it was far worse than it had been all week. Now she had begun to see that perhaps, once upon a time, there had been a totally different Edmond, that perhaps the Lord Edmond she knew had been shaped by guilt and rejection and grief and other factors that she knew nothing of.

But she wanted to see none of those things. She wanted to marry Lord Goodrich. She wanted to be quiet and contented with him. She wanted to have a family with him before she was too old. She did not want to be thinking of Lord Edmond Waite at all.

But try as she would to direct her thoughts toward the future that had been definitely offered to her that evening, she could think only of Lord Edmond as she tossed and turned on her bed. And she could dream only of him after she had fallen asleep—strange, frightening dreams. In one of them he was on horseback and laughing at her as she soared over the high gate that he had just cleared. Except that she was not on horseback, and she was falling slowly, and he was running—on foot, not on horseback—slowly, much too slowly, to try to break her fall. She woke up before she touched the ground—or his outstretched arms.

Two weeks went by, weeks during which the heat of July became more oppressive in the city. And yet they were not unhappy ones for Mary. Her friends Hannah and Penelope both left, one for the North, the other for Brighton. But the viscount remained and continued his almost daily attentions. He did not renew his marriage proposal during that time, but both of them behaved as if they had an understanding.

True to her word, Lady Eleanor sent an invitation to dinner for both Mary and Lord Goodrich, and they discovered that there was only one other guest, an elderly baronet of Lady Eleanor's acquaintance, who had been invited to make up the numbers, she explained, without seeming to offend her friend.

It was a pleasant evening, followed by a pleasant drive home. And if Mary's treacherous mind kept making comparisons, then she ruthlessly suppressed them. She was becoming accustomed to the unwelcome images and memories and was learning not to fight them too ruthlessly, but to patiently and determinedly replace them with others.

She was succeeding, she believed, until one morning when she was going through her mail—much diminished now that the Season and its flood of invitations was at an end. She looked more closely at a letter with unfamiliar handwriting, only to discover that it came from Hampshire, where he had his estate. She slit the seal with impatient and shaking hands and spread the letter on the breakfast table before her. Her eyes went first to the signature, large and bold at the bottom of the page—"Edmond."

Mary drew in a deep breath and closed her eyes. It was not a long letter, she had noticed. She opened her eyes again.

"My dear Mary," she read, and paused before reading on. "Contrary to what you may suppose, I did not arrange it. I knew nothing of it until my own invitation arrived this morning. I am inclined to accept because she is my aunt and has always been kind to me. And she will have only one sixtieth birthday, I suppose, unless she refuses to grow any older. However, if you have already accepted your invitation or want to do so and do not wish to see my face again, I will make some plausible excuse. All my tenants and servants can come down with smallpox or some such calamity. May I beg the favor of an immediate reply? Your obedient servant, Edmond."

Some mysterious invitation from his aunt to a sixtieth-birthday dinner? Mary frowned and thumbed through the rest of the pile of mail, and there it was. She opened the letter with the already familiar handwriting and read the note.

But it was not an invitation merely to dinner or an evening party. It was an invitation to spend a week at Rundle Park, Lady Eleanor's country home in Kent, in celebration of her sixtieth birtday. A few other family members and friends were to be there too, Lady Eleanor explained. She very much hoped that Lady Mornington could be among their number. She had sent an invitation to the Viscount Goodrich too, she added.

Mary folded the invitation and tapped it against her palm as she stared off into space.

It would be courting disaster to meet him again when she

did not have to do so. She could easily find an excuse to refuse the invitation. She would not even have to resort to dooming all her servants to an attack of smallpox. She smiled unwillingly at the thought. She would be meeting him, if she agreed to do so, in the close confines of a country party. It was a quite undesirable situation.

But if she saw him again, if she spent a whole week in company with him, then she would surely be able to lay a few ghosts finally to rest. She would be able to see quite unmistakably that whatever he might have been as a very young man, before the death of his brother, now he was a man to be neither liked nor respected.

Nor loved.

She would think about it. She would discuss the invitation with Simon when he came later in the morning to take her shopping and to the library.

But she knew already what her answer would be. What it must be.

And she must write to him before the day was out. She must not keep him waiting for his answer.

It seemed so long. She closed her eyes. It seemed so long since she had seen him last.

10

HE DID NOT particularly want to be doing this, Lord Edmond Waite thought as he descended from his carriage and hugged his aunt. He was always pleased to see her, of course, and normally he would have been quite happy to give a week of his time to celebrating a birthday with her, especially as there was to be other company. He had spent several summers at Rundle Park as a boy, when his uncle was still alive, and had pleasant memories of it.

But it had been hard to leave Willow Court just when he was settling there and finding that living in the country in his own home, surrounded by his own land, and served by his own servants, had a certain charm after all. And a certain soothing influence on a turbulent heart.

Yet now he had to face her again after making such a prize idiot of himself the evening of the garden party. She had not taken his hint that perhaps she should refuse her own invitation, since, as Lady Eleanor's nephew, he felt pretty much obliged to accept his. She had written back to say that she had no objection to meeting him at Rundle Park if he had none.

If he had none! Did she not have the sense—or the sensitivity—to realize that he would really rather face the devil than her?

And Goodrich had been invited too. His mistress and bastard brood were going to have to live without him for a whole week, Lord Edmond thought nastily. Was Mary betrothed to him yet? If she was not, doubtless she soon would be. Perhaps this week in the country would provide a suitable environment for the announcement. Perish the thought!

"Edmond!" his aunt said, hugging him and kissing him on the cheek, "can I believe the evidence of my own eyes?

You are a day early, when you are almost always late.''

"Just say the word," he said, grinning, "and I shall take myself off and put up at the village inn until tomorrow, Aunt. Are there any new barmaids there?"

She clucked her tongue. "You will stay here where I can keep an eye on you," she said. "Do come inside, dear. It is an unexpected pleasure to have you all to myself for a whole day before anyone else can be expected to arrive. Perhaps I can talk some sense into you."

"That sounds ominous," he said, setting an arm about her waist and walking up the horseshoe steps with her to the double front doors. "And what the devil did you mean by sending me a partial guest list with my invitation?"

"Watch your language, dear," she said. "I thought you might be pleased to know that I was inviting Lady Mornington too."

"And Goodrich as well," he said. "I fell all over myself with eagerness to accept your invitation when I knew that he had been invited too, Aunt. Has he accepted?"

"Both of them have," she said. "I believe they are quite an item. It will be a good match for her."

"She will have the devil of a lot of his attention," Lord Edmond said. "What with the two legitimate sons and his mistress and five bastards. Did you know about them?"

"I always think it unkind to use such a word to describe children born out of wedlock," she said. "They cannot help their birth, after all. Apparently he provides well for them and has a secure future planned for each of them."

"You do know," Lord Edmond said. "Then what the devil are you about, saying that he will be a splendid match for Mary? Any woman deserves better."

"Goodness me," she said. "Your language does leave something to be desired. It is possible that she knows about that other family. Some women do not mind, you know. It enables them to have all the comforts of marriage without any of the, ah, excesses."

Lord Edmond snorted. "Mary would mind," he said. "Believe me, she would mind."

Lady Eleanor looked interested. "Well, then, dear," she

said, "perhaps you think you would be a better match."

"Me?" He laughed. "Poor Mary. It would be rather the choice between the devil and the deep blue sea, would it not? At least Goodrich has respectability. He is very discreet about his other life, and that makes it quite acceptable, of course."

"Pour yourself a drink, dear," Lady Eleanor said. She had led him into a downstairs salon. "Who is the devil and who the sea, I wonder."

"No, thank you," Lord Edmond said. "I would prefer tea, Aunt. If you are having some, that is."

She raised her eyebrows but said nothing. She crossed to the bell rope and pulled it. "I thought you had something of a *tendre* for her," she said. "Now I am sure of it."

"For Lady Mornington?" he said scornfully. "A *tendre*, Aunt? What put such a ridiculous notion into your head?"

"A certain way you had of looking at her when you were in Richmond," she said. "And a certain hostility toward a gentleman who we both agree is quite respectable and quite an eligible suitor for her."

"Nonsense," he said. "Anyone with any decency would feel distaste at the idea of a poor woman contemplating marriage with a man while knowing nothing of the very domestic and long-standing arrangement he has with a woman of another class."

She smiled. "I have not heard any speeches of moral outrage from you in many years, Edmond," she said. "Welcome home, dear."

He frowned but said nothing as the door opened at that moment to admit the butler and a maid with the tea and cakes.

"And talking of home," she said when they were alone again, "tell me what you have been doing at Willow Court in the past few weeks. Getting to know your property, I hope, and astounding your bailiff with your interest. And do sit down, dear. You look rather like a cross bear standing there."

Lord Edmond sat.

She would really rather not be doing this, Mary thought as the carriage completed its long drive through the park leading to Rundle and turned in the direction of the horse-shoe steps. Normally she would have been delighted at the prospect of a week in the country during the heat of August, especially as her hostess was to be someone she liked.

But she would have to meet him again just at a time when she was beginning to persuade herself that she was putting him from her memory. And just at a time when she believed Simon was preparing to renew his offer for her and she was preparing to accept.

She was going to accept. Definitely. She had decided that.

"Here we are at last," Lord Goodrich said from beside her. She had agreed to travel with him, since the journey from London to Rundle Park could be made in a single day. "You will be glad to refresh yourself and have some tea, I am sure, Mary."

"Yes." She looked fearfully from the window, but the double doors at the top of the steps were only just opening. No one had yet emerged. "It has been a tiring day."

The viscount was already handing her down onto the cobbles when Lady Eleanor came from the house and down the steps, followed by Sir Harold Wright, the same gentleman who had been at Richmond when they had dined there. There was no one else, Mary saw in some relief, except servants.

"How wonderful!" Lady Eleanor smiled at Lord Goodrich and hugged Mary. "Now everyone is here and yet it is still not quite teatime. All my guests can become acquainted before the afternoon is out."

Mary shook hands with Sir Harold, who was asking the viscount politely about the journey.

"Do come inside, dear," Lady Eleanor said, taking Mary's arm. "I shall take you to your room myself, and you may take some time to freshen up. It always feels good to change one's gown and wash one's face after a journey, does it not? And on such a hot day too. Is the weather not glorious? I just hope it holds for the week so that everyone can find plenty of entertainment outdoors. Ah, good. I see that your luggage and your maid have arrived. And Lord Goodrich's valet, is it?"

Mary smiled and looked about her in interest at the neatly tiled hall of the manor. She had always wished that she had a home in the country. But Lawrence, though he had left her comfortably well-off, had not been a wealthy man.

"You are not quite the last guests to arrive," Lady Eleanor said. "But the others are not to arrive for a few days yet and are to be kept a secret." She smiled mysteriously. "Being sixty years old, Lady Mornington—I am going to call you Mary if you do not mind—makes one bold. One realizes that there is not limitless time left and that certain things that need doing and perhaps have needed doing for years must be done now if they are to be done at all. Along here, dear. I have given you a room facing across the park to the front. I have always preferred this view to that of the hills and trees at the back, though many people prefer the wilder aspect there. Here we are."

"How lovely," Mary said, looking about her at the Chinese wallpaper and screens of her room and at the floral curtains and bed hangings.

"I knew you would like it," Lady Eleanor said. "I shall leave you, dear, and send my housekeeper in half an hour to direct you to the drawing room for tea."

"Thank you." Mary smiled at her hostess and wandered to the window after she had been left alone. The driveway ran very straight behind formal gardens, flanked on either side by rolling lawns and stands of trees. It was all very green. Very beautiful. She would have a country home, she thought suddenly, if she married Simon. *When* she married Simon.

Some of the guests were to arrive a few days later, Lady Eleanor had said. Perhaps he was one of them. Perhaps she would not have to face him that day. Perhaps there would be a few days first in which to relax.

There was hope in the thought. And also, inexplicably, a twinge of disappointment. She wanted the meeting over with. If it had to happen, then it might as well be now.

Her maid arrived at that moment with a manservant carrying her trunk, and Mary turned her mind to getting ready for tea.

* * *

They had arrived. Together. He had watched them from an upstairs window, alighting from their carriage and greeting his aunt and Sir Harold. They were quite an item, his aunt had said. Well.

Lord Edmond ensconced himself in the corner of the drawing room farthest from the door and exchanged reminiscences with Peter and Andrew Shelbourne, nephews of his uncle, no blood relations of his at all. He had met them often at Rundle Park when they were all boys. Peter's wife, Doris, sat silently at her husband's side. She disapproved of him, Lord Edmond thought, and did what he often did under such circumstances—he fixed her with a steady look until she lowered her eyes. Now she would be a little afraid of him too. It was so easy to intimidate women.

There were twenty-one guests in all, including Sir Harold Wright, his aunt's faithful friend since long before his uncle's death. Rumor had had it once upon a time that they were lovers, but if it were true, they were very discreet about their affair and had made no move to marry after his uncle's death. Perhaps they were just friends, Lord Edmond thought. Perhaps it was just that gossip could not accept anything so dull and unscandalous as a platonic relationship. Anyway, it was none of his business.

It was a larger gathering than he had expected, but he welcomed the numbers. It would be easier to keep his distance from her. And apart from her presence, it was an unthreatening gathering. He had always been a little afraid at his aunt's parties that he would unexpectedly run into some other member of his family. But she had always been tactful. She had never tried to entertain his father or his eldest brother and him at the same time. He was the only guest at the party from her own family.

But then, she had always declared quite openly, even when he had been a puny and bookish and quite uninteresting boy, that he was her favorite. Bless her heart.

And then, just when he was chuckling over some long-forgotten memory with Peter and Andrew and was feeling quite off his guard, she came into the room. He knew it even though he was not looking directly at the door at the time. And sure enough, when he did look, there she was. Their eyes locked almost immediately. She had come into the room alone—without her watchdog.

He favored her with his expressionless stare, since he could not at the moment quell from his mind the memory of the abject misery with which he had taken his leave of her the last time he had seen her. She lifted her chin and then inclined her head. She did not smile.

Well, he thought, turning away to resume his conversation with his childhood friends, that was that, then. He had seen her again and he was still feeling relatively sane. The room had not crashed about his head. Many of those present— Doris Shelbourne, for example—would undoubtedly derive huge amusement from the knowledge that he had been waiting in fear and trembling for the arrival of one small, not particularly beautiful lady. Well, it was over.

He thought of an escapade that had got him and Peter into some trouble many years ago—one that the poker-faced Doris would not find quite proper—and began to tell it. To hell with the woman, he thought. If she expected vulgarity from him, then he was more than willing to oblige her.

Goodrich had entered the room and was standing beside Mary, their shoulders almost touching. He was smiling at her possessively. He looked almost as if he might set an arm about her shoulders at any moment. If he tried it, Lord Edmond thought, he would have to go about for the rest of his life minus one arm. And catching the drift of his thoughts, he redoubled his efforts to make the telling of his story quite as outrageous as he could. Peter and Andrew were already chuckling. Doris had not cracked a smile.

Devil take it, Lord Edmond thought as that arm came briefly about Mary's waist to turn her to greet a couple who were approaching them. Hell and damnation! Was he to be subjected to this for a week? He muttered something to his companions and strolled across the room.

"Ah, Mary," he said in his haughtiest manner, quite rudely ignoring the viscount and the couple with whom they were speaking, and not at all caring about the impression he was making. "So you have come to rusticate, have you?"

"I would hardly call spending a week in the country at a party with more than twenty other guests rusticating, my lord," she said, turning toward him so that his rudeness to the other three would not seem quite so obvious.

"Would you not?" he said. "What would you call it, then? A great yawn? It keeps you from your books and your poets and your politicians. It must seem like a massive waste of time."

"Heavens!" she said. "What a strange impression you must have of me. Life has more to offer than just books and intellectual conversation, my lord. And more than idle amusement too. Life has an infinite variety of experiences to offer, and I like to sample all of them."

"All?" He widened his eyes and looked down deliberately at her mouth.

"Very well, then," she said, flushing. "Many. Words should be chosen with care, as you have just implied."

"I wish you had meant the *all,*" he said, his eyes caressing her.

"You are trying to put me to the blush, my lord," she said calmly.

"And succeeding," he said. "Did you cry, Mary?"

"Cry?" She looked at him inquiringly.

He smiled at her arctically. "My only regret," he said, "was that I could not follow you invisibly into the house. But I will wager that you cried. Women cannot resist a broken heart, I have found, especially when they think themselves the breaker."

"You did not mean a word of what you said, then?" she asked.

He raised his eyebrows. "Did you think I did?" he asked. "Poor Mary. If I was to endure the mortification of a rejection, I felt justified in meting out a little punishment in return. I succeeded, did I?"

"You flatter yourself," she said. "It has been obvious to me from the beginning of our acquaintance that you are quite incapable of experiencing any of the finer feelings, not to mention love. Your charade would not have convinced an imbecile."

"Mary of the acid setdowns," he said, his head to one

side. Her fine gray eyes lent her whole face beauty when they were flashing with indignation, he thought. "You really must give me lessons one of these days."

"You forget," she said, "that we are to have no future dealings at all, that you have a promise to keep. I believe this gathering is large enough that we can keep from having to exchange any future words, my lord."

"At which point I am to crawl abjectly back into my corner, I suppose," he said. "Mary, Mary, when will you learn that a libertine and a rogue is without honor? I needed to be in the country for a few weeks. Tedious business to attend to and all that. I have scarcely stopped yawning since I left town. Did you really think that I was keeping my promise to you?"

"Yes, I did," she said. "It was one small thing—one very small thing—for which to respect you."

He shook his head. "And with that short speech you expect to blackmail me?" he asked. "I don't want your respect, Mary, remember? I don't care a damn for your respect." He lowered his voice. "I want your body. And the campaign is about to resume, my dear. Remember that I have the added incentive of knowing that you also wanted mine on the return from Richmond. Very badly, as I recall."

"It seems, then," she said, "that I am a better actor than you, my lord. I convinced you?"

He grinned suddenly. "That was unworthy of you, Mary," he said. "It was not even a good try. You have merely made yourself look remarkably foolish."

She blushed and had no answer, he was interested to note.

"Why the letter?" she asked. "Why the warning, if you were planning to be so unscrupulous?"

"Ah," he said. "I know something of human nature, Mary. I thought the letter would pique your curiosity. I thought you would not be able to resist casting your eyes on a man sick with love for you. And behold you here. And behold me, your lovesick swain."

"You are despicable," she said. "If you will excuse me, my lord, there are other people I should be talking to."

As if on cue, the Viscount Goodrich, having managed to

finish his conversation with the other couple, drew Mary's arm protectively through his and nodded stiffly to Lord Edmond.

"Waite," he said.

"You had better hang on to her," Lord Edmond said conversationally. "I had plans for ravishing her in the middle of my aunt's drawing room, Goodrich."

"Such sentiments, flippant as they are, are not for a lady's ears," the viscount said. "And I can imagine what your plans are, Waite. Forget them. Mary has me to protect her, and I will do so, though I would much regret any public unpleasantness during the festivities for your aunt's birthday."

"But you would not regret private unpleasantness?" Lord Edmond pursed his lips and considered for a moment. "Neither would I. It can be arranged anytime you so choose, Goodrich."

"Please." Mary's voice was quiet, but Lord Edmond knew, though she showed no outward sign, that she was furious. "Enough of this. There will be no wrangling over me and no fighting. Are you two schoolboys to be coming to fisticuffs over nothing at all? And am I a youthful beauty to be fought over? Lord Edmond, you are doing this deliberately, and it will not succeed. Simon, escort me across to the tea tray, if you please."

Lord Edmond watched them go. Her back was very straight. Her hips swayed pleasingly, though without any conscious provocativeness, beneath the loose folds of her muslin dress.

He wondered what on earth had possessed him. Some demon quite beyond his control. He had not planned any of the things he had said to her. And everything had been a pack of lies.

Good Lord, he thought, the wise thing for him to do was to pack his bags and return to Willow Court as fast as horse could gallop. Otherwise there was no knowing to what dishonorable depths he would fall with regard to Mary or what asinine sort of duel he would end up fighting with Goodrich. He might even find himself telling Mary about the plump

mistress and the brood of bastards, and despising himself
for the rest of his life.

"Ah, Edmond," his aunt said, linking an arm through his.
"I did not wish to interrupt you while you were renewing
your acquaintance with Mary, but now that you are alone
again, you really must meet the Reverend Samuel Ormsby
and his wife—she was Phillip's cousin, you may remember.
Samuel believes you and he were at Oxford together for a
while."

"Oh, Lord," he said.

"Precisely, dear," she said. "I am surprised that he has
recognized you."

Instead of rushing from the room to pack his bags, Lord
Edmond allowed himself to be led toward the gentleman in
the clerical garb, who was beginning to look somewhat
familiar.

Oh, Lord. It was like something out of another lifetime.
Out of another era. Another universe.

"The air feels good," Mary said, closing her eyes and
breathing it in with the scent of flowers. "There is the
suggestion of evening coolness already."

She was strolling in the formal gardens with Lord
Goodrich, tea being over and most of the guests having
dispersed to their rooms.

"I knew he was Lady Eleanor's nephew," he said. "I
suppose it should have struck me as a possibility that he
would be a guest here too. But I would have expected her
to show better taste than to invite him with decent people.
I would not have brought you here if I had known, Mary,
I do assure you. I am sorry."

"But you did not bring me here," she pointed out. "We
each accepted our separate invitations. I think perhaps it
would be better, Simon, if you did not show such open
antagonism to him. It goads him on into being more
outrageous than he would otherwise be, I believe."

"I will be antagonistic to anyone who treats you with
anything less than the proper respect," he said.

She smiled at him.

"No," he said, "the best way we can handle this, Mary, is to become betrothed without further ado. He will not argue with a fiancé's rights, believe me."

"It is a rather strange reason to become betrothed," she said.

He stopped walking and took both her hands in his. "Have I given the wrong impression?" he said. "You know otherwise, Mary. You know that I have chosen you as the woman I want beside me as my wife for the rest of my days. And I believe you are ready to accept my suit now, are you not? I have felt it in the past few weeks. Why not make it official now, when there is a good reason?"

"But it is Lady Eleanor's birthday celebration," she said. "We must not try to take some of the attention from her, Simon."

He squeezed her hands. "Somewhere in those words I found reassurance," he said. "Do I take it that you were not saying no but only that the timing is poor?"

She thought. "Yes," she said, "I think that is what I was saying."

"You will marry me, then?" he asked.

"Yes," she said. "I think so."

"Think?" he said.

She drew a deep breath. "I believe I must have been unmarried for too long," she said. "The thought of taking such a step, of voluntarily giving up my freedom again, frankly terrifies me, Simon."

"Then we will not rush into marriage," he said. "I shall give you time to accustom yourself to the idea. Agreed?"

"Agreed," she said after a small hesitation. "But, Simon, I don't believe we should say anything this week."

"Only if Waite proves troublesome," he said. "If he does, Mary, you must allow me to tell him in no uncertain terms that you are affianced to me and that any insults to you, however slight, will be answerable to me. Agreed?"

"Agreed," she said again after another hesitation. "But I think it would be better to ignore him, Simon. He thrives on the sort of attention you give him."

He squeezed her hands once more. "Leave such matters to me," he said. "Relax and enjoy the party."

"Yes." She smiled at him.

"We are betrothed, then," he said, looking at her in some satisfaction. "I am happy about it, Mary."

"And I," she said.

He bent his head and kissed her chastely on the lips.

11

MARY FELT HAPPY for the rest of the day and for most of the following morning. Everything she had hoped would be accomplished during the week at Rundle Park seemed to have been accomplished during the first day.

She was to be married. She was to be the Viscountess Goodrich, and her main home was to be a country estate. There she would live out a life of security and contentment with a man she liked and respected. She was only thirty years old. There would be children—two perhaps, even three. She would like to have a son, though of course Simon already had his heir. And a daughter too. She would like at least one of each.

She was glad that he had asked again and that she had had the courage to say yes. And she was a little sorry during the evening that she had asked for their betrothal to be kept a secret during the week. She wanted to tell everyone. She was fairly bursting with excitement.

And that other had been accomplished too. She had seen Lord Edmond Waite again and the spell was broken. All the unwilling feelings of attraction and regret had fled, and as she had hoped, she could see him again for what he was. He was an unprincipled scoundrel.

She was so glad she had come and had not refused her invitation, knowing that he would be there too. It was true that he had declared himself to be in pursuit of her again, but she did not care about that. Once he knew that she was betrothed to Simon, he would have no choice but to leave her alone. Besides, she would put up with the nuisance of his attentions now that her greatest dread had been put to rest—that she was falling in love with him.

He made no effort to seek her company during the evening, being seated at quite the opposite end of the table from her at dinner and contenting himself with a few amused glances across the drawing room at her afterward as she and a few other ladies played the pianoforte and sang. He directed his attentions to Stephanie Wiggins, the shy young daughter of one of Lady Eleanor's friends. He did so, Mary suspected, only because the girl's mother was looking on with almost open alarm.

And the following morning, when Sir Harold led several of the guests on a ride to a distant hill, from which there was a pleasing prospect of the surrounding countryside, Lord Edmond expressed a preference for billiards. Mary rode at the viscount's side with a feeling of enormous relief. Those words at tea the previous afternoon must have been spoken merely to tease her. It seemed that he was going to be civil after all.

It was a beautiful day, as every day for the past three weeks had been. They would have to pay for such a glorious July and August, Doris Shelbourne said gloomily. Doubtless they would have an early winter. Mary smiled to herself. She had learned during the brief years of her marriage that the moment of happiness had to be seized. Certainly troubles were ahead—they always were, just as more happiness was ahead. But why cloud the joy of the happy times with a fear of the unhappy?

"I cannot imagine a lovelier day or more pleasant surroundings," she said, turning her head to smile at the viscount.

"You have been nowhere else but England except for Spain," he said. "There are lovelier climes and far more spectacular surroundings, Mary."

"But I don't think any could bring me greater happiness than England," she said.

"That is a typically insular attitude," he said, smiling at her. "I shall persuade you to change it. I plan to take you to every corner of Europe on our wedding journey. I shall keep you away from these shores for a whole year at least, Mary. Perhaps two or even three. Paris, Vienna, Rome, Venice—you shall see them all, and more."

"Mm," she said with a sigh. "How wonderful it will be.

I will have to pinch myself to believe that it is all real.''

"Oh, it is real," he said. "I promise you."

"But you did exaggerate." She laughed. "A whole year, Simon? You could not enjoy being away from home so long, surely. And away from your sons?"

"They are at school," he said. 'And they have relatives with whom to spend the holidays. They are beyond the age of having to be coddled. I never did encourage them to be dependent on me.''

She pulled a face. "But you must be a little dependent on them," she said. "Your own sons, Simon. You do not have to feel obliged to take me on an elaborate wedding trip, you know. Just to be with you and at your home will be happiness enough.''

He smiled at her. "Ah, but I intend to make your happiness the main goal of my life," he said. "We will travel, Mary, and when we return, we will always be where it is most fashionable to be. There will always be something to amuse you.''

"I am thirty years old, Simon," she said. "Did you know that? I am sure you must have. I make no effort to try to hide my age." She flushed. "I cannot delay too long if I am to give you a family.''

"I have a family," he said. "You do not have to worry about that tedious duty, Mary. I have no intention of burdening you with children.''

"Burdening?" she said. "Oh, no, Simon. It would be no burden. It would be a joy.''

They did not argue the matter. They were riding in company with other people, and soon it became necessary to converse with others. Besides, it was very early in their betrothal. Such matters could be discussed with more seriousness later. There would be time enough to convince him that domestic joy for her meant a country home and a husband and family of her own.

Nevertheless, a little of the joy had gone out of the morning. What if their goals for happiness should really prove to be incompatible? But she pushed the thought from her mind.

* * *

His aunt was trying to throw them together. She was matchmaking. He had suspected it right from the day of the garden party, when she had unexpectedly invited them to stay to dinner. She liked Mary and for some strange reason had conceived the notion that she would make him a good wife.

He had suspected even more strongly when he had received his invitation to this week at Rundle Park and his aunt had mentioned specifically that she had also invited Mary and Goodrich. He had been even more sure of it after he had arrived and talked with her.

If she was hoping to match the two of them, of course, there were those who would have thought it strange that she would also invite Goodrich, since in her own words he and Mary had become an item. But that was just the way his aunt worked. She confronted problems head-on. By inviting the three of them into the country, she hoped that he would oust Goodrich from Mary's affections and that she would see that he was the better man.

Ha! The better man.

What his aunt had done was force him into becoming a blackguard. Or into remaining a blackguard. He did not have much honor or reputation left to lose, if any.

He tried. After that disaster of an opening tea, he did try to keep his distance from her. He even looked over the slim pickings of unattached females at his aunt's party and tried determinedly to show a gentlemanly interest in Miss Wiggins, though the girl was almost young enough to be his daughter and seemed never to have heard the word "conversation." And he denied himself the pleasure of a morning ride merely because Mary was to be one of the party.

But in the afternoon he could no longer avoid being in company with her. His aunt had filled up two carriages with guests interested in the ancient Norman church and church-yard in the village. She had craftily offered Goodrich the seat next to her before the man realized that only those who could fit into the two carriages were to go. Mary was not among them.

For those guests who remained, Lady Eleanor suggested a walk across the pasture and through the trees past several follies to the lake. She was sly, Lord Edmond thought. Not by the merest hint had she suggested that both he and Mary join the walkers. Certainly there was no evidence that she had even dreamed that they walk together. But she had set the scene nicely, he had to admit that. He caught Goodrich's eye as the viscount escorted his aunt out to the waiting carriages, and inclined his head. He noted with the greatest satisfaction the tightening of Goodrich's jaw.

And the rest was inevitable. He was one of the first of the walkers to arrive downstairs, and Mary was the first unattached lady to put in an appearance. Perhaps he might have hung back and waited to offer his arm to Miss Wiggins or to the widowed Lady Cathcart, who had been married to his uncle's cousin. But Mary made the mistake of catching his eye and raising her chin stubbornly. His very self-respect set him to sauntering across the hall to her side.

"Mary?" he said. "You are walking and have reserved no one's arm on which to lean? Allow me to offer mine." Which he proceeded to do with a courtly bow.

"Thank you," she said, her voice chilly. "But I am not sure I will need anyone's arm."

He raised one eyebrow and looked at her.

"Very well," she said, one foot beating a light tattoo on the tiles. "Thank you, my lord."

Everyone else came downstairs in a large and noisy body.

"Doris and I will lead the way," Peter Shelbourne said. "This was the route of many a childhood romp. Remember, Andrew? Edmond? I could do it with my eyes closed."

"A rather pointless though impressive offer," Lord Edmond said. "Go ahead, then, Peter. Lady Mornington and I will bring up the rear so that we can rescue any stragglers who happen to get lost."

"Nicely done," Mary said as they descended the horse-shoe steps at the back of the group. "I suppose you intend to lag so far behind that you will have me all to yourself."

"It is a fine idea," he said, "though it had not occurred to me until you mentioned it."

"And I suppose you arranged it that Simon go on the drive," she said, "so that I would be unprotected."

"Far from it," he said. "My knees are still knocking from a certain nocturnal visit I was paid last night."

She looked at him in inquiry.

"It seems I am to keep my eyes and my hands and every other part of my body off you," he said, "since you are now someone else's possession."

Her jaw tightened. He wondered at whom her anger was directed.

"I gather that my jaw and my nose and several other parts of my anatomy are at risk if I choose to be defiant," he said. "I believe that even a bullet through the heart or brain would not be considered excessive punishment."

"Well," she said, "at least now you know."

"I do indeed," he said. "Mary, are you really going to marry him?"

"I am," she said. "I have been a widow long enough. I want the security and contentment of marriage."

"Ah," he said. "And I thought that it was a new lover you were in search of. No wonder you rejected my suit, Mary. I should have offered you marriage."

"How ridiculous!" She looked at him scornfully. "As if I would have married you. And as if you would have offered marriage. You would be quite incapable of the type of commitment that marriage calls for. Fidelity, for example."

"Do you think so?" he said. "Though perhaps you are right. I had not the smallest intention of being faithful to Dorothea had I married her. And she was too civilized to have expected it. She would have preferred me to reserve all amorous activities apart from the begetting of an heir for a mistress, I suspect. On the other hand, I did intend to be faithful to Lady Wren. She was the most exquisite creature I have ever seen. Yourself included."

"Thank you," she said. "I have never had any illusions about my own beauty."

"I could have been faithful to you, though," he said, his eyes roaming her face. "I don't believe I would have ever wished to stray from you, Mary."

"Nonsense!" she said. "We have nothing whatsoever in common."

"Oh, yes," he said. "There was something."

She looked about her. "Why are we walking around the formal gardens instead of through them like everyone else?" she asked.

"A question unworthy of you, Mary," he said, though he had not noticed until that moment that they were not following the others, "when the answer is so obvious. So that we may fall farther behind, of course."

"If you think to seduce me," she said, tight-lipped, "you have a fight on your hands, my lord."

"A tempting thought," he said. "But let us be civil. Talk to me, Mary. Tell me how you like this house and what you have seen of the park."

She relaxed somewhat as they rounded the end of the formal gardens and proceeded after the others in the direction of the stile leading to the path across the pasture.

"Oh, I like it very well," she said. "I cannot imagine why anyone with a country home can bear to leave it in order to live in town."

"The pursuit of pleasure," he said, "and company. The escape from self. One does not have to come face-to-face with oneself so often amid the clamor of town entertainments."

"Is that why you live almost all the time in town?" she asked.

"As usual, Mary," he said, "you know unerringly how to wound. You think I find facing myself unpleasant?"

"Do you?" she asked.

He lifted her hand away from his arm so that he could climb over the stile and turn to help her over. He could not resist lifting her down and lowering her close to his own body. She flushed, but she smoothed out her dress calmly enough and took his offered arm again.

"Why should I?" he asked. "I have almost everything a man could ask for in life. I have wealth and property and position. I have had a great deal of pleasure in my life."

"And peace of mind?" she said. "And self-respect? And a place to call home, and loving people to fill it?"

"Ah, you would be enough for that, Mary," he said.

"No." She looked up at him and shook her head. "Absolutely not. For whenever I am with you, my lord, I am doing what you always object to. I am wounding you, if it is possible for you still to feel wounded. I am your conscience. You are a fool if you think you could ever be happy with me."

He sighed. "My small attempt to keep the conversation light and general has failed, has it not?" he said. "We are back to the wrangling. Tell me, why exactly are you marrying Goodrich? Is it just that you think you are of an age when you ought? Is it just for security and contentment? They are very dull words. Is there no love, no fire, no magic?"

"My reasons are my own concern," she said, her voice frosty.

"By which words I understand that there are none of those elements in your relationship," he said. "You are not the sort of woman who can live permanently without any of the three, Mary."

"Oh," she said crossly, "how can you pretend to know anything about me? You know nothing beyond the fact that I am terrified of thunderstorms and behave very irrationally when one is happening."

"I know you, Mary," he said. "I know you very well, I believe."

She clucked her tongue. "Everyone else is across the pasture and in the woods already," she said. "I think it ungentlemanly of you to keep me so far behind, my lord."

"You will insist," he said, "on telling me I am no gentleman on the one hand and expecting me to behave like one on the other. Is he going to take you to live in the country? You will like that, at least."

"He wants to take me traveling," she said. "He wants us to spend a year and perhaps longer traveling about Europe after our wedding. He wants to make my happiness the focus of his life, he says."

"Then you should be ecstatic," he said. "Why are you not?"

She was looking ahead to the ancient trees that made up the woods surrounding the lake. "I want a home," she said. "I did nothing but travel during my first marriage. We never had a home at all except for a tent and sometimes some rooms for a billet. And though I have my home in London now, it can sometimes be lonely."

"So the traveling holds no lure for you," he said. "If your happiness is indeed his main concern, Mary, then all you will have to do is tell him so."

"But he seems so set on it," she said. "And so set on making pleasure the object of our life together. I want a family, but he says he will not burden me with children."

"He is set on bringing himself pleasure," he said quietly, "and on not burdening himself, Mary."

Her eyes flew to his suddenly and she flushed rosily. "Oh," she said, "how did you do it? How? What on earth could have possessed me to confide such things to you? To you of all people?"

"Sometimes a sympathetic ear can loose even the most tightly knotted tongue," he said.

"Sympathetic!" She looked at him in distaste. "What use will you make of these confessions, I wonder. You will tell everyone, I suppose. You will make me the laughingstock. And you will anger Simon."

He swung her around to face him and grasped her by both arms. "When have I ever made public anything I know about you?" he asked. "At least absolve me of that, Mary. And is it so shameful anyway to admit that you want a home and family with the man you are planning to marry?"

She laughed bitterly. "At least," she said, "you can be thankful that I did not somehow maneuver you into offering for me. Can you imagine a worse hell than living with a woman with such lowly ambitions?"

"I have a country home I might have offered you," he said. "If it is solitude and domesticity you crave, Mary, you would like it. I have neglected it for years. It needs redecorating and refurnishing from stem to stern. I have just been there for a few weeks. It needs a woman's touch. But it is cozy. Not as large as Rundle Park or Goodrich's estate,

I will wager. It was the smallest of my father's properties—a suitable one to which to banish me. I might have offered it to you.''

"So that you might neglect me too?'' she said. "What nonsense you speak. Sometimes I think you almost believe your own words. Do you know yourself so little?''

He released one of her arms to set the backs of his fingers lightly against one of her cheeks. "And you might have had my seed,'' he said, "as you did that one night. I might have been able to offer you babies, Mary.''

She opened her mouth to speak, but the muscles of her face worked somewhat out of her control for a moment.

"Only you could possibly say such a very improper thing to a lady who is not even your betrothed,'' she said.

"We might have changed that too,'' he said. "If only I had met you fifteen, sixteen years ago. You were a child then, were you not? And I too, Mary. I was the veriest child until my twenty-first birthday, and a man the next day. What a coming of age it was. The weight of ages.''

"You merely reaped the consequences of drunkenness,'' she said.

"Yes.'' He dropped his hand from her cheek. "So I did. You are in the right of it there.'' He turned to walk on, his hands at his sides.

She hurried to catch up to him. "Why did you not stop,'' she asked, "after the accident? Did it not teach you a lesson?''

He wanted to stride away from her suddenly. He wanted to be alone. But he could neither stride nor leave her. They were among the trees and had to wind their way carefully to the site of Apollo's temple with the circular seat within and the view down to the lake.

"If you had killed your brother, Mary,'' he said, "would you slap yourself on the hand and promise that you would never be bad again? Would you promise to be a good little girl for the rest of your life? With your brother dead at the age of twenty-three? No life left at all? No second chances? And for you one mistake and a lifetime of hell to face before death brought the real thing for the rest of eternity.''

"One mistake," she said. "Was it the only time you drank? Or was it the only time that you brought nasty consequences?"

He felt inexplicably like crying. His nose and his throat and his chest ached with the need. He clasped his hands tightly at his back.

"It was the only time," he said. "The first. You would not believe what I was like, Mary. An innocent. A prude. A bookworm. A moralizer. I lived with my head in the clouds. And so they set themselves to get me foxed for my birthday. Not Dick, but the others—Wallace, my father, my friends. They succeeded beyond their wildest dreams. I was still foxed the morning after, when I lifted him up from the ground with his broken neck and stroked his hair and told him all would be well and scolded him for doing anything as foolhardy as to attempt that gate."

She had stopped walking. She was looking at him, her eyes wide.

"You look as though you had seen a ghost," he said. "Do you want to take my arm again?"

"Oh," she said. "I did not know. Though I might have begun to guess. Is it true, then? *Were* you different before the accident? You were at university? You were going to be a clergyman?"

He laughed. "The joke of the century, is it not?" he said.

He watched her swallow. "And you have never been able to forgive yourself?" she asked.

"For murder?" He shrugged. "It was all a long time ago, Mary, and I am what I am. Perhaps it is as well that you despise me so. If you liked me just a little, you would be trying to reform me. Women are famous for that, are they not? I am thirty-six years old. Beyond reform."

"It was not murder," she said. "There were others equally to blame, including your brother himself. Your aunt was right when she explained a few things to me—it was just a terrible accident."

His smile was twisted. "Pat me on the head, Mary," he said, "and I will feel all better. Where the devil is everyone else?"

They had reached the temple, only to find it deserted, though there was the sound of distant voices.

"Ahead of us," she said. "You deliberately planned it so that we would lag behind."

"Did I?" he said. "Was I planning to steal a kiss from you?"

"Probably," she said.

He indicated the stone seat inside the folly and sat down on it himself. "I have probably incurred the undying wrath of your betrothed already anyway," he said. "I suppose I might as well try to deserve it to the full. If you would care to move a little closer, Mary, I will attempt that kiss."

"I was right, was I not?" she said. "You do hate yourself."

"Devil take it," he said, reaching out and taking her hand in a firm clasp. "Do we have to have this conversation? What does it matter if I am not overfond of myself? At least I thereby make the opinion of the world unanimous."

She took him completely by surprise suddenly by sliding along the seat until she was close beside him. She had not pulled her hand from his. "I am sorry about Dick," she said, "and sorry about the hell you have carried within you ever since. I truly am sorry about the nasty and unfeeling things I have said concerning that incident. But hell need not be eternal unless one chooses to make it so. Did your brother love you?"

"Dick?" he said. "He was deservedly everyone's favorite. There was not a mean bone in his body. Why do you think he came galloping after me? No one else did. They all watched me on my way with laughter. Dick came to save me, the fool."

"He came to save you," she said. "Would he have condemned you to fifteen years of hell and perhaps a whole eternity?"

He got abruptly to his feet. "Enough, Mary," he said. "Who mentioned hell anyway? Me? I tend to overdramatize sometimes. Had you not noticed that about me? There are many men who would give a right arm for a share in my particular type of hell, you know." He reached out a hand to draw her to her feet.

"Yes," she said. "The more fool they."

"Does he kiss you?" he asked. "Do you respond to him as you have always responded to me?"

She shook her head. "Don't," she said. "Please don't."

"Don't what?" he asked. "Ask those questions? Or kiss you?"

"Both," she said.

But she did not fight him as he drew her against him. Her breasts pressed against his coat, and her hands, lightly clenched into fists, rested against his shoulders. She lifted her face to his and closed her eyes.

He kissed first her eyes, feathering his mouth across them before lowering it to brush her lips lightly. He deepened the kiss, savoring the softness and warmth of her, parting his lips only slightly.

And he hated himself anew and ached with his love for her.

She opened her eyes and looked up into his. It was a look of naked vulnerability. She was his in that moment, he knew. And the temptation was almost overwhelming.

"So, Mary," he said, "what is the answer to my question? Does he kiss you? Does he arouse passion in you? Does he bed you?"

"Don't," she said. "Don't look at me like that."

He did not know how he was looking at her. Only that he was steeling himself against temptation.

"Don't sneer," she said. "Sometimes I think I glimpse someone—someone I might like, someone wonderful—behind your eyes. But I am mistaken. There is no one, is there? Perhaps there was, once upon a time. But no longer. I wish there was not this."

"This?" he said.

"This attraction," she said. "This longing for you to kiss me properly, not with the restraint you just showed." She pushed herself away from him suddenly and straightened the ribbons on her bonnet. "Where are the others? Shall we follow them?"

"A good idea," he said. "More invitations like that, Mary, and you might well find yourself being tumbled on the hard ground and complaining bitterly to me afterward about my lack of restraint. If you want me, you have but to say the word and we can make the proper arrangements. But I like my mistresses in civilized surroundings.''

"In scarlet rooms," she said. Her voice was scornful. "And mistress, did you say? Not wife any longer?"

'Why marry you," he said, "when you seem so very available without benefit of clergy?"

She drew away from him and began to walk along the path toward the next folly, a tower which had been built ruined. Miss Wiggins was standing fearfully at the top, on the very safe ruined parapets, clinging to the arm of Andrew Shelbourne, and everyone else was either looking up at them or gazing out across the lake, which was close by.

"I have quite lost touch with you over the years," the Reverend Samuel Ormsby said to Lord Edmond. "Ever since you were sent down from Oxford most unjustly."

"It was hardly unjust," Lord Edmond said. "I did call such a hallowed personage as a don an ass, you may recall."

"At a time when everyone knew you were beside yourself with grief over the passing of your brother and the grave illness of your mother," the Reverend Ormsby said. "Several of us signed a petition on your behalf, you know. But it seemed to do no good. What have you been doing with yourself since?"

"Perhaps you should tell me about yourself first," Lord Edmond said.

Mary, he noticed when he turned to look at her, had joined a few of the other guests. Yet others were going in search of the grand pavilion, which was hidden away among the trees farther along the shore of the lake.

12

LADY ELEANOR gave a few interested guests, mostly ladies, a guided tour of the greenhouses the following morning. Not that there was a great deal of attraction in the greenhouses, she explained to them, when it was summer and the gardens were bright with flowers. The winter was the time to wander in the warmed buildings and enjoy the summer beauties of nature while all was winter bareness outside.

Mary hung back as everyone else strolled from the last of the greenhouses on the way to the rose arbor.

"Ma'am?" she said as their hostess made to follow them. "May I have a word with you?"

Lady Eleanor smiled at her and closed the door. "What is it, Mary, my dear?" she asked.

Mary fingered the velvety leaf of a geranium plant. "I need to know . . ." she said. "That is, there are certain gaps in my knowledge. It is really none of my business, of course, but . . . I need to know," she ended lamely.

"Of course you do, dear," Lady Eleanor said, and she took Mary's arm and began to stroll with her back along the length of the greenhouse. "Sometimes we cannot order our lives as we would wish, can we? We should be able to secure our own happiness with logical planning, but life does not always work that way. You have planned well, and look to be succeeding admirably—on one level. On another you wonder why it is you cannot force yourself to feel happy. Of course you need to ask more questions."

"You know?" Mary said.

"It was very obvious to me the first time I saw you together," she said. "An exceedingly odd couple, I overheard someone say, and I would wager that she was not the only one to say it that afternoon. But not as odd as it would seem, dear, to one who has known and loved Edmond all his life."

"I do not wish to have any interest in him at all," Mary said. "I have fought against his persistence and against my own feelings."

"It would be strange if you had not," Lady Eleanor said. "Edmond is probably the most disreputable member of the *ton* now gracing its ranks. He is fortunate that he is still being received at all. Only his title and his fortune have saved him from complete ostracism, I believe. No lady in her right mind would willingly fall in love with him."

"I did not say I have fallen in love with him," Mary said hastily. "Only that I—"

Lady Eleanor patted her hand. "If only you knew for how many years I have waited for him to meet you, Mary," she said, "or someone like you. I had almost given up hope. Dorothea, of course, was all wrong for him. And Lady Wren too, though I heard about his attachment to her and was pleased at first. She is a beautiful lady and must have had a dull marriage to her elderly first husband, though I never heard a whisper of scandal surrounding her name. But she was in love with her Mr. Russell, and Edmond could not see it."

"Please," Mary said, "I did not mean to give the impression that I am going to—"

"Of course not," Lady Eleanor said, and turned at one end of the greenhouse so that they could walk back along its length again. "What exactly did you need to know?"

"Yesterday," Mary said, "he told me much the same story about his brother's accident that you had told. Except that he added that his father and his eldest brother had deliberately set out to get him drunk. It must have been easy. He had never drunk before, he said."

"Very likely," Lady Eleanor said. "I would not doubt the truth of that."

"They laughed when he insisted on going riding the next morning," Mary said. "They thought it all a great joke, even though he was still drunk."

"Unfortunately," Lady Eleanor said, "we often laugh at those who are inebriated, my dear. There appears to be something funny about people behaving differently from their normal selves. Seeing Edmond foxed must have seemed hilarious. He was always so very serious, so very much in control of himself.''

"But if that is all true," Mary said, 'they were more to blame for what happened than he was.''

"I have always thought so," Lady Eleanor said, "though I was not there at the time to know exactly what happened. They were not a vicious family, Mary, none of them. And they were a very close and loving family, though I used to think that perhaps Edmond suffered from Richard's great popularity. They were alike—both quiet and home-loving. They both adored their mother and looked up to Wallace and my brother as types of heroes. Edmond was by far the more intelligent of the two, but Richard had the gift of sweetness, which Edmond never had. I think perhaps Edmond was a little jealous of Richard.''

"And therefore his guilt would have been stronger," Mary said. "He would have felt as if unconsciously he had wanted his brother dead.''

"Oh, dear," Lady Eleanor said. "Yes, I suppose that is altogether possible. Edmond always looked inward far too much for his own good. He always had too tender a conscience.''

"He was banished, he said." Mary frowned. "He was cast out from the family. And yet it was not his fault, or at least it was no more his fault than anyone else's. How could they have treated him so cruelly?''

"Tragic accidents need scapegoats," Lady Eleanor said. "At first, of course, it must have seemed that Edmond was entirely to blame. He was the one who had been drunk and reckless. He was the one who had not listened to Richard's pleadings. Of course they turned on him. It was cruel, naturally, and unjust and despicable. But people are never quite rational at such times. And they did not heap more blame on him than he heaped on himself.''

"Did they not realize?" Mary swallowed, surprised to find that her voice was not quite steady. "Did they not realize that they were destroying him? Have they never realized that they lost both brothers on that terrible day?''

"Oh, if you are talking in the present tense," Lady Eleanor said, "then I think the answer must be at least partly yes.

At the time, they were too consumed by their grief for Richard and by their concern at the complete collapse and rapid decline of my sister-in-law. And Edmond's running away and his expulsion from Oxford and his failure to put in an appearance at either funeral did not help his cause. Those absences angered even me at the time. It is hard to understand and make allowances for human nature when one's own emotions are raw.''

"But now?'' Mary said. "They will have nothing to do with him?''

"Overtures were made years ago, I believe,'' Lady Eleanor said. "But we are talking about human nature here, Mary. I did not read any of the letters that passed, but I know my brother and I know Edmond quite well. My guess is that there was too much pride on both sides, and too much willingness to assume guilt on the one side and not enough on the other. And then, as invariably happens with family quarrels, too much time had passed.''

"They have never met one another since?'' Mary asked.

"Both sides are at great pains not to do so,'' Lady Eleanor said. "London is understood to be Edmond's domain, the north of England my brother's and Wallace's. Whenever I issue invitations, I have to be careful to issue them separately. For years my brother would always ask if I had invited Edmond too, and Edmond always asked if I had invited his father or Wallace. Fortunately they gave up asking some time ago, confident in the belief that I would never distress them by bringing them together unexpectedly.''

"There must be so much need of healing,'' Mary said. "On both sides. Perhaps too much need. Perhaps it is too late.''

Lady Eleanor opened the door of the greenhouse and motioned for Mary to precede her out onto the dark lawn. "It is a pity to miss the fresh air,'' she said. "We do not know when we are to lose this glorious weather, do we?''

"It is surely the best summer I can remember,'' Mary said.

"I have been saved from lying this time,'' Lady Eleanor said.

Mary looked her inquiry.

"Had either side asked this time if the other was to be here for my birthday," Lady Eleanor said, "I would have been forced to lie, Mary. I am sixty years old, or will be in just a few days' time. My brother is four years my senior. We are getting old. We cannot delay much longer."

Mary's eyes widened. "He is coming here?" she asked. "Lord Edmond's father?"

"And Wallace and his family," Lady Eleanor said. "They should arrive sometime tomorrow. Perhaps I am doing entirely the wrong thing, Mary, especially with other guests at the house. Sparks may fly at the very least. But it is time, I believe. Much past the time, in fact."

Mary said nothing.

"Now, tell me I am right," Lady Eleanor said. "Please tell me I am right, my dear. I respect your opinion."

"Yes." Mary drew a deep breath. "You are right, ma'am. Whatever the outcome, you are right. I do not know the Duke of Brookfield or his eldest son—I am afraid I do not know his title."

"Welwyn," Lady Eleanor said. "The Earl of, my dear."

"I do not know them," Mary said. "But as far as Lord Edmond is concerned, I do not believe more harm can be done. On the other hand, good may come of it."

Lady Eleanor squeezed her arm. "How wonderful you are, my dear," she said. "I waited with bated breath for your verdict. I was very much afraid I had done the wrong thing. And it is still possible, of course. Perhaps they will not even alight from their carriages tomorrow if they discover that Edmond is here. And perhaps he will leap onto the back of the nearest horse and gallop for London when he sets eyes on them. Who knows? One can only try."

"Yes," Mary said. She hesitated. "Was your invitation to me all part of your master plan?"

Lady Eleanor laughed a little ruefully. "It is a gamble, I must admit," she said. "I merely wanted you to see your two men together for a whole week, Mary. I wanted to set your reason at war with your heart. And I have succeeded, have I not? But again, I do not know if I have done the right thing. What if your heart wins and you end up living unhappily ever after? It is entirely possible. I am not altogether sure that Edmond is capable of having a loving relationship with anyone.''

Mary turned her head and smiled at her hostess. ''I will not have you feel guilty,'' she said. ''I must tell you that since my arrival here I have accepted Lord Goodrich's offer of marriage. It is what will be best for me, I am sure. And Lord Edmond has never offered me more than *carte blanche,* you know. Does that shock you? I would not accept either that or a marriage offer from him. I could not possibly be happy with him—or he with me either. But at least I do not despise him as I used to do, and I am glad of that. You are partly responsible, ma'am, and I am grateful to you. And for this lovely week in the country. Sometimes I pine for the countryside.''

''You are very gracious, my dear,'' Lady Eleanor said. ''Very. *Carte blanche,* indeed. Does the man have no sense left whatsoever? Does he think to satisfy those needs with you and waste everything else you have to offer him? Men! Sometimes I could shake the lot of them.''

Mary smiled.

He was not enjoying himself. And that was an understatement of the first order. He wished himself back at Willow Court, if the truth were known. He had never had much use for his country estate, finding life there far too dull for his tastes, but he had found a measure of peace there during the past few weeks, and he longed to be back. Alone. Away from people. Away from her.

For all his worst suspicions had been confirmed during the past couple of days. He was not only in love with her. He loved her. And that changed everything—everything by which he had lived for fifteen years. All his adult life.

Ever since he had rammed the barrel of a dueling pistol into his mouth late on the date of his mother's funeral and had sweated and shaken and finally thrust the weapon from him and cried and cried until there were no tears left and no feeling either—ever since then he had decided that love, family, commitment to other people could bring nothing but pain and disaster. And so he had lived for himself, for pleasure. Pleasure had become the yardstick by which he measured all the successes of his life. If he wanted something, he reached for it. And if it brought him enjoyment, then he clung to it until the pleasure had cloyed.

Perhaps the nearest he had come to being selfless in all the years since had been his comforting of Mary at Vauxhall. Even when he had mounted her there, he had done so not from any selfish desire for personal gratification but from the desperate need to shelter her from her fear. He had drawn her as close as one human being can draw another.

He cursed the chance that had brought him that invitation to Vauxhall and the whim that had made him accept. For it had changed his life as surely, if not as dramatically, as Dick's death had done. And he did not want his life changed yet again. He had grown comfortable with it. Almost happy with it.

He loved her. And so he could no longer even try to take advantage of her. He could easily do so. She had actually told him that she was attracted to him, and her body had told him as much every time he had touched her. Her eyes told him the same story every time he met them, even though she masked their expression with coldness or disdain or hostility.

He could have her if he wanted her. It would take very little effort on his part. And he did not think he was being merely conceited to think so. He could have her.

Devil take it, he could have her.

And yet she did not want him. Every part of her except the basely physical recoiled from him. And justly so. She should not want him or like him. Or love him. And if she did, or thought she did, he would have to disabuse her. For he could not take her in any way at all. He loved her, and he was the last man on earth he would wish on her.

And yet there were four days of the country party left, and he felt obliged to stay at Rundle Park despite the longing to get away. Four days in which Mary would see him and perhaps continue to be troubled by her unwilling attraction to him. And four days during which he must fight the temptation to dally with her or to try to ingratiate himself with her.

And yet, he thought, riding out alone during the morning while several of the ladies, Mary included, were touring the greenhouses, perhaps his very best course was to pursue the first of those temptations. Perhaps he should dally with her, as he had done to a certain extent the afternoon before. Perhaps he should make himself quite as obnoxious as he possibly could. It should not be at all difficult. He was an expert at being obnoxious.

He had told her too much the day before. He had felt her sympathies begin to sway his way. It was strange, perhaps, when he had never felt the compulsion to tell anyone else about that worst of all days in his life. He had never felt the need to justify himself or to try to give anyone a glimpse into his personal hell. Only Mary. But of course he loved Mary, and against all the odds and all the urgings of his better nature—if there were such a thing left—he wanted her to love him.

But he did not want her sympathy or her affection. It would be too unbearable to know that her feelings had softened toward him at all. It would be better by far if she continued to despise and even hate him as she had always done. And there was only one way to ensure that that happened.

Lord Edmond laughed rather bitterly to himself. He would probably end up fighting a duel with Goodrich before the four days were at an end.

But it would be worth it. Once he had made her hate him in true earnest, then she would be safe from him. And he from her.

He smiled to himself and spurred his horse into a gallop across a fallow field, heedless of the possibility of rabbit holes or other irregularities in the ground. If there were a high gate to be jumped, he thought with grim humor, he would jump it without a second thought, since there was no one coming along behind him to imitate his foolhardiness and break his neck.

And this time he was not even foxed!

"We are going to get storms out of this weather before

it changes, you mark my words,'' Doris Shelbourne assured the people within earshot of her later that evening. "And then summer will be over. We will have an early autumn. We cannot expect to enjoy weather like this and not suffer for it.''

"Storms," Mrs. Leila Orsmby said, looking up at her husband, who was standing beside her chair. "I do hope not. The children are terrified of them."

"Children usually are," Viscount Goodrich said, one hand on Mary's shoulder as he stood behind her chair. "The best medicine is to ignore both the storm and their wailing. They quickly learn that there is nothing to fear."

"That is easily said," Leila said, "but it is more difficult to do. When children are crying and they are one's own children, one feels constrained to comfort them."

"Then one is merely making a rod for one's own back, if you will forgive my criticism, ma'am," Lord Goodrich said. "Children must be taught fortitude."

"I am not sure that fortitude can be taught in that way," Mary said quietly. "The fear of storms is a dreadful thing and one must remember that there is something very real to the fear."

"Nonsense!" Lord Goodrich said. "Pardon me, Mary, but I must disagree most strongly. A little healthy thunder and lightning never did anyone any harm."

"It killed four soldiers in the tent next to my husband's and mine in Spain," she said. "Since then, I have not taken storms so lightly."

"In fact she is driven into a blind terror by them."

Mary looked up at Lord Edmond, who was lounging against the wall in Lady Eleanor's drawing room, his arms crossed over his chest. He was half-smiling down at her in a manner that suggested that they shared some very personal secret. It did not soothe her indignation to remember that they did indeed. But only the day before he had declared quite seriously that she must absolve him of ever having shared any personal knowledge of her with anyone else.

"I have seen it happen," he said.

Mrs. Bigsby-Gore was playing determinedly on the pianoforte for several dancing couples, Lady Eleanor having been persuaded by the young people to have the carpet rolled up so that they might have an evening of informal dancing.

"Yes," Mary said, lifting her chin. "I am afraid of storms. I can sympathize with your children, Mrs. Ormsby."

"Mary." Lord Goodrich squeezed her shoulder. His tone was teasing. "You should be ashamed of yourself. You cannot spend the rest of your life quivering at the approach of a storm just because you once had the misfortune to be close to men foolhardy enough to get themselves killed by one. What were you and they doing in tents during a thunderstorm anyway?"

"Trying to keep dry," she said more tartly than she had intended. "We were bivouacking, Simon. Camping. We were part of an army on the march."

"And the army could do no better for you?" he said. "That is quite shameful. Surely there must have been buildings available. Your husband was, after all, an officer. You ought not to have been subjected to the unpleasantness of being so close to those deaths."

"I do agree that the four poor devils who did not survive the storm should have had the good taste to die elsewhere," Lord Edmond said. His voice, Mary noticed, was heavy with boredom. "As for Mary's fears, Goodrich, you should perhaps thank providence for them. She likes to be held tightly. Ah, very tightly."

Mary's eyes blazed at him briefly. How could he! But she was aware of Leila Ormsby's and Doris Shelbourne's discomfort at the suggestiveness of his last words.

"I know it is a foolish fear," she said. "I do my best to conquer it and almost succeed if I am safely inside a large building. But, anyway." She smiled brightly at Doris. "I hope your prediction does not come true after all, Mrs. Shelbourne. I hope that one morning—a long time in the future— we will awaken to good English drizzle and find that our glorious summer has disappeared quietly in the night."

Fortunately, Sir Harold Wright arrived at that moment to ask her to dance and she got gratefully to her feet.

She glanced at Lord Edmond several times while she danced. He continued to stand against the wall, watching her, that half-smile on his lips. She did not like it. It looked malicious. And he had proved himself to be malicious. What possible reason could he have had for saying what he had about her behavior during storms? The comfort he had given her at Vauxhall was almost the only kindly memory she had of him. And now he had tarnished that.

She felt very cross with herself. She realized suddenly that ever since the day before, and especially since her talk with Lady Eleanor that morning, she had been looking for redeeming points in him. She had been looking for something to like, something to excuse the way she felt about him physically. Despite everything, she had been trying to change her opinion of him.

It was foolish in the extreme, she realized. Perhaps he had been very different once upon a time—undoubtedly he had. And perhaps the fault for what had happened to his life was not entirely his own. Perhaps he was to be pitied. But those facts did not excuse him for present obnoxious behavior. They did not make him more likable or more worthy of respect.

For the past day she had allowed feelings to obscure judgment. But she had not liked his contribution to the conversation on storms. She had not liked it at all. And she would not forget again, she decided.

She was standing with the viscount and the Reverend and Mrs. Ormsby later in the evening when Lord Edmond touched her shoulder.

"Waltz, Mary?" he said. "Mrs. Bigsby-Gore is playing one, I hear. And you dance it awfully well, I remember. Though the last time we danced it, I believe we did not spend the whole time, er, dancing. However, there is, alas, no balcony outside the drawing room here, and no large concealing potted plants on the nonexistent balcony." He smiled.

The viscount drew breath to make a reply. He was going to make a scene, Mary thought, in front of the reverend and his wife.

"Thank you," she said quickly. "It would be pleasant to dance, my lord."

She hoped that her smile was as arctic as it felt.

13

IT WAS NOT by any stretch of the imagination a ball. There was merely a lady seated at the pianoforte, her playing making up in enthusiasm what it lacked in finesse. And merely a few couples dancing about the cleared floor of the drawing room, while others stood or sat about watching or conversing. It was certainly too confined an atmosphere for a quarrel.

Mary schooled her features to bland amiability. "You have just surpassed even yourself in vulgarity," she said.

"Have I, by Jove?" he said. "Thank you for saying so, Mary."

Still that half-smile, she noticed. She would have liked—oh, yes, she really would—to slap it from his face. "What do you mean," she said, "by suggesting that you have held me tight during a thunderstorm and dallied with me behind a potted plant?"

"Suggested?" His eyelids drooped over his eyes and he looked down to her lips. "Suggested, Mary? If I remember correctly—and I am quite, quite sure I do—I held you very tightly indeed during a certain storm. I do not believe I could have been closer to you if I had tried. The female body is capable of only a certain degree of penetration, you know."

Her eyes widened as she willed herself not to flush. "You are disgusting," she said. "Perhaps you would like to return to the group and repeat those words there. You missed a grand opportunity to sink a few degrees lower in public esteem. Better still, perhaps you would like to stop the music and make a public announcement. It is too delightful a detail to share with only a select group."

"Smile, Mary." His voice drawled annoyingly. She hated men who drawled. There was such affectation involved. "Unless you want the world to witness your indignation, that is."

She smiled. "If I were just alone with you for a single minute," she said, "I would have your ears ringing before I was done with you. Be thankful, my lord, that we are not alone."

"Thankful?" he said. "I could dream of no greater bliss. But it would have to be for longer than a minute, Mary. Considerably longer. Even on a certain tabletop, I believe it took me longer than a minute. Smile!"

Mary smiled. "I choose to end this conversation," she said. "We will dance in silence, if you please."

"You may credit me with some sense of propriety," he said. "You may safely trust me not to make public the fact that we have enjoyed the ultimate intimacy together. No, no, close your mouth. You have just expressed your desire to dance in silence. You need not say 'Enjoyed!' with all the venom and hauteur that you planned. You did enjoy it, Mary, much as you may wish now that you had not. There is no point in denying it. I was there, if you will remember."

She clamped her teeth together and smiled.

" 'As if I could possibly forget,' " he said. "You see? I am even supplying your side of the conversation. Mary, what sort of an ass would ask you what you were doing in a tent in Spain in the middle of a thunderstorm when he knew you were with Wellington's army? I almost asked him myself, but I remembered your objection to my use of that particular word in your salon."

"You will leave the name of my fiancé out of this conversation—no, out of this monologue, if you please," she said.

" 'Ass' is more suitable than his name anyway," he said. "Is he good, Mary? Rich he certainly is, if rumor is correct on the matter. Have you slept with him? I believe I have asked you that question more than once, but you have never answered it. Have you?"

She gave him a glance of cold contempt before looking away to smile vaguely at the room at large.

"Do you sleep with him here?" he asked. "If not, perhaps you would care to leave the door of your bedchamber unlocked, Mary. Is it ever locked, by the way? What I mean is that I could come to you at night and you could explore the full extent of this attraction you claim to feel toward me.''

She drew in her breath slowly.

"Was that an indication of assent?" he asked. "Tonight, Mary? We could do together all those things we did in a certain scarlet room. And there are far more things I want to do to you and with you, and far more things that I want you to do to me.''

"I am betrothed.'' They were the only words she was capable of at that particular moment.

"That will not worry me," he said. "I will not think about it while we are about our business. I am not quite the three-in-a-bed type, but I believe I can learn to share you, provided I have you alone in bed when it is my turn.''

"Does this particular tune go on and on forever?" she said. "Will it never end?''

"Oh, it will," he said. "Patience, Mary. The night will come. And I will come with it. All you need is a little patience.''

She looked fully at him and forgot the need to smile. "I have been a fool," she said. "An utter fool. For the past day I have been trying to convince myself that if you were human once upon a time you must still be so deep down. But you are not. You spoke yesterday to arouse my pity, did you not? So that I would climb into your bed to comfort you.''

"I have never wanted your pity, Mary," he said. "Anything and everything but that.''

"I despise you now more than ever," she said. "We are all ultimately responsible for our own words and actions, my lord. Perhaps circumstances cause major changes and stresses in our lives, and perhaps we can be excused for crumbling beneath the weight of those circumstances—for a certain time. But the real test of the strength of our characters lies in our ability to go forward with our lives unbroken, to rise above circumstance. I lost a dear husband in all the useless cruelty of war. I found his body myself. He was naked on the battlefield after the local peasantry had completed their stripping and plundering of the dead and wounded. My husband, who had died for their freedom. You are not the only one to have suffered.''

For a moment he gazed into her eyes, his face drained of all color and expression. But only for a moment. He sneered.

"I suppose your point is that you have greater strength of character than I," he said. "Well, I will not argue the point, Mary. You are undoubtedly right. But I will wager that I have had greater pleasure from life than you."

"Pleasure!" she said. "That is all that matters to you. Pleasure! Not pride or honor or joy or happiness. Just pleasure."

"You see?" he said, drawing her to a halt with a firm hand at her waist. "While your mind was otherwise occupied, the music came to an end after all. Time does pass, you see. Tonight, Mary?"

"I will not lock my door," she said, looking steadily into his eyes. "I will not cower behind locked doors. But if you set so much as a finger on the knob outside my door, my lord, I shall scream so loudly that even the most distant groom will come running. And if you believe that I am afraid of the scandal that would be caused, then try me."

He smiled and raised his hand to his lips. "Fascinating," he said. "Has she told you any of these stories of Spain, Goodrich? Thank you for the dance, Mary."

"Simon." She smiled up at him as he came up beside her and set an arm protectively about her waist.

"All the rest of the dances this evening are mine, Waite," the viscount said. "I believe my meaning is clear?"

"I always hate that question," Lord Edmond said. "It is quite impossible to say no, and yet one feels remarkably foolish saying yes. One always wishes one could think of some witty reply. Ah, I do believe my aunt is calling me. If you will excuse me, Mary? Goodrich?"

And he sauntered away to quite the opposite corner of the room from where Lady Eleanor was deep in conversation with Sir Harold and Lady Cathcart.

"I warned him," the viscount said. "I went out of my way to do so quite privately and civilly so that there need be no public unpleasantness. But such a man is quite impervious to the decencies, it seems. He did not repeat any of his vulgarities while you danced with him, Mary?"

"No," she said. "He was quite civil, Simon."

But in truth she seethed and she mourned. Seethed at his outrageous behavior that evening, far outstripping anything else she had suffered from him since their acquaintance began. And mourned for a love that had been born and struggled for existence, only to die just when it had seemed that perhaps it would survive and grow after all. And she castigated herself for even allowing that love conception and birth when it was a hopeless and an undesirable thing. For once something had been born and died, it had existed. It had been a part of one's life and must be forever a part of one's memory and therefore a part of one's very being.

She had loved him for a day. For a day she had let down her guard and loved him.

And dreamed. She had allowed herself to dream. Foolish, foolish woman.

Deny it as she would, she had allowed both to happen. For a day. For a permanent part of her life.

He had probably given her a sleepless night, he thought as she came rather late into the breakfast room the following morning. Her face looked pale and a little drawn. She had probably lain awake waiting for the sound of his hand on the doorknob. And of course, being Mary, she would have scorned to lock the door merely so that she could sleep without fear.

If only she knew how long he had lain awake fighting the temptation. Part of him had wanted to go and had rationalized his wish. If he went and she screamed as she had promised to do, then there would be a dreadful scene and he would be forced to leave. He would have his excuse to return to Willow Court, to be done with her once and for all.

And if he went and she did not scream—and he did not think she would—then they could renew their argument. He could find more and more outrageous words to disgust her. He could try to seduce her. Perhaps he would even succeed. He believed he had enough power over her physically that she would succumb to his caresses if he set about the seduction with enough determination. Either way, her hatred of him would be intensified once it was over and she had returned to her senses. His goal would be accomplished.

If he went and she did not scream, then he would have one more chance to talk with her privately, one more chance to touch her, perhaps to kiss her. Perhaps to make love to her.

Perhaps to impregnate her.

The thought had put an abrupt end to his dreaming. He had remembered that she wanted children, that she felt herself almost too old to begin a family, that Goodrich was unwilling to saddle himself with yet another family—seven children, it seemed, were quite enough for him. And strangely, Lord Edmond had thought, he himself had wanted children too while she had talked to him—children by her body, children to make her happy, and himself too. He had never thought of children except in terms of an heir. He had never wanted children.

He had stayed away from her and resigned himself to a sleepless night and imagined her sleepless too. He watched her now the following morning pick up a plate and fill it from the dishes on the sideboard. Though "fill" was not quite an accurate word. The plate was almost as empty when she sat down—as far from him as she could find an empty chair—as it had been when she picked it up.

"Another sunny day," Andrew Shelbourne said. "Is this England? Can it be England?"

"It can be and is," Lady Eleanor said firmly. "I put in a special order for another week of fine weather during my prayers last Sunday. So everyone can relax and enjoy it. Such prayers are always answered, are they not, Samuel, my dear?"

The Reverend Ormsby grinned. "I cannot answer for God," he said, "but for myself, I would consider it quite uncivil to ignore such a prayer."

"It seems that God is a civil gentleman," Andrew said.

"Even so," Doris said after the general laughter had died away, "I am not sure that we should be venturing as far as Canterbury today. Fourteen miles." She frowned. "It would be a treacherous journey in a storm, and a storm is going to be the inevitable outcome of this long spell of heat, mark my word."

"Doris is going to be thoroughly disappointed if she proves to be wrong," her husband said with a twinkle in his eye.

"And my children will be worse than disappointed if she is right," Leila Ormsby said with a sigh. "Especially if I am from home. Should we perhaps stay, Samuel?"

The Reverend Ormsby laughed. "We might be at home forever, Leila," he said. "They will have their nurse in the unlikely event that the weather does break in the course of the day, and a whole army of other servants in the house."

"And me too, dear," Lady Eleanor said. "I will be unable to come to Canterbury, I am afraid, though I love it above all places on this earth."

There was a chorus of protesting voices about the table.

"I am expecting some callers," she said, "on this very day. Annoying, is it not? I invited them, and I cannot put them off without seeming quite rag-mannered."

"What a shame," Mrs. Wiggins said politely. "Perhaps we should postpone our drive until tomorrow."

"By no means," Lady Eleanor said. "You are all to go and enjoy yourselves. I live close enough, after all, that I can go to Canterbury any day of the year."

The trip had been suggested during the course of the evening before, and the idea had been received with enthusiasm by all the guests, who were about equally divided between those who were eager to shop and those who wished to view the cathedral.

Lord Edmond was tempted not to go at all. He would stay and keep his aunt company and make himself agreeable to her callers, he thought. But he changed his mind again. Perhaps Mary was not yet convinced. Perhaps somehow she had persuaded herself that his behavior the evening before had not been so bad after all. Perhaps his failure to make any attempt to enter her room during the night had redeemed him somewhat in her eyes. He would take this one more day to convince her. And then he would leave her alone. He would stay as far away from her as it was possible to when they were both guests at the same country home.

"What?" he said to a question Mr. Bigsby-Gore had just asked him. "Oh, yes, assuredly I am going. I would not miss such a pleasure trip for the world."

* * *

There were two days still to go to Lady Eleanor's birthday and the grand celebration she had organized for the occasion. And then one more day after that before the party was at an end. It was not long. But it was far too long. Mary would not be able to endure that long. She would have to leave, return to London.

She sat in one of the carriages on the return from Canterbury late in the afternoon and let the conversation of the other three ladies flow about her without participating in it to any great degree. She felt weary, sick, and quite unable to face another three days at Rundle Park.

She could not do it. She had been foolish enough to love him for one day, and now the persistence and vulgarity of his attentions were no longer merely offensive. They were nauseating. Literally nauseating. She wanted to retch and retch and then cry herself dry and empty. She wanted to sleep and to forget. She wanted to get away. She had to get away. Away from Rundle Park and away from him. And, yes, away from Simon too. She was not sure of anything at all any longer. She needed to be alone. She needed to think. She needed to lick her wounds.

It had been a horrid day. Somehow there had been a minor misunderstanding between herself and Simon, with the result that when they had arrived in Canterbury and she had been handed from the carriage—the ladies had traveled in carriages, while the gentleman had ridden—he had already comitted himself to escort a group of shoppers, whereas she had attached herself to a party set to view the cathedral.

It had not seemed a serious matter. After all, even when they were married, they would not expect to be inseparable. And if he preferred to shop while she preferred to feast her eyes on history, then it was perfectly desirable that they go their separate ways for an hour or two. It had not seemed serious, because Lord Edmond, unmannerly brute that he was, had attached himself to neither group, but had stridden off alone as soon as his horse had been stabled.

But he had reappeared at the cathedral, as she might have expected he would. And he had attached himself to her left side until the gentleman with whom she had been walking moved off from her right to hear some comment that Stephen Wiggins was making.

"You like these old, cold, moldering edifices, Mary?" Lord Edmond had asked.

But she would no longer believe either his ignorance or his lack of taste. "And so do you, obviously," she had said, "or you would not have come here quite alone, with no coercion at all."

"Ah," he had said, "but I came here to be with you, Mary, having guessed that you would choose this rather than the shopping trip. Had I made my intention clear, Goodrich would have been here, hanging on your arm like a leech."

"What a very unpleasant simile," she had said.

"Like a watchdog, then," he had said with a shrug. "Isn't Chaucer or someone buried there?"

"No," she had said. "He is buried in Westminster Abbey, as I am sure you are very well aware. You are thinking of the *Canterbury Tales.*"

"Ah," he had said. "Memories of school days and forbidden readings of 'The Miller's Tale.' A fine story. Have you read it?"

"You are becoming very predictable," she had said. "If I had had to guess one story from the *Tales* that you would choose as your favorite for my benefit, it would have been that. What else?"

"And no blushes?" he had said. "A shame."

Their conversation had ended at that point as the whole group came together to stroll about and see all that was to be seen.

It had not been bad—only the sort of encounter she was learning to expect. What had been bad—and especially bad when she considered that they had been inside a church—was the way he had grasped her arm as everyone went outside, and twisted her around so that her back was against a heavy stone pillar and she was suddenly quite out of sight of anyone who was not making a deliberate search. She had been taken so much by surprise that she had made no resistance at all to the press of his body to her own and to his practiced kiss, which immediately opened her mouth so that his tongue could thrust inside.

Looking back on the embrace as she rode home in the carriage, now totally oblivious of the conversation of the other ladies, she could find no way to describe it except with the word "carnal." It had been horrible. None of his other embraces had been like it. There had been no tenderness, no gentleness, no teasing or persuasion or . . . or anything except the most nauseating lust. His hands had grasped her breasts, hurting them. His groin had ground itself against her, parting her legs and setting her off-balance.

His eyes had been glittering when he had lifted his head to look down at her. "You see now why I wanted to separate you from the leech?" he had said. "You see, Mary? I want you. And you want me. Admit it."

She had done the only thing she had been capable of doing. She had imposed relaxation on her body, though the lower half of his own was still pressed against her, and she had stared back at him, her face expressionless.

The half-smile had been back on his face, the expression that helped her to hate him. "You are a coward, Mary," he had said. "We could have so much pleasure together that we would have to invent a new word for it. But you are afraid to admit to anything as unladylike as sexual desire. 'Attraction' was the word you used. It is a weak euphemism for what you really feel, my love."

"I have nothing whatsoever left to say to you, my lord," she had said, her voice flat. "Not reproach or pleading or denial. Nothing. You will do what you must to pursue your own pleasure, but you will find no more pleasure from me. There will be no further response to whatever approach you care to take with me. You might as well pursue a fish. Now, shall we go? Or would you like to press more kisses on me while you have me imprisoned here? If so, proceed. I have nothing to say."

"Mary." His voice had been amused, but he had pushed himself away from her. "I could arouse response in the snap of my fingers if I so chose. But the time and place are not quite right, are they? Later, my love. Later."

"If you say so," she had said.

He had bowed before her just as if he had been treating her the whole time in the most courtly of manners. "Shall we rejoin the others?'' he had asked. ''Take my arm?''

''If you wish.'' She had turned toward the doors. ''And if you insist.'' She had taken his arm.

She closed her eyes in the carriage. It had been a dreadful day. Dreadful. And she could take no more. She had had enough. If she had to face one more of those scenes, she would surely crack.

She was going to have to leave. Rude as it would appear, and much as she hated to throw any sort of blight on Lady Eleanor's birthday celebrations, she was going to have to go away.

14

HE WAS FEELING rather sick. Physically nauseated with self-disgust. It was rather a new feeling. He supposed that Mary had been right when she said that he hated himself. When he thought about it, he had to admit that she had a point, though he had never consciously hated himself through the years—not since the rawness of pain and guilt over Dick's death and his mother's had receded, anyway. Rather, he had turned the feeling outward and looked on the world and all that made it meaningful to many people with contempt. His most habitual expression, he guessed, though he rarely looked at himself in a mirror, was a sneer.

So this disgust with himself was a new thing. He would not use even the most degraded whore with the coarse vulgarity he had accorded Mary in Canterbury Cathedral—in a church, of all places. But the setting was perhaps a fitting one for him. The final degradation. The final thumb at the nose to the world and to God and what they had done to his life—to what *he* had done to his life. There was no point in starting to blame God. He had never done that. At least he had never become a whiner.

He was riding beside Andrew Shelbourne as they turned onto the driveway to Rundle Park, Peter and Bigsby-Gore close behind them. Two of the carriages were ahead, one of them containing Mary. He had not participated a great deal in the conversation on the way home.

He was going to have to leave. He did not want to do so. He loved his aunt and he owed her a deep debt of gratitude. He was not quite sure how he would have fared if all ties to his family had been broken when he was so young. But there were two days to go to her birthday. He could not hold out that long. Two days was an eternity. And he did not know how he was to face Mary again.

He eased his horse to the back of the group as they approached the house. The ladies would need to be helped from the carriages. Only Goodrich and Wright were up ahead. Perhaps he would not help at all, he thought. Perhaps he would disappear in the crowd and withdraw to the stable block. After all, most of the ladies did not expect perfectly courtly behavior from him anyway.

But before he could suit action to intention, his aunt appeared at the top of the horeshoe steps, and with her another lady and two gentlemen—doubtless the callers for whom she had had to stay at home. Lord Edmond glanced at them with little curiosity. He did not know the lady. She was perhaps his own age, perhaps a little older. She was elegantly, if quietly, dressed. His eyes moved on to the elder of the two men, the tall white-haired one—and then jerked quickly to the younger man, whose hair was only beginning to gray at the temples.

And then he was off his horse and thrusting the reins into the hands of he knew not whom and striding he knew not where. He was looking for someone—he did not know whom. Desperately looking. Looking in a panic. And then he saw her and he was beside her and his hand clamped onto her wrist.

"Come with me," he said, and he jerked her into motion so that she almost fell.

"Take your hand off me," she said coldly.

"By God, Waite, you will answer to me for this," Lord Goodrich said, his voice low and furious. "Take your hand off Mary this instant or this whole gathering will witness the breaking of your jaw."

Lord Edmond did not even hear either of them.

"Come," he said. "Come."

Mary looked up at the top of the steps and back to Lord Edmond. "It is all right, Simon," she said. "I will go with him."

"Mary!" the viscount protested.

"It is all right," she said.

But Lord Edmond did not hear the exchange. His eyes were on the corner of the house at the end of the terrace. He knew only that he had to reach the corner and round it. His hand was like a vise on Mary's wrist, but he did not know it. She had to take little running steps to keep up with him.

She should dig in her heels and stop. She should demand release. She should rant and rave at him, scream if necessary. She had had enough of him. More than enough—a raging excess. She should claw and kick at him.

But she did none of those things. She had looked up and seen the two unfamiliar gentlemen with Lady Eleanor and she had understood. And she had looked into Lord Edmond's face and seen the whiteness of it and the wildness of his eyes. And she did none of those things. She half-ran beside him around the corner of the house and down the side, past the rose arbor, and diagonally across the back lawn toward the closest of the trees.

At first there was pain in her wrist and then numbness, and then pins and needles in her hand. But he did not release her or relax his hold on her. And she said nothing. She hurried along at his side.

They were among the trees at last, and he swung them around behind the huge trunk of an ancient oak, set his back against it, and pulled her hard against him. One arm came about her waist like an iron band. The other hand tore at the ribbons of her bonnet, tossed it carelessly aside, and cupped the back of her head. Her face was against his cravat, pressed there so that there was no possibility even of turning her head to one side in order to breathe more easily.

"Don't fight me," he said, though she had done no fighting at all. "Don't fight me."

She closed her eyes and relaxed against him. He was leaning backward slightly against the tree. Her weight was all thrown forward against him. She breathed in the warmth and the scent of him, and she listened to the wild thumping of his heart.

She did not know how long they stood there thus. Perhaps it was five minutes, perhaps ten. It felt much longer even than that. But in all the time, his hold on her did not relax at all, though his heart gradually quieted.

She did not care how long it was. Although her mind was

quite calm and quite rational, she knew only that she was where she had to be, where she was needed—and where she wanted to be. She knew without panic or horror—they would come at some future time and in some future place, but not now—that she loved him. That despite everything, she had to be with him—for now, at least.

His hand behind her head relaxed finally and joined the other at her waist, and she raised her head and looked up at him. His own was thrown back against the tree trunk, his eyes closed. His face was as white as it had been when he first grasped her wrist.

And then pale blue eyes were looking down into hers, dazed, not quite seeing her until they gradually focused and he lowered his head to kiss her.

It lasted for several minutes. But it was not at all a kiss of passion. It was one of infinite tenderness and need—the need for human closeness and touch. And she gave back gentleness and tenderness and love, holding her mouth soft and responsive and slightly open for him. She set both arms up about his neck and held him warmly.

"Do you know what this is all about?" He lifted his head away from hers eventually and set it back against the tree again, staring off somewhere over her head as she lowered her arms to rest her hands on his shoulders.

"Yes," she said.

"Ah." His voice was expressionless. "Then it was no accident. It was planned. And you knew about it, Mary, and did not warn me? But why should you? You must have been privately gloating."

"No," she said.

"No?" He ran the fingers of one hand absently through her hair. "And what am I to do now? Run off, dragging you with me? Abduction to add to my other crimes? Would you kick and scream the whole way, Mary? Why have you not been kicking and screaming now?"

"It is time to go back," she said.

He laughed, but there was no humor in the sound. "There is a whole wealth of meaning in those words, is there not?" he said. "You do not mean just to the house, do you, Mary?"

"No," she said.

"Time to go back," he said. "We can never go back, Mary. Only forward. There is no point in going back. The past can never be changed. My brother was not Lazarus, nor I Jesus."

"Sometimes we have to go back," she said. "Sometimes we have lost the way and need to go back."

His eyes looked down into hers again. "Is that what happened to me, my wise, philosophizing, sermonizing Mary?" he asked. "Have I lost the way?"

"Yes," she said.

"Fifteen long years ago," he said. "Too long ago. All the highways and byways will be overgrown with weeds so high they will have become forests."

"Edmond." She touched his jaw lightly with the backs of her fingers. "You must go back. There is nothing ahead if you do not."

"Edmond," he said. "You say it prettily, Mary. Have I made you blush? Had you not realized that you were using my name for the first time? And is my case so desperate? You make me sound like a lost soul."

"You are a lost soul," she said.

He smiled at her slowly and lazily. "It cannot be done, you know," he said. "I cannot be made over into the sort of man who might be worthy of you."

"I am not thinking of me," she said. "You need to become a man worthy of your own respect. Don't smile at me like that."

He continued to smile. "How do you come to be here with me?" he asked. "Did I bring you?"

"I have the bruise on my wrist to prove it," she said.

He took her hand in his and ran his fingers over the still-reddened wrist before raising his eyes to hers. "I have done nothing but bruise you in the past two days," he said. "I should take myself off, Mary, away from them and out of your life. It is what I intended to do on my return from Canterbury."

"No," she said. "You must go back. You must."

"Tell me," he said. "Were they as surprised as I? Did they know that I was here?"

"No," she said.

"So my aunt is playing devil's advocate," he said. "Well, there is no reason why we cannot all be civil to one another, I suppose. It was all a very long time ago."

"Yes," she said. "You must go back."

"But only if you will come with me," he said. "My feet will not know how to set themselves one before the other across that lawn if you are not there to hold my hand, Mary. You must come with me. Will you?"

"Yes," she said.

"Holding my hand?" He chuckled. "The leech's face will turn purple at the sight, I would not wonder."

"Don't," she said. "He is my betrothed."

He sobered instantly. "Yes, he is," he said. "But no more worthy of you than I, Mary. At least my crimes are all open ones. Promise me that you will look more closely into his background and history before you marry him."

"Let's go back," she said, trying at last to pull herself upright and away from his body.

But he caught at her waist and held her to him, "Promise me," he said.

"If there is something about him that I need to know," she said, "then perhaps you should tell me. But not mere spite, please."

"Promise me," he said.

"Very well, then," she said. "I promise. Let's go back."

He released his hold on her and she moved away from him, brushing the creases from her dress and bending to pick up her bonnet. He was still leaning against the tree as she tied the ribbons beneath her chin. His smile was somewhat twisted.

"Do you have any inkling of how hard this is for me, Mary?" he asked. "I feel paralyzed in every limb. I don't believe it can be done."

She held out her hands to him and he looked at them, surprised, and set his own in them.

"Yes, it can be," she said, "because there is nothing else to be done." She tightened the pressure of her hands in his.

"Well." He squeezed her hands before releasing them and finally straightening up away from the tree. "Perhaps you are right. And perhaps at some future time, when I have your back to a bed and I am between you and the nearest door, I shall say the same words and you will admit the truth of them as meekly as I have just done.''

''I would not count on it,'' she said.

''Let us go and face this unfaceable situation, then,'' he said. But when she would have taken his arm, he took her hand in his, laced his fingers with hers, and tightened his hold. ''After which I may well throttle my aunt.''

They stepped out from the cover of the trees and began the walk back across the lawn to the house.

The drawing-room doors were open and a buzz of sound issued from inside. The guests were partaking of refreshments, though it was far too late for tea, yet too early for dinner.

Lord Edmond Waite fixed a footman standing outside the doors with a steely eye. ''Her ladyship is inside?'' he asked.

''Yes, m'lord.'' The servant bowed.

''Then ask her to step outside, if you please.'' His fingers were still laced with Mary's.

Lady Eleanor appeared no more than a minute later. ''Edmond, Mary,'' she said brightly. ''Where on earth did you disappear to after such a long journey?''

''They are inside there?'' Lord Edmond asked curtly, nodding in the direction of the drawing room.

The brightness disappeared from Lady Eleanor's face. ''No,'' she said. ''They are upstairs. It was as much as I could do to prevent them from calling out their carriage and loading up their unpacked trunks again.'' She smiled fleetingly.

''And you have Mary to thank that I am not twenty miles off by now,'' he said. There was no softening in his expression. ''Why did you do it, Aunt?''

She looked helplessly at Mary and then back at her nephew. ''Because I will be sixty years old,'' she said, ''in two days' time. Because I have one brother and two nephews. Does that make sense to you, Edmond? Probably not.''

He looked stonily at her. ''Well,'' he said, ''there is no

avoiding the matter now, is there? Let us have it over with, then. Will they see me?''

"They are in my sitting room," Lady Eleanor said without really answering the question. "Will you come up now, then, Edmond?''

"Now or never," he said. "This is not easy, you know, Aunt. Did you expect it to be?"

"Nor for me, dear," she said. "And no, I did not expect it to be easy for anyone. Even for myself. I did not know—I *do* not know—if I am perhaps bringing even worse disaster on anyone. But there is no worse, is there?" She looked at Mary, smiled at her briefly, and turned to lead the way up the stairs.

Mary stood where she was and tried to free her hand, but Lord Edmond's tightened about it.

"Mary comes too," he said firmly. "I will not do this without her."

Lady Eleanor looked back, her expression interested. "Very well, dear," she said. "If Mary wishes it."

"She has talked me into it," he said, his voice grim. "She had better wish it."

"Such a gentlemanly way to ask, dear," Lady Eleanor said, clucking her tongue, but Mary had moved up beside Lord Edmond again, drawn by the pressure of his hand, and was accompanying him up the stairs.

"I will come," she said quietly.

His aunt preceded them along the upper hallway to her suite of rooms. Lord Edmond did not look at Mary. Indeed, he was almost unaware of her presence at that moment. But he did know that if she once released her hand from his, he would lose all courage. His aunt opened the door into her sitting room and stepped inside. He drew Mary to his side and entered with her.

It was rather like a carefully arranged tableau, he thought irrelevantly. His father stood with his back to the room, looking out of a window, down onto the formal gardens. His brother stood behind and to one side of an easy chair, his hand on the shoulder of the lady who must be his wife. No one was moving or smiling or talking.

"Well," Lady Eleanor said brightly. "Here is Edmond returned at last, Martin."

His father turned to look at him. He was so very much the same, even after fifteen years, except that his hair, which had been partly dark, partly silver then, was now completely white. People had always said that Edmond looked like his father—tall, inclined to thinness, the face long and austere, the nose prominent, the lips thin. His father looked the picture of elderly respectability.

Edmond had a sudden image of his father standing straight and immobile beside the bed on which Dick had been laid out the morning after his death. His father's face had been stern, more like a mask than a face. He had looked across to the doorway where his youngest son had appeared.

"Get out!" he had hissed so low that the words had seemed to reach Edmond by a medium other than sound. "Murderer! Get out of my son's room."

The last time he had seen his father. The last words he had heard him utter.

"Sir?" he said now, and he was aware with one part of his mind of Mary flinching beside him. He eased the pressure of his fingers against hers. He inclined his head into what was not quite a bow.

"Edmond?" His father's mouth scarcely moved. There seemed to be as little sound as on that morning in Dick's bedchamber.

"And Wallace is here too," Lady Eleanor said heartily. "And Anne. You will not have met your sister-in-law, Edmond."

They had married almost thirteen years before. Although they had had a big wedding, he had not been invited, of course.

"He called me murderer." Edmond had staggered to his eldest brother's room and thrown the door open without knocking. "He called me murderer, Wally."

"And what would you call yourself?" Wallace had been standing at the window, his hands braced on the sill, his shoulders shaking with the sobs that had racked him.

Edmond had stood there for a few moments, cold and

aghast. And then he had left. His mother had been too sick to see him. Or so her maid had told him. But he had heard his mother's voice tell the maid not to admit him. She never wanted to set eyes on him again.

So he had left, taking nothing with him but his horse and his purse and the clothes he had stood in.

"Wallace?" he said now. "Ma'am?"

"Edmond?" his brother said.

There was something farcical about the conversation, that part of his mind that had learned to look on the world with scorn and amusement told him. But he felt no amusement.

"Edmond?" his sister-in-law said, getting to her feet and coming across the room toward him. She was a little over-weight, he noticed, elegantly dressed, rather plain. She held out a hand to him. Her chin was up and she looked very directly into his eyes. "I am delighted to make your acquaintance at last."

And finally he had to relinquish Mary's hand in order to take his sister-in-law's.

"And I yours," he said. "Anne."

Anne smiled and looked a little uncertainly at Mary. Lord Edmond set an arm about her waist and drew her closer to his side. "May I present Mary, Lady Mornington?" he said. "My friend." He looked at his father belligerently. "And that is not a euphemism for any other kind of relationship."

His father's elegant eyebrows rose. "I would not dream of suggesting otherwise, Edmond," he said. "How do you do, Lady Mornington?"

Mary curtsied. "I am well, thank you, your grace," she said.

"My father, Mary," Lord Edmond said. "The Duke of Brookfield. And my brother, Wallace, Earl of Welwyn. And my sister-in-law, Anne."

"Well," Lady Eleanor said when the civilities had been exchanged, "now that the first awkwardness is past, shall we all sit down while I order up refreshments? I am sure my guests downstairs can entertain themselves for an hour or so."

And incredibly, Lord Edmond thought, they did sit down.

And they conversed on a variety of safe general topics. A little stiltedly, it was true, but nevertheless they talked—all of them. Perhaps the ladies were most to be thanked. Anne talked about her three children, two sons and a daughter, and Mary talked about Canterbury Cathedral, and his aunt talked about mutual acquaintances and the weather. He asked his father about his health and Wallace about their journey. And they asked him about Willow Court.

It seemed unreal. How could they be sitting there, the three of them, conversing together politely about nothing of any importance when they had parted fifteen years before with a bitterness that had completely broken close family ties? And yet that was exactly what they were doing.

Was that that, then? he thought when his aunt rose to announce that it was time to retire to their rooms to change for dinner. Had Dick's death and his mother's and the fifteen years since been of so little significance that the past half-hour had erased all the unpleasantness, all the suffering, all the guilt? Was there nothing of any more importance to be said and settled? There was a feeling of anticlimax to succeed the utter panic that had seized him on his return from Canterbury, when he had looked to the top of the steps and seen them standing there with his aunt.

And then too there was another strange feeling of emptiness, of something not quite completed, when Anne left the room with Mary and both disappeared in the direction of their bedchambers. He stood looking after them for a moment before hurrying off to his own room to avoid having to walk there with his father and brother, who were coming out of the room after him.

Nothing was finished at all. Nothing was settled. He and his father and brother were polite strangers. And Mary? What had been happening with Mary in the past couple of hours? He had worked hard in two days to give her enough of a disgust of him that she would quell any attraction that she felt toward him. And yet as soon as he had seen that danger to all the protective armor he had built up around himself in fifteen years, that threat, he had forgotten everything except his selfish and overpowering need of her.

Even his love for her could not redeem him, then. Selfishness, it seemed, was ingrained in him, and he had just put her in a difficult situation indeed. "My friend," he had told his father, setting an arm about her waist.

And he did not believe that he had the heart to spend another evening and another day tomorrow making her hate him all over again.

He just did not have the heart. He was too selfish. His love for her obviously was not a great enough force.

15

SO WHERE WAS she now? Mary wondered. Her hatred for Lord Edmond had wavered, as had her resolve to leave Rundle Park without further delay. Far worse, she was somehow deeply involved with him now, aware not only of the fact that she loved him but also of the fact that he needed her.

She could not forget the way in which he had dragged her off with him, not even aware of what he was doing, and of how he had held her as if she had been the only firm and solid thing left in his world. And of how he had kissed her, not with the coarse suggestiveness of his embrace in Canterbury Cathedral, but with warm need. And of how he had clung to her hand for a long, long time, even taking her in to the momentous first meeting with his father and brother. And of how he had introduced her as his friend.

His friend! Surely she was anything and everything but that. And yet somehow, in the course of just a few hours, they had become friends. Mary frowned at the thought. Was it possible? Was there any way in which she and Lord Edmond Waite could be friends? And yet they were.

And now Simon was angry with her—and justifiably so, she had to admit. She was his betrothed. They were in the drawing room, with several of the other guests, awaiting the call to dinner.

"I was shamed, Mary," he said, "left standing there like that while you rushed off for a walk with Waite. How must it have looked to everyone else?"

"No one knows we are betrothed," she reminded him.

"But everyone must realize that we have an understanding," he said. "It is in the poorest taste to give another man your private time. And what on earth could you have been doing to have been gone so long?"

"I told you," she said. "He was shocked to see his family after such a long period of separation. He needed to recover himself before meeting them. And then he wished to present me to them."

"Why?" He frowned. "They are staying, are they not? We will all be presented to his grace and the earl and countess in time. Why did you need a special introduction? Is there something you are not telling me, Mary?"

She felt annoyed until she remembered again that he had a right to ask such questions.

"I am sorry, Simon," she said. "I suppose that in some way Lord Edmond thinks of me as a friend."

"A friend?" he said, his brows drawing together. "A friend, Mary? He has strange notions of friendship. I don't like it. I want you to stay away from him, do you hear me? And I want no more of this calling me off when I am dealing with him, just because you fear there will be a scene. Sooner or later there is going to have to be a scene, or the people here will believe that I do not know how to protect my own."

"Simon," she said, setting a hand on his arm, but Doris Shelbourne and Mr. Bigsby-Gore approached them at that moment.

"A wonderful day," Mr. Bigsby-Gore said. "A most impressive cathedral, would you not agree, Lady Mornington? I had not seen it before, strange as it may seem."

Mary took gratefully to the new topic of conversation.

A few minutes later Lady Eleanor entered the room on the arm of her brother, the Earl and Countess of Welwyn behind them. There was a buzz of renewed animation as the other guests were presented to the new arrivals.

"Lord Edmond resembles his father," Doris said quietly to Mary. "Is it true that they have not met since Lord Edmond killed his brother? The meeting today must be very awkward for his grace. Have they met yet, do you think?"

"I would have to say that it is very decent of his grace to be willing to stay at the same house as Lord Edmond," the viscount said, "considering the life of dissipation he has led since the killing."

"Perhaps we should not judge without knowing the whole

of the inside story," Mary said, and won for herself a cold stare from her betrothed.

Lady Welwyn smiled when she saw Mary, and slipped her hand from her husband's arm. "Lady Mornington," she said, "how pleasant to see a familiar face, though I met you only an hour or so ago. I am afraid that we have kept so much to the north of England since my marriage that I know almost no one from the south. This is something of an ordeal."

Mary smiled. "But I am so glad that you have come," she said.

"For Edmond's sake?" Anne said. "It is high time that old matter was cleared up, as I am sure you would agree. Are you the Lady Mornington who is famous for her literary salons in London?"

"Am I famous?" Mary said. "But, yes, my habit of inviting literary or political figures to my weekly entertainments has attracted many regular visitors."

"My friend Lydia Grainger has spoken of you," Anne said. "How fortunate you are to live in town. Sometimes I pine for it, though I must not complain. The country is wonderful for the children, and we have many close friendships with our neighbors. And Wallace takes me to Harrogate for several weeks almost every year."

Mary warmed to Lord Edmond's sister-in-law.

Lord Edmond was late for dinner. He came wandering into the dining room when everyone was already seated and the footmen were bringing on the first course.

"So sorry, Aunt," he said, waving a careless, lace-bedecked hand in the direction of Lady Eleanor. "My valet could not seem to get my hair to look quite disheveled enough. It was looking too unfashionably tidy."

His words won a titter from Stephanie and some laughter from the gentlemen. The duke's lips thinned, Mary noticed, glancing hastily in his direction, and the earl frowned and looked down at his plate. She could have shaken Lord Edmond. If he wished to make a good impression on his father and brother, could he not at least have been on time for the first meal he was to share with them? And did he have to make such a foolishly foppish excuse for being late?

But of course, she thought, forcing herself to relax and turning to make conversation with the gentleman on her left, it had all been quite deliberate on his part. Just as so much of his behavior was deliberately designed to give people an unfavorable impression of him.

He was, she realized fully at last, a man who wore a mask. And she realized too, perhaps, why she loved him against all reason. She had seen behind the mask.

She looked curiously at him as he took the empty chair between Mrs. Wiggins and Mrs. Ormsby. He looked along the table at her as he did so and winked.

He winked! Heavens, Mary thought, whatever next? But a quickly darted look across the table assured her that the viscount was deep in conversation with Lady Cathcart and had not noticed.

Lord Edmond was out early the following morning, riding alone as was his custom. He would have been on his way home now, he thought with some regret, if it had not been for the totally unexpected arrival of his father the afternoon before. And yet, he had to admit, perhaps it was for the best after all. He had always had the feeling that he could not expect to go through the rest of his life without meeting his family again. Now the dread meeting was over, and really, apart from the inevitable embarrassment, it had not been so very bad.

They had met and been polite to one another. They had spent an evening, first in the same dining room, and then in the same drawing room, and been polite to one another. There was one day to his aunt's birthday, two to the end of this country visit. If they were all careful—and polite—those days could be lived through without any major confrontation, and forever after they would not all live in dread of being brought face-to-face with one another.

And as for Mary—well, there were two days during which he could avoid her as much as possible and be polite to her when he could not avoid her company. It could not be that difficult a time to get through if he set his mind to it.

As luck would have it, there were two ladies walking in the formal gardens as he made his way back from the stables, and one of them was his sister-in-law. He somehow never expected to encounter ladies until close to noon at the earliest. She saw him, raised a hand in greeting, said something to Lady Cathcart, and made her way toward him. Well, at least, he thought, neither Wallace nor his father was in sight. And he had liked Anne the day before.

"Good morning," she said, smiling at him. "Have you been riding? I wish I had known. I would have come with you. Or do you prefer to ride alone?"

"I would have been happy to have your company," he said politely. "Do you always rise early?"

"Oh, always," she said, laughing. "I'm a creature of the country, not the city, Edmond. I am so glad your aunt arranged this little surprise. I have wanted to meet you since long before my wedding."

"The black sheep?" he said. "The skeleton in the closet? The prodigal who did not come home?"

"The missing part of Wallace's family," she said. "The member rarely spoken of but always missed." She laughed. "I have always said that Nigel is like his grandfather, and everyone has always been quick to agree. But he is far more like his uncle. So like that I cannot help but laugh when I look at you."

"Nigel?" he said.

She clucked her tongue. "The estrangement has been almost total, has it not?" she said. "And quite foolish. Nigel is our older son. He is eleven years old. And then there are Ninian, nine, and Laura, six. They are here with us. You must meet them. You are their only uncle on their father's side."

Lord Edmond looked somewhat uncomfortable. "I did know that Wallace had children," he said. "I am afraid I have never had a great deal to do with children."

"It is not obligatory in order to get along well with them," she said with a laugh. "We all were children ourselves, after all."

"Not I," he said.

"You always had your head in a book, did you not?" she said, looking closely at him. "I have learned some things about you over the years, you see, from chance remarks that have been made. You did not play a great deal."

"I have made up for it since," he said. "I have done nothing but play since I reached my majority."

"Oh, yes," she said. "You do not need to look at me with that deliberately cynical look, Edmond. The fame of your reputation has reached us in the north of England, believe me. Each detail is like a knife wound to Wallace and your father."

He shrugged. "Each one convincing them that I am incorrigible?" he said. "Well, I am, Anne. You are not about to try to find redeeming features in me, are you? Females have a tiresome tendency to do that."

"Oh, dear," she said, "one would hate to aspire to the mediocrity of being a typical female. What I meant was that each detail of your . . . your wildness, I suppose I must call it, reminds them of their own guilt, though they would not admit to that even if the Inquisition were let loose on them, of course. I hope the three of you do not mean to be polite to one another for two days. That would be a dreadful anti-climax."

"It is just what I have been hoping for," he said. "Would you prefer that I was rude to them, Anne? I can be dreadfully uncivil when I want to be. And dreadfully annoying too. I have cultivated the art with great care."

"Like insisting on having disheveled hair before appearing at dinner," she said.

"Oh, that was real enough," he said. "You do not know how lowering it would be for a London gentleman to appear unfashionable, Anne."

She laughed. "Your aunt has said that this is to be a free day," she said. "Everyone may arrange his own entertainment. Wallace and I are to take the children for a picnic with your father. Will you come with Mary?"

"With Mary?" he said.

"I like her," she said. "Do you notice how we are on a first name basis already? And if she is your friend, Edmond,

I cannot think you quite beyond hope. She is a very sensible and interesting lady. So it will be a waste of your time trying to shock me or make me frown on you. I shall merely laugh. Will you come?"

"I think you have the wrong connection," he said. "It is Mary and Goodrich, Anne."

"The viscount?" she asked, turning her head to look at him. "Oh, no. That would be a disappointment. Are you sure?"

"I had personal and private notice from his own lips," he said, "that they are betrothed. You had better not try to matchmake, Anne. He might challenge you to a duel."

"How alarming!" she said. "Would the choice of weapons be mine? I should choose knitting needlles. I shall have to invite them both to the picnic, then, and another lady. Whom shall I ask?"

"No one," he said. "I shall stay at the house and challenge someone to a game of billiards."

"Coward," she said. "You must come, if only to meet your niece and nephews. And why did you bring Mary to meet us yesterday if she is only a friend and betrothed to someone else? You looked to be squeezing her hand hard enough to hurt, Edmond."

He narrowed his eyes and looked down at her. "You see altogether too much," he said. "I was terrified, I would have you know. Shaking in my boots. Knees knocking. Teeth clacking. If I had not been clinging to Mary's hand, I would probably have disgraced myself and tripped over a rose in the carpet or something equally foolish."

Her smile softened on him. "They were terrified too," she said. "Wallace's hand was like a vise on my shoulder, so that for a moment I wondered if Mary or I would be the first to scream with pain. And your father had been pacing the room enough to wear a hole in the carpet for you to trip over. You must come this afternoon, Edmond. The time has come, you know. It can no longer be avoided."

He looked at her broodingly. "You talk just like Mary," he said. "If it were not for her, I would probably still be running straight due west. And now you are trying to make me jump right into the hornet's nest, just when I have been hoping to tiptoe about it for the next two days."

She smiled. "You will come, then," she said. It was not a question. "And we might as well go today. If Mrs. Shelbourne is to be believed, this glorious weather is bound to break with earth-shattering storms any minute now."

"She has been telling us so *ad nauseam* ever since we came here," he said. "I don't know why the woman cannot simply enjoy the sunshine."

"For some people, happiness consists in waiting for some disaster to overtake them or the world," Anne said. "It takes all types to make life interesting, Edmond. Would you really rather I did not invite Mary?"

He gave her a sidelong look and did not answer. He should answer, he knew. But he did not.

"Ah," she said. "I heard you loudly and clearly. I am to please myself, and then any blame for what happens must fall on my shoulders. Well, they are broad ones. I am not as slender, alas, as I was when I married. I can hardly believe that I have met you at last, Edmond, and am strolling with you here just as if you were any ordinary human being and not the monstrous skeleton in the family closet that you mentioned earlier. Good old Aunt Eleanor."

"Old fiend Aunt Eleanor, I would be inclined to say," he said. "But I am pleased to have met you, Anne. Wally made a good marriage, I can see. But then, he was always the most sensible of the three of us."

"I must go to my children," she said as their strolling brought them to the foot of the horseshoe steps. "I shall look forward to this afternoon, Edmond."

"Likewise," he said, releasing her arm and making her a bow.

But he felt rather like a condemned man who has just learned that his execution is to take place that very day. A whole afternoon with no one else for company except his family—a father and brother from whom he had been estranged for fifteen years, two nephews and a niece whom he had never met, and a sister-in-law whom he liked but who seemed determined to force a confrontation. And perhaps

Mary and Goodrich, though their company would be no consolation to him at all.

Perhaps he should, after all, have left for Willow Court that morning, he thought.

Mary was feeling a little guilty, though it really was not her fault that she was spending the afternoon as the sole outside member of a family picnic while Simon was driving off with several of the other guests to explore a ruined abbey six miles away. Well, almost not her fault anyway.

The countess had found her writing letters in the morning room and had invited her to join the picnic.

"I intend to invite Lord Goodrich too," she had said. "I understand that he is your fiancé?"

"Oh," Mary had said, "it is not official yet. Nothing at all is settled." She had felt a little guilty over the last sentence, since it was not strictly true. She had said it only because for some reason she did not want Anne to know the full truth.

The countess had looked strangely pleased. "Ah, I have heard wrongly, then," she had said. "But I shall invite him anyway. Will you come?"

"I would love to," Mary had said. But she had guessed that Lord Edmond would also be a member of the group, and she knew that perhaps she should have made some excuse.

Just before luncheon she had met the viscount and asked him if he had had his invitation to the picnic.

"After I had already agreed to join the party to the abbey," he had said. "I was relieved, of course, to have an excuse not to accept. It would be a pleasure to become more closely acquainted with his grace, but since Waite is to be of the party, I am thankful that we are not."

"But I am going," she had said. "I accepted Anne's invitation, since she was going to ask you too."

"She did, but too late." He had frowned. "But I have said you will be coming to the abbey, Mary."

"I am sorry," she had said. "But I cannot go back on my word now, Simon."

A brief argument had ensued, which had left him angry that she would go on a picnic that included Lord Edmond without his escort, and which had left her indignant that he was trying to order her life before they were even married. Both had kept to their original plans.

And yet she felt guilty. She understood that Anne had not issued the invitation to Simon until the abbey party had been all arranged. Had Anne held back deliberately, hoping to separate them? Because she, Mary, had denied that there was a betrothal, perhaps? Mary sensed that Anne liked her and was prepared to like her brother-in-law too. However it was, she was part of the picnic group and Simon was on his way to the abbey.

The picnic was to be at the lake, and they were retracing the route by which a larger group had come there a few days before. His grace was going with the carriage and the food by an easier and more direct route. But this time it was the earl who helped Mary over the stile. Lord Edmond and Anne were up ahead with the children. Lord Edmond was in close conversation with the older boy, Nigel.

"You have known my brother long, Lady Mornington?" the earl asked politely.

"Not very," she said. "We were members of the same party to Vauxhall one evening just this spring. Then Lord Edmond attended one of my literary evenings and took me a couple of weeks later to meet your aunt, who was eager to make my acquaintance and has since also come to my salon. Hence my invitation here."

"Edmond attended one of your literary evenings?" he said in some surprise. "Is that not out of character for him?"

"Mr. Beasley was expounding on some of his radical social theories," she said. "Lord Edmond was the only guest present willing to argue against him. Everyone else was awed by his fame, I believe. It was a lively evening." She did not know quite why she spoke of that evening as if Lord Edmond's behavior had been exemplary.

"He is so very different," the earl said. "I scarcely recognized him, Lady Mornington. Oh, the physical differences are not so great, except that he has aged as one would expect a man to do in fifteen years. But in every other way. I expected it, of course. We have heard enough about him. But I suppose I still expected the old Edmond when I met him again.''

"What was he like?" Mary could not resist asking the question of yet another person who had known him.

"Quiet. Serious." The earl thought for a moment. "He loved the world of books. He used to write poetry. He lived more in his imagination than in reality, I believe. And yet I am not sure that is quite true either. He always had a strong sense of justice and fairness, but a grasp of the realities of life. He used to feel that the wealthy and privileged had a great responsibility to the poor and downtrodden.''

"He was at university," she said.

"Yes." There were another few moments of silence as he thought back. "He never seemed to know how to have fun. Poor Edmond. We used to worry about him. We used to plan ways to force him to enjoy himself." He laughed without amusement. "We need not have worried if we had been able to look into the future, need we?''

"Did you plan his twenty-first birthday party?" she asked.

He looked uneasy. "We all did," he said. "It seemed fitting that he enter full adulthood in a more manly way than with his nose buried in a book. Unfortunately, Lady Mornington, he was unable to hold his liquor. But enough of that. Your late husband fought in the Peninsular Wars? Did you follow him there?''

They talked about Spain and Waterloo and Wellington and the peace for the rest of the walk to the lake.

But the Earl of Welwyn, Mary decided after their brief conversation about Lord Edmond, probably felt as guilty about the death of his younger brother as Lord Edmond himself did. If only they could talk to each other freely, offer healing to each other. And they were so close—together again for the first time since the day after the disaster. And yet not close at all.

But it was none of her business, she told herself as they reached the lake, glancing at the duke, who was seated already beside the water and was smiling at the children and

beckoning them, ignoring his youngest son, or perhaps not
knowing how to include him in his welcome without great
awkwardness.

Her heart ached suddenly for Edmond. And she realized
that even in her mind she had thought of him by his given
name without his title to prefix it.

16

HE FELT DEUCED uncomfortable, if the truth were known. And if he had imagined that the worst of the embarrassment was over after that first meeting, then he was discovering that he had imagined wrongly. He found himself directing all his conversation toward Anne and his niece and nephews—especially toward Nigel, the elder, who had inexplicably chosen to discuss Latin poetry with him during the walk to the lake. It was a novelty, he was finding, to be an uncle. But he could think of nothing that would not sound trite to say to his father and his brother. And he dared not talk to Mary. He certainly did not want to be alone with her.

"I believe that after that lengthy walk we should eat before exploring the shores of the lake," Anne announced when they had joined the duke on the grassy bank.

"Hoorah!" cried Ninian, who was rather inclined to share his mother's tendency to be overweight, Lord Edmond noticed, looking critically at the boy.

And so blankets were spread on the grass and the baskets carried from the carriage by the footman who had accompanied it from the house. And the children waited impatiently for Anne to hand around the food.

Lord Edmond could have sat beside his father, who had Laura seated on one side and him and empty blanket on the other. He sat down instead close to Mary, not looking at her, addressing some remark to Anne.

They sat thus through most of tea, seated close to each other, turned slightly away from each other, conversing with other people. It was the most uncomfortable meal he had ever taken, Lord Edmond thought. The food tasted rather like straw. Though perhaps that was unfair to his aunt's cook. The truth was that he did not taste the food at all. He would not have been able to say afterward what he had eaten.

And then, halfway through the meal, he set his hand down on the blanket to brace himself, to find that Mary's hand was there too, their little fingers almost brushing. He should move his hand, he knew. He expected her to move hers. And yet neither moved until a couple of minutes later their little fingers rested quite unmistakably against each other.

Lord Edmond had to concentrate his attention on his wine when the thought struck him that the light brushing of two fingers could be as erotic as the most intimate of sexual contacts. He would not answer to what might have happened if there had not been three other adults and three children present.

"May I go and play, Mama?" Ninian asked impatiently when the adults seemed to be lingering over their meal.

"As long as you promise to stay away from the water's edge," Anne said. "Let Nigel and Laura go with you. I do not trust you otherwise not to get at least your shoes and stockings wet."

"I want Grandpapa to come with us," Laura said.

"Grandpapa is still eating," the earl said.

"I am merely enjoying more of Cook's good food than is good for me," the duke said, getting slowly to his feet. "Where do you want to go, little poppet?"

Lord Edmond had a feeling that his father was relieved at the excuse to get away from the uncomfortable atmosphere on the blankets.

When after several more minutes and another glass of wine Anne suggested a walk to the pavilion, Lord Edmond got to his feet quickly and stretched out a hand to help Mary up. But he did not quite look at her. He was hoping that the walking arrangements could be as they had been earlier. He did not want to walk with Mary. He turned to Anne.

"Have you seen the pavilion?" she was asking Mary. "It is supposed to be almost as large and splendid as the house. In which direction is it, Wallace?"

"Around there," the earl said, pointing off to the denser trees and the bend in the lake. "But you exaggerate somewhat, Anne. I daresay it is not one tenth the size of the house."

"Large enough for the birthday tea and celebrations anyway,"Anne said with a laugh. "Come along, Mary. We will explore."

And Lord Edmond found that the situation was much worse than the one he had feared. He was to walk with neither Mary nor Anne, but with his brother. And already the ladies were striding off along the bank of the lake, in the opposite direction from that taken by his father and the children. He clasped his hands behind his back and pursed his lips.

"Trust Aunt Eleanor not to do anything as uncomplicated as organize a dinner and dance at the house," his brother said.

"Her love of the unexpected has always been one of her greatest charms," Lord Edmond said. "Do you remember the time when she had a group of traveling players performing at the house, and had them stay for several days afterward, mingling with the other guests just as if it were proper for them to do so? Mama almost had a fit of the vapors when she knew we had been subjected to that. I think she thought that perhaps your virtue had been assailed by some of the actresses. Dick and I were too young and too uninterested in such matters to worry about."

The earl made no comment.

"Of course," Lord Edmond added, hearing his words almost as if they issued from his mouth independently of his brain or his will, "as it turned out, I am the one she should have worried about. Actresses are far more interesting offstage than on, in my experience."

He had the dubious satisfaction of seeing his brother's lips thin. "Hardly a matter for general conversation," he said.

"General?" Lord Edmond looked at his brother in surprise. "But I am talking to you, Wally. You used to like to regale us with tales of your exploits at Oxford and all the delights that were in store for us there. Not the intellectual ones, of course."

His brother flushed. "For God's sake, Edmond," he said. "We were puppies then. We are middle-aged men now. Some of us have taken on responsibilities and have answered the demands of respectability."

Lord Edmond winced. "Middle-aged," he said. "Is that what we are, Wally? And no longer capable of enjoying ourselves? Is that what one gives up with youth?"

"Obviously you have not," the earl said, his voice low and furious. "Your excesses seem to grow with your years, Edmond. I just hope that you do not try to corrupt my children."

Lord Edmond's nostrils flared. His voice was icy when he spoke. "Actually," he said, "on the walk here I was enlightening Nigel on the sensual pleasures that Eton will have to offer him—with not a woman in sight, of course. I shall try to have the same conversation with Ninian on the return walk. As for Laura, I must take her aside within the next day or two and give her some early instructions on how to entice her man away from courtesans. Girls can never learn too early, can they?"

His words were interrupted when his brother's hand grabbed him by the cravat and swung him around to face him.

"It was not enough, was it," he said through his teeth, "for you to kill poor Dick and Mama? But you must destroy Papa too with your wildness and your debaucheries. And now you must attempt to sully my family with the products of your vile mind. Leave here, Edmond. Do something decent in your rotten life and leave today."

Lord Edmond made no move to release himself. He spoke quietly. "Sometimes, Wally," he said, "when people expect certain behavior of someone, he will oblige them. If you expect the worst of me, then devil take it, the worst you will get. What did you expect, you and Papa—and Mama too, though she never said it in words—when you called me a murderer? What did you expect when you drove me away? That I would finish my studies, become a clergyman, and spend the rest of my days doing pious penance? Is that what you expected?"

"That is what anyone with a sensitive conscience would have done," the earl said.

Lord Edmond laughed and brushed his brother's hand away. The ladies had already disappeared among the trees, he saw. "Then perhaps I do not have a sensitive conscience," he said. "Do you?"

"I beg your pardon?" The earl's voice was haughty.

"How did you absolve your conscience for getting me foxed for the first time in my life and laughing at the spectacle I made of myself?" Lord Edmond asked. "How did you forgive yourself for allowing me to take that ride, and even thinking it a huge joke, and for not stopping Dick from coming after me?"

The earl was nodding his head. "Oh, yes, I see how it is," he said. "I might have expected it. It is often the case, I believe, that a guilty man will try to shift the blame onto someone else's shoulders."

"No," Lord Edmond said. "I was as guilty as sin. I killed them just as surely as if I had taken a gun and shot them. But I was not quite alone in my guilt, Wally. And I certainly do not need you to point out to me how rotten my life has been. I know it better than anyone—I have lived it. But I do not like to mire innocents in my hell, for all that. Your children are safe from me. You may rest easy."

The earl seemed uncertain of what to do with his anger. He clasped his hands behind him and swayed on his feet. "We did not drive you away, Edmond," he said, his voice uneasy. "You went. We searched for you and you were gone. And we wrote to tell you of Mama's passing. You might have come for the funeral."

"When the letter told me that the shock of Dick's pointless death as a result of my drunkenness had driven her to a premature end?" Lord Edmond said. "It was scarcely an invitation home, Wally."

"Neither was it a command to stay away and break Papa's heart with a rapid decline into dissipation," the earl said. "You might have come home, Edmond. You might have made your peace with us. You might have found us ready to forgive."

Lord Edmond's laugh was more sneer than laughter. "Perhaps I was not ready to forgive you," he said.

"Good God, Edmond!" The earl's voice was exasperated. "How were we to know that you would be so little able to hold your liquor? You were twenty-one years old. A man, or so we thought. It seems we were wrong. You proved quite unable to control either your liquor or your life."

Lord Edmond laughed again. "I was a boy," he said. "A little bookworm of an innocent and naive boy. It is not easy for a boy to adjust his life to the sudden fact that he is a murderer and has lost his family. I needed you—you and Mama and Papa. I needed you to tell me that all would be well, even though it could not possibly be true with Dick gone. I needed you to tell me that you loved me, even though my part in his death would have made it a strain to do so. I needed you to tell me that we were still a family and that nothing could ever change that, even though Dick was gone. I needed to cry. I did so finally alone on the day of Mama's funeral. And if there is a worse misery than crying alone, Wally, I wish you would tell me what it is so that I can direct all my energies to avoiding it for the rest of my life."

"If you had just written and told us that," the earl said, white-faced. "If you had just come, Edmond. Do you believe that we would really have turned you off? Things would have been strained for a long time, but we had always been a family. We would have come through it together. Instead we were left to believe that you did not care at all. First of all getting yourself expelled from Oxford and then all that followed it. And finally humiliating Lady Dorothea and running after a woman who did not even want you, by all accounts. What were we to think, Edmond? The evidence was all against you."

Lord Edmond smiled. "I suppose I have always made the mistake of believing that other people have imaginations as acute as mine," he said. "We had better walk on, Wally. The ladies will be thinking we have both fallen in the lake."

"Anne set this up," the earl said. "I know her quite well enough to be certain of that, Edmond. And you may be sure that before you leave here there will be a similar confrontation arranged with Papa. Anne does not realize that after fifteen years the rift is beyond healing."

"Women," Lord Edmond said, "are incurable romantics. They believe that if only two people can be made to talk, all their problems will be solved. Mary is the same."

"What in the name of all that is wonderful is she doing in your life?" the earl asked. "She is an intelligent and a decent lady, Edmond."

"Thank you," his brother said dryly. "And I will not wait for you to add hastily that you did not mean the words exactly as they sounded, because you did. She is too good for me, you think? Far too good? On that we are agreed. The lady will not be long in my life. I meant it when I said that I do not like to corrupt innocence. And if you think the renunciation will be easy, let me add this. I love her. Do you understand me? I do not mean that I lust after her, want to bed her. I mean that I love her."

He instantly regretted the anger that had made him speak the words aloud. His love for Mary was to have been a private matter, locked deep within the most secret recesses of his heart.

His brother sighed. "I thought you were gone completely, Edmond," he said. "Apart from your looks, which tell me unmistakably that you are my baby brother fifteen years after I saw you last, I have found nothing to recognize in you. Almost as if someone else were in possession of your body. But there spoke Edmond for the first time. Ever the idealist, ever the romantic."

"Romantic?" Lord Edmond frowned in puzzlement.

"Loving," his brother said, "and renouncing that love from the noblest of motives. You did it with Sukey Thompson once upon a time. Do you remember?"

"Sukey?" For the first time Lord Edmond's laugh had a tinge of amusement in it. "With the blond ringlets and the big blue eyes and the pout?"

"You were deeply, painfully in love with her," the earl said. "You were seventeen, if I remember correctly, and she was nineteen. You renounced your love for her because you had nothing to offer her of greater value than the life of a country parson, and even that quite far in the future. You were heartbroken for days, perhaps even weeks. You wrote reams of poems."

Lord Edmond snorted. "And she did not know I existed," he said. "Did she not have a *tendre* for you, Wally? Do you know, I had not thought of that girl for years and years."

Both brothers laughed. Then they looked at each other rather self-consciously.

"Perhaps it was partly my fault," the earl said quickly.

"Do you think I have not always been plagued by the thought? Only the way you turned out reassured me, Edmond. You must have been heading for bad ways, I have always thought, and we had just not seen it. But perhaps part of the guilt was mine. No." He passed a hand over his eyes. "There is no perhaps about it, is there? I wanted to see you foxed—grave, serious Edmond making an idiot of himself. It was great fun. Perhaps it was all my fault."

"I did not have to drink," Lord Edmond said. "Neither you nor Papa nor anyone else at that infernal party ever held me down and poured liquor down my throat. I drank because I wanted everyone to see that I was now a man. I wanted to be like you—grown-up and self-assured and popular with the ladies. You were always my hero—everything I could not seem to be. All I could do was hide behind my books and pretend that life perfectly suited me that way."

"Oh, God!" The earl closed his eyes and passed a hand over them again.

"I am afraid I was not nearly a man," Lord Edmond said. "I was still a child despite my twenty-one years. A child who played with fire and got burned."

"Edmond," his brother said wearily, "how it is possible to go back? It has been so long and the damage has been so great. And not only to you. We all lost a family on that dreadful day. You more than Papa and I, is it true. But we all lost. At least that is what Anne has been telling me for years. But how can we go back?"

"I think we just have," Lord Edmond said. "Perhaps you will never know, Wally, what it means to hear you admit that you were a part of the whole guilt surrounding Dick's death. What it means to hear you say that I was not the only loser. It makes me feel that I have been missed, that perhaps I was of some importance in your lives."

"Of some . . . ?" The earl looked at his brother with mingled incredulity and exasperation. "What the devil are you talking about?"

Lord Edmond shrugged. "You were as I have described you," he said. "Dick was more like me, but gentle and sweet—everyone's favorite. And then there was me, with nothing but my proficiency in Latin to commend me."

The earl stared at him. "Did you not know how much we were all in awe of your learning?" he said. "How Mama and Papa almost burst with pride every time they could boast of you to someone new? We all basked in the glory of your accomplishments."

Lord Edmond laughed rather shakily. "Well," he said. "Well."

"I think we had better go and find the ladies," his brother said, "before we do something that would embarrass us both, like falling into each other's arms or something."

"Quite right," Lord Edmond said. "And I have to go through something like this with Papa too, you say?"

"I will wager that Anne will arrange it somehow," the earl said.

Lord Edmond grimaced and looked down at the hand his brother stretched out to him.

"Shall we at least shake hands?" the earl asked. "Will you at least do that, Edmond, to show that you forgive me for my cowardice through the years? I have let you bear it all alone."

Lord Edmond stared at the hand for a long moment before placing his own in it. And then after all they were in each other's arms, slapping each other's backs, wordlessly choking back the tears that would have made their humiliation complete.

"Nigel is keen on the classics," the earl said, frowning as they drew apart and each tried to pretend that nothing out of the ordinary had happened. "I have always boasted to him about how his uncle was such a Latin scholar. He has not begun to pester you about it yet, has he?"

Lord Edmond laughed. "All the way here," he said. "Though I would not describe his behavior as pestering. Actually I have been tickled pink to think that anyone would consult me as a Latin expert. My intimates in town would roar with laughter and not stop for a week. I would never live it down."

"Edmond—" his brother began.

"I am not going back," Lord Edmond said quickly. "Not for a long time, anyway. I am going home after this party, Wally. I was there for a few weeks before coming, and rather fancied myself as the country squire. I am thinking of taking to striding about my property with a stout staff in my hand, a foul-smelling pipe in my mouth, and a faithful shaggy hound at my heels.''

His brother chuckled.

"Besides," Lord Edmond said, "Mary lives in town.''

"It is truly magnificent," Anne said, "and a total folly to have it built out here in the middle of nowhere, glorious and wondrous as that nowhere is. We are agreed, Mary?''

"Oh, yes," Mary said. "And a wonderful if improbable setting for a birthday party.''

"And having said as much to each other in a dozen different ways during the past fifteen minutes or so," Anne said with a smile, "shall we confess to what is really on both our minds?''

"Are they not coming here?" Mary asked. "Have they turned back?''

"Either way," Anne said, "I can only read hope into their absence. If they had continued embarrassed and tongue-tied in each other's company, they would have hurried along on our heels, would they not, for fear of being left alone together?''

"You think they have talked?" Mary asked. "And come to some sort of an understanding?''

"Or bloodied each other's noses," Anne said with a laugh that sounded a little nervous. "I have wished for this for so long, Mary, that I hardly dare hope. Wallace has never been quite happy. Always, even at our most joyous moments— our wedding, the birth of the children, their christenings, a few other occasions—always I have been aware of something. And I have known him long enough to be quite aware by now of what that something is. It is guilt and grief. Grief fades when a person is dead, Mary. You would know that as a widow. But it does not go away when the person grieved for is still alive.''

"I have not known Lord Edmond long," Mary said, "and cannot pretend to know him or understand him well. But I am sure that it is guilt and this family rift that have . . . oh, that have kept him from being the person he might have been.''

''You love him, do you not?'' Anne asked quickly.

Mary stared at her. ''I am betrothed to—'' she said.

Anne waved a dismissive hand. ''Oh, yes,'' she said. ''But you are not serious about that, Mary. You will not make the mistake of marrying him, I think. And I must confess to some guilt of my own. I maneuvered this situation—him going to the abbey and you coming here. Am I not dreadful? You love him, do you not?''

''Lord Edmond?'' Mary said. She hesitated. ''I have grown fond of him.''

Anne chuckled and then sobered. ''Oh, here they come,'' she said. ''We must pretend to be admiring this pillar, Mary. Corinthian, is it? I have never been able to remember what name goes with which kind of pillar.''

''It is Corinthian,'' Mary said.

They both glanced with disguised curiosity at the two men when they came up, but absurdly they all admired and conversed about first the column and then the whole of the domed round pavilion in which Lady Eleanor's birthday party was to take place the next day.

Five minutes or more passed before Lord Edmond grabbed Mary by the wrist, rather as he had done the afternoon before on their return from Canterbury, and drew her outside to look down on the lake.

''Well, Mary,'' he said, ''you insisted that I go back. I went back yesterday and I have been back today.''

''And?'' she said.

''And I believe I have a brother,'' he said, gripping her wrist so tightly that she began to lose the feeling in her hand.

She drew in a deep breath but said nothing.

''And a damned managing sister-in-law,'' he said. ''It seems that nothing on this earth can stop her from setting up a similar ordeal with my father.''

She looked at him and smiled.

''And what the devil do you mean by that damned smirk?'' he asked her.

''It is a smile,'' she said. ''And your language belongs in the gutter, my lord.''

"Which is where I live and picked it up," he said. " And we are back to 'my lord' again today, are we?"

"Yes, my lord," she said.

"Ah." He looked out at the lake and said nothing for a while. "It is as well. If you called me by my given name again, I would as like be trying to steal kisses or more from you again, Mary. And it would not do with the good, rich man waiting to lead you to the altar, would it?"

"No," she said.

His grasp shifted to her hand suddenly and he raised it to his lips before releasing it entirely. "Thank you, Mary," he said. "Thank you for making me go back."

17

IF IT WERE POSSIBLE, the day of Lady Eleanor's birthday party was sunnier, more cloudless, and warmer than any other day of the glorious summer so far. Everything was perfect, everyone agreed, for the day of celebration. All morning, servants made their way to and from the pavilion, doing last-minute-cleaning and taking the food and the punch. An orchestra, a surprise addition to the party, arrived from Canterbury and made their way to the lake after taking refreshments at the house.

It was bound to storm before the day was out, Doris Shelbourne declared. She could just feel it in the air. But everyone either ignored her or politely agreed that it was a distinct possibility, but perhaps some other day.

Many of the guests walked to the pavilion during the afternoon. Others rode there in carriages. A few select neighbors had been invited. It was difficult to put a name to the entertainment, Lady Cathcart complained to Mary as they strolled across the pasture. It was not strictly a tea, since they were expecting to stay at the pavilion until dusk or perhaps even later. It was certainly not a dinner, since no hot meal was to be served. Though of course a veritable feast had been taken from the house, so they would not starve by any means. Had Lady Mornington observed the extent of it?

Lady Mornington had.

It was too formal for a picnic, Lady Cathcart declared. Yet it was not a ball, was it? There would not be enough guests. Besides, they were wearing day clothes, not nighttime finery. But there was the orchestra. Merely to entertain them as they ate and conversed? Or was there to be dancing? Had Lady Mornington heard?

Lady Mornington had not.

"It is all very provoking," Lady Cathcart said. "One likes

to be able to give a name to the type of entertainment one is attending, does one not, Lady Mornington?''

"Whatever it is," Mary said with a smile, "we are all certain to enjoy it. Just the weather and the surroundings are sufficient to lift the spirits. Add the pavilion and the orchestra, the food and the company, and I believe Lady Eleanor has excelled herself."

"Do you believe so?" Lady Cathcart asked doubtfully.

Mary smiled. But in fact she was not convinced. It was true that all those ingredients for a happy day were there, and true too that if anyone did not enjoy himself, then the fault must be entirely his. But she was not expecting to enjoy what remained of the afternoon or the evening.

She had been overhasty earlier in the week. Her desire to be married again, to enjoy all the security that marriage could bring, had clouded her judgment. Affection had been the single most prominent factor in her first marriage. She had not given enough attention to it in her plans for the second. Worst of all, perhaps, she had accepted Simon's offer as much to escape from feelings she wished to deny as to embrace a life she did want.

It was true that no public announcement of her betrothal had been made, but her private word had been given. And she was sorry for it. Oh, it was as good a match as she could hope to make, and it had everything to offer her that she had ever dreamed of—security, a home in the country, a husband who appeared to care for her. Everything except children, perhaps. She had not broached the subject with Simon again, but she feared that perhaps they could never be in agreement on that point. For him two sons seemed to be family enough.

That important difference notwithstanding, she would be mad, she thought, to end the betrothal. The only possible reason she could have for doing so was that she loved another man. Though when she verbalized the fact in her mind, she had to admit that it was a very major reason indeed for ending an engagement.

And so end it she must. And she feared that it would have to be done on the day of the birthday party. With her decision firmly made, she did not believe she could dissemble for a whole day. Besides, it did not seem fair to do so. Simon had a right to know of her change of heart.

The opportunity did not come until well into the evening. From the start the party was a great success. There was music to listen to and food to eat and punch to drink and conversation to be enjoyed. Later, there was dancing. There was the bank of the lake to be strolled along. The guests mingled freely so that there was little chance of any private *tête-à-tête.*

Mary stayed away from Lord Edmond, a task not difficult to accomplish, since he seemed equally intent on avoiding her. She also stayed away from the viscount as much as she was able, and acknowledged to herself that she was being cowardly, deliberately avoiding the moment that she knew must be faced.

But he finally sought her out and suggested that they join the Ormsbys, Stephanie Wiggins, and a gentleman from the neighborhood in a stroll up through the woods. It seemed that the moment could be avoided no longer, Mary thought, smiling at him and taking his arm. Though there was perhaps safety in numbers.

They walked up past the follies to the edge of the trees and the beginnings of the pasture.

"Oh, dear," Leila Ormsby said, pointing to the west. "That is why the heat is still so oppressive though it is evening already. Look!"

She did not need to point. They could hardly avoid seeing the heavy dark clouds banked in the western sky.

"Rain will be welcome," the Reverend Ormsby said. "Though it would have been better timed had it waited until tomorrow. Perhaps the clouds will pass us by after all."

"Those are rain clouds if I ever saw any," Mr. Webber said, shading his eyes.

"At least Doris' predictions of a storm are unlikely to prove right," the Reverend Ormsby said. "There is not a breath of wind."

"That is the very fact that makes me expect one," his wife said. "Do you think we should hurry back to the house, Samuel, to be with the children?"

He laughed. "And miss the rest of the party?" he said. "There are so many servants at the house, my love, that our presence would be supremely redundant. I suggest we get back to the pavilion in case the rain does come over."

"I would look a perfect fright if I got wet," Stephanie said, pulling on Mr. Webber's arm and turning back to the woods.

The Ormsbys followed them, but Mary and Lord Goodrich by common but unspoken consent strolled out into the pasture.

"I have had so little time alone with you in the past few days," he said. "Country parties are not the best occasions to enjoy a new betrothal, especially a partly secret one."

"No," she said. "Simon—"

"I am selfish, Mary," he said. "I want you to myself. Waite has seen more of you than I. You are sure he did not harass you yesterday? I was more than annoyed at the unhappy chance that sent us in different directions."

"It was a pleasant family picnic," she said. "Lord Edmond spent much of the time with his brother. It seems that they are reconciled, and I can feel nothing but happiness about that."

"I suppose so," he said. "Certainly they went off riding together this morning. I cannot help feeling, though, that Waite is making a dupe of Welwyn."

It was so easy when something unpleasant was to be said, Mary was finding, to grasp at any conversational straw, to put off the evil moment.

"Simon—" she said.

He covered her hand on his arm with his. "You are not really enjoying that party, are you, Mary?" he asked. "I expected something altogether more glittering and formal. I thought we would go to the house and spend some time alone together."

They were halfway across the pasture, she noticed. She also noticed at the same moment a distant flash of lightning from among the heavy clouds. The old terror clamored for attention. Her breath quickened.

"It is going to storm," she said. "Did you see that?"

"All the better," he said, smiling down at her. "The others

will stay at the pavilion until it is well past. We will have the house to ourselves, apart from the servants.''

There was a low rumble of thunder, so distant that it was felt more than heard.

''Perhaps we should go back to be with the others,'' she said.

There was a suggestion of coolness against their faces. The trees off to their right, at the edge of the pasture, were beginning to rustle in the breeze.

''Nonsense!'' He chuckled. ''Are you really afraid of storms, Mary? I will protect you, you know. It would be my pleasure.''

Vivid images of Vauxhall flashed into Mary's mind with the next fork of distant lightning. ''Simon,'' she said, ''let's go back.'' She held on to rationality. She tried not to want to reach the safety of Edmond.

''Look,'' he said, laughing, ''we are at the stile already. Come, Mary. We will be at the house before the clouds move over or the storm really begins. By that time I will have you warm and safe in my arms.'' He vaulted over the stile, disdaining to use the stepping stones, and he held out a hand to help her up.

''Simon.'' She stayed on her side of the fence and gripped the sides of her dress. ''I have been trying to say something all the way across the pasture. I cannot seem to force the words out.''

He looked at her closely and dropped his hand.

''I am afraid I have to go back on my promise,'' she said. ''I cannot marry you. I cannot feel comfortable with the idea, and it would not be fair to marry you just for the security I crave.''

He stood staring at her for a few moments and then extended his hand again. ''Come over the stile,'' he said, as she set her hand obediently in his. ''It is absurd to talk in this manner.'' He lifted her down when she had swung her skirt carefully over the top bar. ''Is it persuasion you want, Mary?'' He drew her to him and kissed her.

''No,'' she said, turning her head away. ''I am sorry, Simon. I know I am treating you shabbily, but there is no decent way to break a betrothal. I am sorry.''

"It is Waite, is it not?" His voice was tight with anger. "You prefer to sink to the gutter than to marry me, Mary?"

"Please," she said, "let us not get unpleasant."

"I was willing to take you despite a sullied reputation," he said. "And I am to be rejected in favor of London's most notorious libertine? And you expect me to smile and wish you well, Mary?"

She had stiffened. "A sullied reputation?" she said.

"Everyone knew you were Clifton's whore," he said. "I was prepared to overlook that fact."

"Perhaps you should not have done so," she said quietly. "You cannot expect honorable behavior of a whore, can you?"

"Obviously not," he said.

He looked up at the sky, drawing Mary's eyes up too. The clouds had moved fast, and the breeze was now steady on them and increasing into a wind. Lightning flashed even as they watched.

"There is no time to go back," she said regretfully. "We will have to make a run for the house."

"Yes," he said grimly, and they hurried side by side, not touching, in the direction of the house.

They reached it in time, though it would not be long before the rain came down and the storm moved overhead, Mary guessed. She turned to her companion when they were inside the hall.

"I am afraid we should have turned back to the pavilion earlier, Simon," she said. "Now you are stuck in the house alone with me and the servants and a broken engagement. I have managed things badly. I am so sorry."

"For my part," he said, "I have no intention of wasting the evening, Mary. I am returning to the pavilion."

"But you will be soaked." Her eyes widened.

"Perhaps." He shrugged. "I believe there is still a little time before the rain begins in earnest. But better a soaking than remain here to an evening of boredom."

She drew a deep breath. "So I am to be left all alone," she said.

"As you said, there are plenty of servants." His expression and voice were cold, and despite her fear of the storm, Mary was suddenly glad that she had had the courage to speak up. Life with this man would not have been easy, she saw. He did not like to have his will thwarted.

"Yes," she said, "and so there are."

But there were none in the hall, which seemed large and dark and frightening after the doors had closed behind the viscount and she was left alone. Most of them would be either at the pavilion or belowstairs enjoying some free time, with family and guests away.

Mary hurried up to her bedchamber and closed the door firmly behind her. She could always summon her maid, she told herself. She need not be entirely alone. But she was determined at least to try to remain alone. She was in a large, securely built mansion. She was quite safe. And it was time she conquered her fear.

She stood rigidly in the middle of the room, hands clasped firmly to her bosom, as lightning flashed outside the window. She counted slowly, waiting for the rumble of thunder that would follow.

It came about much as he had expected it would. He would have been surprised if the day had passed without its happening. He danced with Anne and at the end of the set she smiled at him and linked her arm through his.

"What a warm evening," she said. "Let us walk down by the lake, Edmond, shall we?"

He put up no resistance, even though he knew what was about to happen, just as if it were a play for which he had written the script. His father was sitting close to the door, talking with Sir Harold.

Lord Edmond smiled and gave her his arm. "That would be pleasant," he said.

He watched with mingled amusement and despair as she pretended to notice her father-in-law for the first time as they were about to pass him.

"Father," she said, delight in her voice, "how fortunate that you happen to be right here. I need a gentleman for my other arm. Do come for a stroll by the lake."

His father looked as delighted by the prospect as he himself felt, Lord Edmond thought. But Anne, he was beginning to realize, must have been a manipulator all her life. A benevolent one, perhaps, but a manipulator nevertheless. Like puppets on a string, the two of them were soon wandering down to the lakeshore with Anne between them.

And of course—oh, of course—after a mere five minutes, despite the fact that it was such an oppressively warm evening, Anne shivered and felt the absence of her shawl and excused herself to go and fetch it. Both Edmond and his father knew that she would not return.

"I do believe she is right," the duke said, squinting off to the west. "There is a cool breeze and those are rain clouds moving in. I hope this does not mean we are to be stranded here for the night. Eleanor would be delighted beyond words."

And indeed all the signs were there, Lord Edmond had to admit when he looked, and thought about the heavy atmosphere of the evening and the freshening breeze. It was not just rain. There was a storm brewing. And despite his embarrassment at being left alone with his father, his thoughts leapt to Mary. There was a storm coming. She would be terrified. She had gone off walking with Goodrich and a few other couples. He hoped Goodrich would have more sense than he himself had had at Vauxhall and would bring her back to the pavilion before the storm started. He would not like to think of her having to take shelter—especially with Goodrich, of all people—in one of the small follies.

"A storm," he said. "Doris is to be proved right, it seems. She will let us all know of it, too, for the rest of tonight, and probably all day tomorrow."

"Edmond," his father said quietly, "I never stopped loving you, you know."

Lord Edmond's body went rigid. He continued to stare off to the west.

"But I have been quite unable to bring myself to talk to you in the past two days," the duke said. "I know myself terribly at fault. I have known it all these years, but not seeing you has made it easier to suppress the guilt. I cannot recall what I said to you to make you run off. It must have been something dreadful."

"You called me a murderer," Lord Edmond said quietly.

"Ah." There was a short silence. "Yes, I knew that. I just hoped it was not true. I lashed out at you from my pain and guilt. And then, when you left and everything else started to happen, I convinced myself that you must truly have been guilty. At least I convinced a part of myself."

"It is old history," Lord Edmond said. "It is best forgotten."

"No." His father sounded sad. "I have ruined your life, my boy. I have known it all these years, although perversely I have only railed against you and half-believed my own condemnations. Too much time has passed. Too much wrong has been done. How can I ever ask forgiveness for the enormous wrongs I have done you? I am sorry, my boy. I will have to go away from here tomorrow and leave you to what I can only hope will be a happier future."

Lord Edmond turned to look at him. "Tell me what you said at the beginning of this conversation," he said. "Say it again."

"That I have never stopped loving you?" The duke looked into his son's eyes. "You want my love, Edmond? After all I have done to you?"

"I want it." Lord Edmond's eyes were intense.

"I love you," his father said. "You are my son. Can you ever forgive me?"

Lord Edmond swore. He stared at his father for a few moments, hesitated, and then drew him into a hug even more bruisingly hard than that he had exchanged with his brother the day before. For perhaps a minute both were oblivious of the people who strolled about them, and of Anne, who appeared briefly in the doorway of the pavilion and then disappeared again.

"You must come home," the duke said at last. "You must come back home, my boy. You have been too long away."

Lord Edmond smiled. "I am going home, Papa," he said. "To Willow Court. I am in the process of learning what it means to be a landowner. But yes, I will come to stay with you and with Wally and Anne and my nephews and niece. Perhaps for Christmas." He laughed. "Or perhaps you can all come to me. Is this really happening?"

The duke looked up at the sky. "It is indeed, my boy,"

he said. "And the storm is about to happen too. Those clouds are moving faster than I expected. Did you hear that thunder?"

They walked back to the pavilion, looking at each other in some wonder when they stepped inside to the brighter candlelight, and smiling rather self-consciously.

"I knew when Anne got you and Wallace together yesterday," the duke said with a chuckle, "that my turn would come today. I have a gem of a daughter-in-law, Edmond. Perhaps I will have another eventually?"

"Perhaps," Lord Edmond said evasively.

But they were separated at that moment when Lady Cathcart called to his grace to make up a hand of cards while the younger people danced.

"It looks as if we might have a long night of it," Lady Eleanor said to Lord Edmond. Predictably she looked thoroughly pleased by the possibility. "Doris is already circulating with the proud tidings that she has been right all along. Will the storm be bad, do you suppose?"

Lord Edmond looked about the room after she had wafted off to talk with someone else. The Ormsbys were dancing. They had gone walking with Mary and Goodrich. Stephanie had been one of the group too, if he was not mistaken. She was sitting with her mama at the other side of the room. There was no sign of Mary or Goodrich. And he could hear rain against the long windows.

Damn Goodrich! He hoped at least that they were inside a folly and not sheltering beneath a tree. Surely they could not be that foolish.

And then he breathed a great sigh of relief. He caught sight of the viscount close to the doors, brushing raindrops from the sleeves of his coat. They had returned just in time, too. The rain outside was becoming a deluge, so that many of the guests stopped what they were doing in order to look toward the windows. There was a buzz of excitement at a flash of lightning.

Lord Edmond wondered if Mary would be frightened in the midst of a crowd. He looked for her. But she was nowhere in sight. He looked more carefully.

He strolled toward the viscount, who was laughing at something Mrs. Bigsby-Gore was saying. "Where is Mary?" he asked, interrupting their conversation without preamble.

"Lady Mornington?" The viscount looked at him haughtily. "Somewhere in the house, I would imagine."

"The house?" Lord Edmond frowned. "The house as opposed to the pavilion? What is she doing there?"

"How would I know?" the viscount said. "I am here, as you see. And I imagine that Lady Mornington's movements are none of your business anyway, Waite. Ma'am, will you dance?" He turned back to Mrs. Bigsby-Gore.

But Lord Edmond clamped a hand onto his arm. "Is she alone there?" he asked. "Did you leave her alone to return here?"

Lord Goodrich looked pointedly at the hand on his arm. "The house is full of servants," he said.

"She is terrified of storms," Lord Edmond said, his eyes narrowing. "With very good reason. You knew that."

"Childish nonsense!" the viscount said. "If you would be so kind as to remove your hand from my arm, Waite, I can lead the lady into the dance."

"You left her," Lord Edmond said, his voice tight with fury, "knowing that." He lifted his hand away from Lord Goodrich's sleeve as if it had burned him. "Your own betrothed."

"Lady Mornington is nothing to me," the viscount said, and he turned away as thunder rumbled in the not-so-far distance.

Lord Edmond strode across the room, but a hand on his sleeve stayed him as he was about to open the door.

"Edmond?" his aunt said, laughing. "You cannot go out there, dear. I fear we are stuck here for many hours to come. Is it not dreadful?" She smiled cheerfully.

"I have to go back to the house," he said. "Mary is there alone."

"At the house?" She frowned. "But Lord Goodrich is here."

"The bastard left her there alone, knowing her terror of storms," he said.

"Oh!" She looked shocked, though not, apparently, at his

choice of words. She lifted her hand from his arm. "Go, then, Edmond. Go quickly, dear. And don't try to come back."

He was gone without another word, shutting the door firmly behind him. Lady Eleanor enjoyed a private smile at the closed door before turning back to her guests.

18

SHE LICKED DRY lips with a dry tongue as she paced. She glanced several times at the bell rope, one tug on which would bring her maid in just a few minutes. But she did not pull it. It was merely a matter of waiting out the storm, she told herself. Storms did not last forever, and usually they were directly overhead for no longer than a few minutes. And storms did not strike large stone mansions or harm the people safely lodged inside them.

She tried to remember how she had used to feel about storms as a child. But she could remember only Lawrence's voice muttering more to himself than to her in their tent in Spain that someone was surely going to get it. And the terrified screaming of horses. And then . . . the rest of it.

She rubbed her hands against the sides of her dress. Moist palms. And a dry mouth. Lightning flashed and she counted only to eight before the thunder followed. She looked at the bell rope again.

And then she swung around toward the door, relief flooding her. Her maid had come without being summoned. Somehow she must have heard that her mistress was at home. The door opened after a quick tapping.

"Oh," she said, and the relief was still there—and something else too. "You look like a drowned rat." She laughed, the sound nervous and almost hysterical to her own ears.

"Hm," he said. "You are supposed to gasp out something like 'My hero!' and rush into my arms."

"Am I?" she said, and bit her lip and smiled at him a little uncertainly. "What are you doing here?"

"Dripping onto your carpet," he said, looking down.

She swallowed. "Did you come because of me?" she asked.

"I seemed to recall that you are susceptible to seduction during thunderstorms," he said. "Of course, I came because of you, Mary."

"Don't," she said. "Don't use that voice. It is the one that comes with your mask."

"Mask?" He raised his eyebrows.

"Oh, Edmond," she said, "do go and change. You will catch your death."

But a particularly loud clap of thunder had her scurrying a few steps toward him before stopping. She licked her lips again.

He dragged off his coat, grimacing as he did so from the wetness of it. He pulled free his neckcloth and began to unbutton his shirt.

"By the time I go to my room and change and comb my hair in a fashion that suits it when wet, and don a few jewels to impress you," he said, pulling his shirt free of his pantaloons and drawing it off over his head, "the storm will be over and I will have lost my chance with you, Mary. Besides, by that time you will probably be a blithering idiot." He grinned at her. "It is going to be overhead soon. I think my arms had better be dry and available for you when that happens. Your teeth are beginning to chatter."

She clamped them firmly together, swallowed as he pulled off his Hessians and moved his hands to the buttons of his pantaloons, and turned jerkily away.

"I shall fetch you some towels from the dressing room," she said. But another flash rooted her to the spot.

"No need," he said. "A blanket from the bed should do. I will be able to cover myself quite decently, I do assure you. If you do not want to watch the next installment, Mary, you had better turn away again for a moment."

She did, and crossed the few feet to the bed to pull free one blanket. He took it from her hand before she turned back to him, and had wrapped himself in it by the time she did.

"Come a little nearer," he said as the storm grew closer and louder and more intense. "But I have had second thoughts about these dry arms holding you, Mary. All this stripping off to the skin and talking of seductions has made me dangerous. Not to mention certain delicious memories of the last storm. Just stand close and we will talk our way through the height of the storm."

She moved closer and curled her hands into fists at her sides.

"Don't you think I should have a laurel wreath for my hair, and perhaps rope sandals for my feet?" he said. "Is that what the ancient Romans wore on their feet? I think this blanket looks distinctly like a toga, don't you, Mary? How did they fasten the things about them? Do you know? They surely did not stride about the streets of Rome clutching them as I am forced to do. How would they shake hands with anyone? Did the Romans shake hands? And what if a particularly nasty gust of wind came along? It could all be a trifle embarrassing, don't you think? You are not being fair, you know, Mary. I have asked enough questions to form the basis for a fifteen-minute discussion, and you have answered none of them. Help me out. It is your turn."

"You were a classics scholar," she said. "You must know all the answers."

"I merely follow the methods of Socrates," he said. "He never told his pupils anything. He merely asked endless questions. Yes, it is close, is it not?" he said as she cringed. "Must I hold you? Don't trust me, Mary. I don't trust myself."

His pale blue eyes gazed intently back into hers when she raised them to him. She was almost past reason.

"I have been trying so hard," she said. "I know it is something I must conquer."

But the lightning and thunder happened simultaneously even as she finished speaking, and she found herself being drawn against warm and naked safety. Strong arms came about her, enclosing her in the blanket. She buried her face against warm chest hair and rested her hands against it too.

"It is all right, Mary," he was murmuring, his cheek against the top of her head. "I have you safe, love. Nothing is going to hurt you."

He rocked her in his arms during the five minutes or so that the storm was overhead. She listened to the rain lashing the windows and to the strong steady beat of his heart. And the terror was suddenly all gone. She could almost enjoy the fury of the elements while she relaxed in her warm and living cocoon.

She drew back her head and looked up at him.

"No," he said. "A big mistake, Mary." And he set one hand behind her head and drew it none too gently against his chest again. "Don't look at me. If you don't look at me, I can pretend you are a frightened maid or my niece or my sister-in-law or some elderly dowager. If you don't look at me, I have a chance.'"

"Edmond," she said.

"Christ!" he said. "And that was no blasphemy, Mary. That was a fervent prayer. What has happened to 'my lord'? Call me 'my lord.' "

Through the thin muslin of her dress she could feel the stirrings of his arousal. And she could feel a tightening in her own breasts. Edmond! She kept very still.

"Whose idea was this blanket, anyway?" he said. "What I should have done, Mary—but hindsight is always point-less—was take you along to my room and stand you with your back to me while I changed into dry clothes . . . into decent armor. You know enough about human anatomy to know very well what is going on here, I suppose? No, don't answer that. You might try to be tactful and say no, you had not noticed, and that would be a dreadful blow to my masculine pride. Why am I the only one babbling?"

"Edmond?" She raised her head again and looked up into his eyes.

He sighed. "You will have no respect for my title, then?" he said. "Listen, Mary, if you do not want what is about to happen to happen, you had better drag up some courage from somewhere and remove yourself from this blanket. And I mean now, or preferably five minutes ago. The storm is moving off, I do believe. Devil take it, woman, I am only human. Too damned human, I'm afraid."

"So am I," she said. "Too damned human."

"Such language," he said, and his head moved down to hers and his eyes closed and he spoke against her lips. "God,

Mary, I have not wanted this to happen. Not any longer. I have been trying to do something decent at last. But it seems one cannot change oneself after all when one has lived a selfish and self-indulgent life for years."

"Then let it be said that I have seduced you," she said, her arms going up about his neck. "You are merely my victim."

He groaned. "There is only one thing more exciting than your naked body against mine, Mary," he said. "I have just discovered it. It is your clothed body against my nakedness. I don't have a chance, woman. I swear I don't."

"I know," she said, and she angled her head and opened her mouth wider, inviting him to deepen the kiss.

He accepted the invitation without hesitation, widening his mouth over hers, teasing his tongue over her lips, up behind them so that she shivered with a sharp ache, and into her mouth, sliding over surfaces, circling her tongue, and finally beginning a firm rhythm of thrust and withdrawal in promise of things to come.

"I have always loved long hair on women," he said against her throat, pushing the fingers of one hand into her hair. "Hair to wrap about the breasts and waist. But your short curls drive me wild, Mary. Don't ever grow them out."

His hands roamed over her, finding the hardened nipples of her breasts, fitting themselves to her small waist, spreading over her hips. And her own hands followed suit. She felt the muscles of his shoulders, the rippling muscles of his back, the narrow waist and hips, the firm, hard buttocks.

"I suppose," he said, "I had better make the ultimate admission of defeat and undress you and lay you on that bed, had I not?"

"Yes," she said.

"You are no help at all, Mary," he said, feathering kisses over her face.

"No."

"So be it, then," he said, and he slipped his hands beneath her dress and shift at the shoulders and slowly drew them down over her arms until, loosened about the waist, they fell away to the floor.

"Ah," he said, drawing her against him again, speaking against her mouth. "Maybe I had better take that back about clothed bodies after all, Mary." The blanket was also in a heap at their feet.

She drew breath slowly. She was far more aware of what was happening than she had been on the Vauxhall night. She could feel him with every part of her body. He was all hard muscle and warm flesh and hair. He was magnificent. And she loved him. She rested her hands on his shoulders.

"Edmond," she said against his mouth.

"You have me persuaded," he said. "You do not need to say more. Onto the bed, love."

She wondered as he turned back the bedcovers and she lay obediently on the bed if he realized what he was calling her. She reveled in the endearment. Even if it were only the occasion that was provoking it, it was enough. The occasion was enough.

"Mary." He came immediately on top of her, his hands moving down her sides, his mouth finding hers. "I don't want to wait any longer. Do you? Say no."

"No," she said.

"Good girl," he said. "I like obedient women. Have I told you how much I like you?"

Like! She smiled ruefully against his mouth. But her body was on fire for him, and her love needed to be fed by him in this physical way—just one more time. One more time would be enough.

"This much," he said, parting her legs with his knees, pushing them wide. "This much." He positioned himself at the entrance to her so that she could hear her own heart beating. "This much, Mary." He came into her, stopping only when he was deeply embedded in her. "I like you this much. Do you like me? Just a little? Tell me you like me just a little. You would not allow this otherwise, would you?"

Light blue eyes looked down into hers in the candlelight. There was a hint of anxiety behind the passion in them.

"I like you." She smiled at him. "This much." She lifted her legs from the bed and twined them about his. "And this much." She pressed her hips into the mattress, tilting herself to him so that he was deeper in her. "And this much." She tightened inner muscles, drawing him deeper still.

"God in his sweet heaven, woman," he said, burying his face in her curls. "Are you trying to prove that I can still perform like a gauche schoolboy? Let me take a few minutes over this, will you?"

She relaxed beneath him, letting his body play with the hum of desire in her own, letting him focus it and build it until she could control her reactions no longer, but tightened her arms about him and twisted her hips, drawing him deep to give her the release she craved.

"Edmond," she pleaded.

"Yes, love," he said, finding her mouth with his again. "Oh, yes. Oh, yes."

And they found it together, that center of the universe, which only lovers experience in the moment of fulfilllment. Her body shook beneath his as his relaxed weight bore her down into the mattress.

"There," he said five minutes later as he moved to her side, drew a sheet up over them, and settled her head on his arm. "So much for reformations of character, Mary. They just do not happen. I am sorry. The temptation was too great."

"Yes, it was," she said.

"I did try," he said. "If only the rain had not made my clothes so infernally wet. I think I might have had a will of iron if I had not had to remove all my clothes."

She chuckled.

"It's not funny, Mary," he said. "Once this storm is over . . . In fact, I think it is already over—have you heard any thunder lately? Anyway, once this night is over, you will realize, as you did last time, just what horrors your terror drove you into. And as usual, I was here to oblige with the grand seduction scene. During the next thunderstorm you had better make sure that you are on a different continent, an ocean between us."

"Edmond." She turned onto her side and touched his cheek lightly with the fingers of one hand. "Don't feel bad. It was not seduction."

"I was not exactly invited into your bedchamber, was I?" he said. "Do you want me to challenge Goodrich? Do say yes. I would like nothing better than the opportunity to draw his cork."

"I broke off our engagement," she said. "I am afraid I have behaved very badly to him. He had every reason to be annoyed with me."

"There is still such a thing as gallantry," he said. "Did you really, though, Mary? It is some relief, anyway, to know that I have not just been bedding someone else's fiancée."

"Have you spoken with your father?" she asked.

He grimaced. "And we cried and slobbered all over each other," he said. "It was in the best spirit of sentimental melodrama, Mary."

"And all is well?" she asked.

"He asked me to forgive him," he said. "*Me* forgive *him.* Can you imagine?"

"I am so glad," she said. "I am so happy for you."

"Are you?" he said.

She nodded and smiled at him.

"Why are your eyelids drooping and your words slurring?" he asked her. "I was not that good, was I? Tell me I was that good."

She closed her eyes. "You were that good," she said. "Now you must return the compliment and tell me that you are sleepy too and that I was that good."

"I am talking in my sleep," he said. "And you were . . . oh, some superlative."

She continued to smile. She loved him. And he liked her. She wondered what he would say if she told him her feelings. She wondered if it would make any difference to anything. But it was surely wiser to keep her mouth shut. She had always considered that they were as far apart as the two poles, in everything except physical attraction. Surely not enough had changed to make any sort of relationship between them a possibility. He was right. It was the storm that made everything seem possible. It must be the storm.

And a good loving.

She fell asleep before she could decide whether or not to say the words aloud.

* * *

He did not sleep. He lay staring up at the moving patterns of the shadows cast by the candles and listening to the rain easing outside and the distant rumbles of thunder. He lay awake memorizing the feel of her and the smell of her.

And regretting fifteen wasted years, years given up to every imaginable excess of debauchery, years in which he had lost reputation and even honor. He had nothing whatsoever to offer a decent woman, nothing to offer the woman he loved. All he could do, all he could look forward to, was making amends in the future, perhaps making something out of his remaining years. Perhaps eventually, although he was already thirty-six years old, there could be marriage and children. Perhaps eventually he would deserve them.

But not with Mary. Too late for Mary. And so the possibilities brought no comfort.

She stirred finally and opened her eyes. She smiled at him.

"You are awake," she said.

"Mary," he said, and he kissed her mouth, tasting her, memorizing the taste, "this is good-bye. You know that, don't you? After tomorrow you will no longer be plagued by me. And it is a promise I will keep this time."

The smile held on her face. Her eyes looked back into his.

"Tell me something," he said. It was something he would rather not think of, but reality was reality. "Is there any chance I might have got you with child?"

She flushed, though she did not look away from him. She appeared to be thinking. "Yes," she said.

He swore.

"Such language," Mary said.

"Listen, Mary," he said. "If it is so, then you must write to me. Promise? I will come to you in London and marry you. I'm sorry about it. I know it would be a dreadful fate for you, but the alternative would unfortunately be worse. Promise that you will write? I would find out anyway."

"I would write," she said after a lenghty pause.

"The rain is stopping," he said. "Even so, it is bound to be hours before the others will attempt to drive home. The thought is tempting."

"Yes," she said.

The look in her eyes and the warm languor of her body told him that she was still amorous after the storm, as she had been in his scarlet room after Vauxhall. The temptation was almost overwhelming. One more time. She was willing. Just one more time.

He kissed her.

One more time. One more chance to plant his seed in her at a time when she was likely to conceive.

He drew his head away, eased his arm from beneath her head without looking into her eyes, and sat rather hastily on the side of the bed.

"Lord," he said. "Wet clothes or the Roman toga. Which is it to be? If I stagger out of here tripping over the hem of the toga, the servants are bound to be lined up outside your door all prepared to enjoy the show."

He walked naked across the room, aware of her eyes on his back, and looked with some distaste at the heap of his clothing, still quite unmistakably wet. His pantaloons were a little apart from the rest. They were damp. Damp and chilly. He drew them on and pulled a face.

"Just what I need to cool my ardor," he said. "The storm has passed. I don't believe it will return. You will be all right, Mary?" He looked back to see that she was sitting on the edge of the bed, wearing a blue silk dressing gown. Her face was flushed and her dark curls adorably rumpled.

"I will be all right," she said.

"Good night, then." He opened the door resolutely after scooping up his wet clothes, stepped through it, and closed it behind him without allowing himself the luxury of a glance back.

She had stood at the window for a long time gazing out into the darkness. Even the final distant flashes of lightning with no sound of thunder had passed. The rain had completely stopped. Soon perhaps the carriages would return, unless the rain had been heavy enough and had lasted long enough to make the roadway slippery with mud.

He had wanted her as his mistress. His bedfellow. His plaything. But he had changed since that time. He had just lived through a turbulent emotional time and it seemed that the rift with his family was healed, and with it all the bitterness and guilt that had blighted his adult life. He was different and seemed to want to make the changes permanent. He no longer wanted her as his mistress. His reluctance to make love to her earlier had been proof of that. She feared that perhaps she really had seduced him.

However it was, there was nothing to suggest that perhaps he would want her as his wife. He liked her, he had said even when he was making love to her. Liked, not loved. Clearly he found her attractive. But attraction was not love. He would marry her if she was with child, he had told her. But that did not mean that he would marry her willingly, that he wished to do so.

Better to leave things as they were, she thought. Better that than to embarrass him by hinting that she loved him, that perhaps after all she wanted a future with him. But not a future as a mistress. As a wife. Perhaps he would feel honor-bound to offer for her if she hinted at any such thing.

But what if his reluctance, his admission only of liking, his good-bye, were all motivated by his belief that she wanted none of him? What if at last he was doing something noble in his life?

What if they lived apart for the rest of their lives because of a misunderstanding? Because neither had the courage to speak the heart's truth? The thought was unbearable.

And so she must risk the hint, she decided, and stood at the window and went through all the arguments yet again—for surely the dozenth time.

But her decision was the same again at the end of it all, and she could not bear to wait until the morning, when she knew she might see everything differently, when the harsh voice of reason might silence her. If her love was to stand a chance—and if she was to risk rebuff and humiliation—then it must be done now.

She turned resolutely from the window and moved toward the door. But she had taken no more than three steps before a swift tap on the door heralded its opening and he stepped inside as he had done earlier. But this time he was wearing a brocaded dressing gown, its blue color several shades darker than her own.

He closed the door behind his back.

"I am a very poor risk, you know, Mary," he said. "Unreliable. Totally undependable. No one would be willing to wager on me. If there were a bet on me in one of the betting books at the clubs, there would not be a single taker for me. Only hordes against. The chances that I will ever make anything meaningful out of my life are slim, to state the case optimistically. You would have to agree with me, wouldn't you?"

She swallowed and said nothing.

"Anyone would be a fool to trust me and take me on," he said.

"Edmond," she said, "I was on my way to your room. Why have you come back here? What are you trying to say?"

"I am going home, Mary," he said. "Home to Willow Court. To stay. I know almost nothing about it except what I learned in the few weeks before I came here. I know nothing about crops and tenants and drainage and rents and all that. But I intend to learn. I am going to become that very dull English type—a country gentleman. So boring that within a year everyone will snore at the mere mention of my name."

He flashed her a grin and she tried to smile back.

"The house is unbelievably shabby," he said, "and the garden too. I don't have any ideas about houses and gardens. All I know is that they look shabby and unlived-in and uncozy. They need a woman's touch."

Mary licked her lips.

"And the house needs children," he said. "Noisy, laughing, mischievous children with muddy feet and jam-smeared mouths."

"Edmond," she said, "I love you."

But he rushed on with what he had come to say. "I cannot offer any evidence that my determination to change will really bring about change," he said. "Perhaps I will fail miserably, Mary. Perhaps it is all so much dreaming. I would not envy any woman who was decent and kind enough to give me a chance. She would be likely to end up hurt and disillusioned. I think that must be right, don't you? Any woman would be a fool.''

"Edmond," she said, "I love you."

"But it is up to you," he said, rushing on. "I am going home, Mary, and I want you to come with me. You would have your home in the country and your children, if I am capable of begetting them. And a husband who would try to love you always as he does today and would try to give you a good life. Will you come? I am sure you would be well advised to say no." He paused and looked at her fixedly. "*What* did you say?"

"I love you," she said.

"It's the thunderstorm," he said. "It does make you a little . . . strange, Mary, you must admit."

"Then you will have to take a risk too," she said. "Will I mean it tomorrow and next week and next year and twenty, thirty, forty years from now? The whole future is a risk. That is the excitement and wonder of life. When do you want me to come?"

There was incomprehension in his eyes. "You are saying yes?" he asked. "After everything I have done to you? After all the aversion you felt for me in London?"

"I was afraid," she said. "I was afraid that I would love where there could be only lust in return, and even that for only a short time. Edmond, I want that home in the country more than I can say. And those children. Plural? Oh, I hope so. And I want all of it with you. Not with anyone else. Only with you."

He laughed. "And I pictured myself hurrying out of this room two minutes after entering it," he said, "with a flea in my ear and a slap on the cheek and perhaps a slipper at my rear end. But I had to come, Mary. I could not risk losing you only because I was afraid to ask for you. You will marry me?"

"Yes." She came across the room to him and set her hands on his shoulders. "When, Edmond? Please soon. Oh, please soon."

"One month from now," he said. "At the very worst, our first child must be no less than an eight-month baby. We can say he was born early and hope he does not weigh twelve pounds. Was tonight really a bad time for you, Mary—or a good time?''

''I think the worst—or the best,'' she said.

''Was it, by Jove?'' he said. ''Is it?''

''Yes.'' She slid her hands beneath the silk collar of his dressing gown and reached up to kiss him beneath one ear. ''That means it will also be the best on our wedding night, Edmond. But speaking for myself, I have no objection to an eight-month baby. None at all.''

''You aren't trying to seduce me again, by any chance, are you?'' he asked her, setting his hands at her waist and arching her body in against his. ''You have a shocking tendency to do that, you know, Mary.''

''Edmond.'' She wrapped her arms tightly about his neck and raised her face to his. ''You said you always want to love me as you love me today. Tell me how much you love me.''

''I'll write a poem about it tomorrow, if you wish, love,'' he said. ''In Latin. For tonight would you not rather that I showed you?''

She thought for a moment and then smiled. ''Yes,'' she said. ''Love me, Edmond, and make me an eight-month baby.''

''God in his heaven, woman,'' he said. ''Is that an invitation or is it an invitation?''

''It is an invitation,'' she said against his mouth. ''Love me.''

''With all my heart,'' he said. ''And that other too, Mary.''

He kissed her and steered her backward to the bed. And he proceeded with slow thoroughness to do both simultaneously.